WHISPER IN THE DARK

SHIFTERS OF MORWOOD: BOOK 1

CHARLENE PERRY

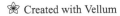

WHISPER

*S*ome days, I love my job.

I take a deep, appreciative inhale of deliciously masculine cologne. A little stronger than I prefer, but distinctly male in that woodsy sort of way. Tousled, dirty-blond hair falls into dark eyes. His body is firm, smooth... tattooed.

His heart's pounding against my chest as I pin him to the wall. I can't resist swaying my hips just a little. He sucks in a breath through clenched teeth, as the corner of his mouth twitches almost into a grin.

Maybe he's doubting my intentions. Maybe he thinks the knife against his belly is just foreplay...

Nah, he knows I'm serious.

I think the second knife pressing into his neck gives it away.

Maybe I'm a teensy bit cruel for dragging this out and letting him think he has a chance. I do love a good fantasy, and imagining he isn't my current mark gives my overactive imagination plenty of room to play.

"What a waste."

I put all my weight behind the six inches of cold steel as it slides effortlessly across his beautiful neck.

What a waste, indeed.

I ignore the buzz-killing final sounds of his death as I slip my knives back into their sheaths at my back and pull out my comm for a quick scan.

Proof of kill and my ticket to a pretty sweet payday.

I stride back out the way I came, past the other two corpses that never got the pleasure of seeing me coming. Just before emerging out of the concrete bunker, I tap into my latest implant. The little red dress that caught my Mark like a deer in headlights fades effortlessly into my standard issue tactical gear. Definitely more my style.

That took a while. Damon's voice comes into my head as I shield my eyes from the glaring, early morning sun. The accusation is thick in his tone, but I just laugh. He knows I like to play with them.

"Like a cat with a mouse."

I earn a thick growl for using his least favorite analogy.

He's still standing guard, keeping his eyes on the surrounding forest and his paw on my discarded pistol. I secure the weapon in its holster on my hip, then lean against his shoulder. The rush of the kill fades from my system as my fingers trail through his lush, velvety fur.

"We're good," I assure him. "The intel was accurate. Mark thought he was home free and only had two guards watching his back. Just another cocky dealer."

You could have waited for him outside. His voice is smooth and deep through our Link implants.

"Where's the fun in that?"

My moody panther Shifter never enjoys the kill missions as much as I do. He's a deadly and efficient assassin when the job requires it, but he's never happy when I take what he considers an unnecessary risk.

I could have waited in the trees for the mark to come outside, but that could have taken days. Besides, one look at his file and I knew I wanted a close-up introduction.

There's no harm in having a *little* fun on the job, right?

Damon tenses under my hand at the same moment I hear the slightest noise behind us. I pivot on my heels, my pistol levelling with the terrified face of a young woman. I don't know what she's more scared of, my weapon or the two-hundred-fifty-pound snarling panther at my side.

I'm guessing the panther.

It's immediately obvious that she's no threat. I motion for Damon to stand down, but I keep my weapon aimed. The intel said nothing about a girl travelling with them. But it did specify to leave no witnesses. This particular drug-trafficking organization doesn't know the Protectors are on to them yet.

"Who are you?"

"I... I'm nothing." She drops her gaze, and I notice that her hair is tangled. Not like morning-after-sex tangled, more like she hasn't had a brush in days. Her face is gaunt, even for her slim form. Her neck is bare, no tats signifying implant tech, though she does have fresh ink on her wrist. She's wearing a gauzy slip of a dress that's seen better days.

"Do you need help?" I lower my pistol to her torso.

She peers up at me through thick lashes, her dark eyes searching mine for some clue she can trust me. "Who are you?"

"My name is Whisper. I'm an Agent with the Protectors."

Her eyes grow larger, making her look even younger than I first suspected. Hell, this girl can't be older than 16.

"But, you're a woman."

"Yes, I am." I put my weapon back into its holster at my hip, and the little shit takes the opening to bolt.

Damon digs his claws in, ready and willing to chase her down.

"Don't."

I flip a small switch on my pistol, take aim, and drop her like a deer. She can take a little nap on the way back to Moridian.

~

IT'S SHORTLY after 8 a.m. when we arrive at Base. The Headquarters of the United Army of Terran Protectors: Ground Division. Also known as 'Base', because nobody wants to spit out that mouthful more than once.

I keep my chin up and my eyes down as we cross the glossy, white tile of the lobby. After a sleepless night on the job, I'm not in the mood for dealing with the stares and whispers. If I see even one person looking at me with that 'what is a girl doing dressed up like an Agent?' expression on their face, I might tell my panther to eat them. Not that he would. Sometimes I like to imagine that he might.

I don't look like much of a threat with my feminine curves on a five-five, one-hundred-twenty-pound frame. But at least my Shifter looks like he could fuck you up. In reality, I'm the one who might just break your face for being a pain in the ass. He's just a big pussy. Pun intended.

I give the receptionist brief instructions about the girl sleeping off her sedative in my back seat. The security gate beeps as I register my comm, and I hold my breath until the elevator doors close behind us.

Now that we're out of the public section of the sprawling, twenty-five story building, I don't have to guard my reactions quite so carefully. Anyone who questions me on this side of the curtain will find out exactly why I have the clearance to be here.

Damon pushes his big head against my side, and I absently run my hand over his head and shoulders. I trace the silvery scar that mars the soft fur of his neck and right shoulder. It's one of many that remind me of the fact that his life began in a shit hole just as dark as my own.

Once the doors open on the twenty-second floor, it's a short walk to the Commander's private office. A quick knock, and I let myself in.

"Hey, Whisp. You're up early this morning." Charles greets me with a smile, then turns back to the pile of papers he's pushing around on his desk. I don't know what he's doing, and I don't care as long as some of those papers mean I've got another payday on the way.

I slide my comm across his desk, earning a frown of annoyance when I mess up whatever organizational method he's got going on. It quickly dissolves into a smile when he realizes what I'm hinting at. He grabs the small device and docks it into his console, reviewing the upload as he nods in approval.

"That job was supposed to take you a week." He shakes his head, passing my comm back across the desk. "How'd you get to him so fast?"

"Guess I just have bigger balls than your other Agents." He shouldn't be surprised, after four years of being my Commander.

He shakes his head again, digging through some of those papers as I hold my breath and hope that he has another job ready for me. If it weren't for Commander Charles Jeffries, I wouldn't be a Protector. I certainly wouldn't be an Agent.

He took me under his wing the moment I showed up at the Academy. No one else would have taken a girl seriously, but he knew my family. He had worked with my father, back when they were both low-level Enforcers. He had gotten a glimpse of the hellhole we called a home, and the assholes that called themselves my brothers. He knew what I had endured. What I had survived. He knew I'd be a real asset to the program, even if everyone else only saw my more superficial assets.

Not that I'm against using those for my own gain, when the situation calls for it.

He got me in the door, but I earned the right to stay. By the end of the two-year program, I graduated at the top of my class. They started me off as an Enforcer, but it didn't take me long to bring in a mark worthy of the Agents. Charles helped me with the red tape, and the rest is history.

"I've got nothing lined up for you yet."

That's definitely not what I want to hear.

"Are you sure? Not even a little one? I'm okay with a side errand if there's nothing big-"

"I've got nothing, Whisp. I'll let you know as soon as I do. What are you saving up for now? You got your little fashion implant already, didn't you?"

"It's a Local Matter Wardrobe, thank you very much. And it has nothing to do with fashion." I cross my arms, feigning insult. "It's a weapon, if you must know."

He looks at me with one eyebrow raised. "I don't think the ability to change your outfit instantaneously counts as a weapon."

"It does on this body." I hair flip for effect. Not because I'm the hair-flipping type, just because I enjoy seeing the exasperation on his face. He has his doubts that I'm being serious, but he didn't see the stun-gun effect that little getup had on this morning's mark. I could have been carrying a rifle and the guy wouldn't have even noticed.

I saved for a long time for that implant, for more than one reason. Mostly, being able to upload any outfit I want and use surrounding matter to manufacture it instantly is just awesome. Goodbye dirty clothes... hello instant outfit. The time it's saved me in laundry alone is well worth the price.

I slide my hand across the side of my neck, over the faint ridges of three small tattoos. Every implant comes with a tat; a small symbol that lets others know what upgrades you're working with. The top one is my Medic implant, given to all Academy grads. It means I can heal crazy fast, which comes in handy often enough in this line of work. The second is my Link implant, which is directly connected to Damon's. We got those when we were matched, after I was promoted to Agent. The third is my new LMW.

"Well, whatever you're saving for, I've still got nothing. I'll reach out as soon as I do. Sound good?"

"Yeah, thanks Charles."

He just shakes his head as we vacate his office and leave him to his paperwork.

Let's go home for some real food, I suggest to Damon, and he picks up his pace with an agreeable purr.

GIDEON

*B*ack in the lobby, I resume my eyes-down got-somewhere-important-to-be pace. I'm out the doors and nearly home free before I'm stopped in my tracks by a vice-like grip on my arm. Damon growls as I grit my teeth and look up into cold, blue eyes.

"Hello, little Whisper." Agent Nutsack leans down so only I can hear him, using his free hand to tuck a loose strand of brown hair behind my ear. Yes, I nickname all my coworkers with genitalia references. Who doesn't? "How would you like to come by my place later? I've got a little energy to burn, and you look like you know how to take it. I bet I could have you screaming my name in under ten minutes."

Okay. Now I'm imagining myself screaming *Agent Nutsack* while in the throes of the orgasmic bliss he's supposedly able to deliver. I'm struggling to keep a straight face, which probably just makes it appear like I'm considering his offer. Not that I would ever consider playing around with an Agent, no matter how maddeningly sexy some of them are, or how many propositions I get. They either want the conquest, want to prove they can handle me, or just want me to let my guard down.

I'm a threat to all of them just by being here. Just by being female. Not to mention the fact that my win rate is top three right about now. I challenge their world, or at least the way they see their world.

Women can't be Protectors. It's not that we aren't allowed to be, no, it's less obvious than that. No woman makes it through the Academy. It's just never happened.

Until me, that is.

I have a superpower. It's not my combat skills or my intelligence, though both of those are highly impressive, if I'm being honest. It's my ability to take a beating. My brothers thought they were making sure I never amounted to anything; that I would never make it out from under their heels. But they taught me a valuable skill, and it gave me the edge I needed to make it through the Academy.

It's not that I roll over and take it. Not by a long shot. But since I was cursed with this small body, it's just inevitable that I'm going to lose when it comes down to brute strength. In the Academy, I lost often. I fucked a few of them up, for sure, but they learned to come at me in groups.

I knew when I had lost; when to stop fighting back. I would go to that quiet place deep inside, never giving them the satisfaction of hearing me beg, or scream, or cry. A trip to the medic for some overnight healing, and I was back in the game the next day.

I was never raped. No fucking way. Even before I knew how to fight, I knew that you kick a man in the nuts the moment he says 'hello'. As soon as I saw where a fight was headed, I took out his weapon of choice. Rape might have been less painful than the bruises and broken bones, but the medic can heal a body, not a soul.

"Well, what do you say, little Whisper?"

Just say the word. Damon's voice is punctuated by his feral growling. I know he'd do it, if I needed him to. He'd take out an Agent to save me, even knowing it would mean his execution.

I don't need to be saved. I just need to use my superpower. I stand perfectly still, not pulling away and not engaging. You can't chase someone who doesn't run.

I could say something that would put him in his place. Hell, with him this close I could have him on his back on the concrete before his next breath, but it would only draw more attention. I might be a little worried if it weren't for the fact that we're doing this little dance directly outside Base.

Nutsack, also known as Agent Daniel Thomas, has been pulling this shit since the Academy, and never once has he summoned the balls to try it without witnesses.

I can hear the snarling of the tawny wolf he's paired with. Damon could take him easily, I'm sure of it. Doesn't matter though. It won't come to that.

"Is there a problem here, Agent Thomas?" A deep, unfamiliar voice cuts through the heavy silence.

The painful grip on my arm releases, and I resist the urge to rub the soreness away. The discomfort won't last long thanks to my Medic implant.

"No, Sir," Agent Nutsack replies immediately, clearly deferring to a superior.

I don't bother to look up. I don't really care who it is, and I sure as hell don't want them to think I required them to save me. I start walking, counting the steps until I can get into my truck and out of here.

"Agent Whisper," the voice calls after me.

I stop in my tracks at the use of my actual title. It's not often someone bothers to have the respect of adding the *Agent* to my name. Against my better judgement, I turn to see the person attached to the voice.

That's the moment my panties catch on fire. Or melt. I'm not sure what's happening down there, but it's really fucking warm.

Gideon. The name is on my tongue instantly, but I keep my mouth closed. This man is a legend. The top of the top. Highest ranked of the highest Protector rank. An Elite. I don't even know why he would be down in Moridian. The Enforcers and Agents work here at ground level. Elites are stationed on the Solars; airborne mega-cities for the wealthy and powerful.

I take a glance around to see if his Shifter is nearby, but I don't see any sign of him. That beauty is just as much of a legend as his Elite. Most Shifters can only shift into other mammals, though some learn to take on reptilian or avian forms. A very rare few, like Tarek, can take the form of mythical or imagined creatures. He's usually in the form of a massive, green dragon.

I've only seen pictures, but imagining this gorgeous specimen of a man riding a dragon is almost as orgasmic as imagining him riding me. Not that I'm imagining either of those things. I'm most definitely imagining *me* riding *him*. Yes, that is definitely the way I want this to go.

I'm still deep into this fantasy when I realize he's a whole lot closer, and his hand is extended in a much more formal greeting than he gave me in my mind.

Settling for G rated, I take his hand and shake. His big palm dwarfs mine, and I let my eyes move up along the thick arm that's attached to it. He's dressed for business, not combat, and his loose button-up shirt doesn't reveal as much as I'd like. Wide shoulders, a chiseled jaw. Clean cut, yet rugged. This guy is all the clichés.

His neck holds my attention the longest. The trail of implant tats stretches from his hairline to his collarbone. I recognize Medic and Link, and there's also Stim, which gives a wicked boost to strength and speed. I see Blender, Comm, O2, VRC, and two others I don't even recognize.

No LMW though... I guess the guy likes to get undressed the

old-fashioned way. Okay, so that one's more for putting clothes on, but I much prefer the mental image of him taking them off.

My eyes finally make their way up to his, and I'm immediately taken aback. His pale green gaze is locked on mine. He's not looking at my boobs, or at my mouth. He's not even giving me a wanna-see-me-naked side eye. I school my raging libido immediately. This man addressed me formally, shook my hand, and now he's looking at me like I'm a fellow Protector.

"Elite Gideon. It's an honor." I address him with the same respect, letting my hand drop back to my side.

"The honor's all mine." A swoon-worthy smile lights up his features. Literally. I might swoon. "I've heard impressive things about your win rates. If you ever think about trying for the Elite program, feel free to throw my name out there."

I open my mouth to respond, but I honestly have no words. He says something else, then turns and heads through the glass doors. Did I just get an offer from an Elite? *The* Elite?

"Damon..."

Put it back in your pants.

Now it's my turn to growl at him, though I'm admittedly not very good at it. He has a point though. As encouraging as that was, a man is a man. He might have a little, okay, a lot more class than the dicks I'm used to dealing with. But he's still a man. The moment I start throwing his name around as some kind of reference, that's the moment I'd owe him.

"Don't worry," I assure him as we head down the road, him in the bed with his big head through the cab window. "We'll get there on our own. We don't need him."

I'm rewarded with a calming purr, and I tilt my head to the side to lean against his cheek.

HOME

I gulp in deep breaths of air, gasping as I claw at hands that aren't there. As reality cuts through the haze of the dream, I feel the warm comfort of Damon's body against mine. He usually sleeps draped across the foot of my bed, forcing me into the fetal position to make room. Whenever my nightmares strike, I wake to find him stretched out along my side, his soft mouth against my ear as he purrs me back to life.

Fortunately, the dreams are always forgotten the moment I wake. If they're half as dark as my memories, I'm more than happy to leave them buried in my subconscious. I've got nothing to fear in this house. One 'perk' of being an Agent is that you get to be on a lot of people's hit-lists. The department foots the bill to have our houses coated in an invisible nano-barrier. Crazy tech from off-world. Not even a grizzly could get through these windows, and heavy artillery would barely leave a scar.

It's my own little minimalist-bohemian fortress. At least, that's what I was going for. It's got more of a dorm-workaholic vibe lately.

When my heart rate slows and I can breathe normally again, I wrap myself around Damon and bury my face in his thick neck.

"I love you, Damon," I say into his soft fur.

I love you, little one.

I've loved Damon since the moment I first laid eyes on his tiny little kitten-face. My first task after being promoted to Agent was to pick out the Shifter I would bond with. I didn't waste any time getting to BioSol Laboratories, where they cook up those strange, awesome little creatures.

The public face of the place is friendly enough, but I don't have any clue what goes on behind the scenes. All I know, all anyone who doesn't work there really knows, is that they implant embryos into big cats, wolves, and bears. They do what they do, and through the magic of genetics, we end up with a bigger, stronger, smarter version of each.

I was there to pick out a wolf pup, but this little runt caught my eye. He was in the cat enclosure, obviously, but he was nearly half the size of the others. They were picking on him like crazy. His creamy fur was matted with blood from wounds on his shoulder, legs and ribs. They were just tearing him up, but the little scrapper was snarling like a demon and showing no sign of giving up.

I asked about him, but apparently the weak are good practice for the strong. Since he barely squeezed by on his aptitude tests anyway, and he was scheduled for culling, they were just 'letting nature take its course'.

It broke my heart. I've never felt such an instant connection to any creature, human or otherwise. Our eyes met, and I just knew that there was more to him. I knew that if he had a chance, he'd show them all.

I wish I could say that was the moment I chose him. I wish I could say that my connection with him had been stronger than my need to prove myself, and that deep down, I'm a good person. The kind of person that rescues another soul just because it's the right thing to do.

But I didn't. If I was going to prove myself as an Agent, keep my place and eventually progress to the Elite program... I needed a badass Shifter by my side. I took a last look at his big, brown eyes, put my name down for a burley, black wolf, and walked out the door.

I tried to put him out of my mind. I prepared to take my oath and refused to let guilt hold me back. I left him to suffer. The same way I'd been left to suffer all those years with my brothers.

I stood at the podium, hand on my heart as I repeated the words that would make me an Agent. When they opened the crate to present me with the Shifter that I had chosen, out walked the missing piece of my heart.

It was the final insult. My pick had been swapped for the broken runt. They knew I couldn't stop it, not without making a scene and ruining the simple yet critical ceremony. That's exactly what they had expected me to do. What they had hoped for me to do, I suppose.

If I felt any disappointment, it disappeared instantly. I picked him up, held him close, and whispered in his ear. *You're so much more than what they see. We'll show them all. Together.*

My little demon didn't disappoint. He might have been physically smaller at first, but he was smarter. He was braver. He was just as determined to prove himself as I was.

When he was old enough to attempt his first shift, he took this big, beautiful panther form. His size, his attitude, and those badass scars combined to ensure no one called him 'runt' again.

I push away from him, moving to sit on the edge of the bed. Rubbing my temples, I try to shake off the last of the sick feeling those dreams leave me with.

"Let's go get a drink," I say to Damon, even though I'm well aware he doesn't drink and I'm merely suggesting he sit outside the bar and wait for me to get mine. He can stay home if he likes, but in the four years we've been together, he's never willingly let me that far out of his sight.

Sleep, little one.

"We can sleep later. Right now, I want some company. Some human company." He knows what I mean, I don't have to spell it out for him, but I will anyway. "I want a man, Damon. Now."

Why would you need a human man? You have me, and I already love you.

I look back over my shoulder, and when I meet his dark eyes, a shiver creeps down my spine. If he could shift into a human body... Fuck. I scrub my hands over my face, trying to erase the mental images. How fucked up am I that I keep fantasizing about my Shifter? It's just wrong. And impossible.

If he tried to take human form, he wouldn't be able to process the depth of thought and emotion. He'd go insane trying to make sense of it all. He'd likely kill himself and anyone near. It's so dangerous, even attempting it is illegal and punishable by immediate euthanasia.

"I don't want love, Dumbass, I want a cock with a driver that knows what to do with it."

With a huff he jumps off the bed, stalking out into the hallway with his ears flat against his head.

I've never shared my dark fantasies with him, not even a hint. What would be the point? I would certainly never consider risking his life just to see him in human form. Plus, he basically has zero sex drive. They don't even make female Shifters.

I head for my closet, almost making it there before I remember my Local Matter Wardrobe implant. My cotton pajamas are immediately replaced by a short, black skirt with a blue, strappy top.

No one's playing hard to get tonight.

HUNT

Thirty minutes later and I'm feeling worlds better already. This is my favorite stool, in my favorite bar. Over the stench of alcohol and too many bodies, I catch a whiff of sweet vanilla perfume. My favorite bartender. Kelsey leans across the counter, her plunging neckline and long, graceful neck combined with a pretty face and cropped blond hair... hell, she's everyone's favorite bartender.

"I'm glad you're here," she says once she's close enough for me to hear her over the noise of the music and patrons. "There's something a little special on the menu for you tonight."

That's my girl. Always scoping out the best options, giving me a head start on my hunt.

"Actually, that shirt is making me think I might take you home tonight." I'm only half joking. It's not like we haven't gone there before, a time or two.

She raises a perfectly curved eyebrow. "I might take you up on that, if you promise to leave the hellcat outside."

"And that's why we can never be together," I pout. "I couldn't be with someone who isn't a cat person."

"I'm not sure he counts as a cat, Whisper." She shakes her

head.

Like most civilians, she's not comfortable around Shifters. I can't really blame her. Shifters aren't generally very friendly with anyone other than their bondmate.

"What have you got for me?" I swivel in my chair to see if I can spot the one she's picked.

Kelsey points, and I immediately see who she's aiming for. Tall, dark, handsome enough. A little scruff and a bit overdue for a haircut. He'll be just fine for tonight.

"And you're sure he's not a Protector?" I double check, even though I know she wouldn't have picked him if she thought he was.

"Definitely not. He's been in here a few times. Works maintenance at the teleports."

"Interesting." I down my drink and give her a wave of thanks as I start toward him.

Halfway across the room, as I'm weaving through bodies, he spots me. I know the moment, because he does a classic double-take. I'm not vain, but I do know that I'm pretty hot. Like, at least a nine. That's not my own assessment. I've been told many times, in varying degrees of sexual context.

But the only opinion that matters right now is Mr. Scruff... and judging by the way he just abandoned his friend mid-conversation, I'm guessing he agrees, too. He meets me in the middle, at the edge of the dance floor. Because I'm far from shy, and I want him to know what he's signing up for, I immediately put my hands on his flat stomach. Defined abs tempt me under his dark shirt, the logo of a band I don't recognize stretched across an equally defined chest.

"My name's Whisper," I offer as I lean in close and raise up on my toes. The music isn't so loud over here, so I keep my voice low, just for him.

A grin spreads slowly across his face. It always amazes me

how the most subtle body language can get a point across. The simple touch, the lean, the slightly lidded eyes combined with parted lips.

"Are you here alone, Whisper?"

"I think I'm here with you." Cue the lip bite, as my hands slide down to tug suggestively at his belt.

He leans in closer and I smell a spiced cologne that makes me want to taste his skin. His hand slides around my waist, a possessive gesture that says he's claimed me.

"Hello again, Agent Whisper." The familiar voice behind me is so out of place here, I almost believe it's a figment of my imagination.

My almost new toy sucks in a breath, removing his hand from my waist as he stands straight. This can't be happening. I turn slowly, plastering a casual, fancy-meeting-you-here expression on my face.

"Elite Gideon." Is it wrong that the only thing I can think about right now is if it's an option to take both of these men home? No, there can't be anything wrong with an image that good.

"Travis McPherson," Gideon greets my toy by name, holding out a hand.

The five-shades-paler Travis shakes his hand, then takes half a step back from me. I can't even be mad that I've apparently just been cock-blocked. If Gideon wants to claim me for tonight, I will happily oblige. Consequences be damned. He doesn't work in my division anyway, so it's not technically breaking my rule.

"Sir," Travis responds after an awkward silence.

"You work on the teleports." Gideon's statement seems to take Travis by surprise. The expression on his face says he has no idea how the Elite in front of him knows who he is. "How's that treating you? Do you manage the airside, or seaside?"

The teleportation systems are used to get people and their crap up to the Solars, or down to the Aquatics. They're pretty expensive, complicated rigs. I don't have a clue how they work. Odds are I'll never get near them anyway. Tickets cost five times as much as just hopping on a carrier or a sub, and even those are out of my price range.

Not that I'd want to go down to the Aquatics anyway. Being that far underwater doesn't interest me one bit. As far as the Solars go, I'll be earning my ticket there sooner or later.

"Seaside." Travis clears his throat and takes another half-step backwards. "I manage the AI interface." He's clearly giving up without a fight. Can't blame him, considering his competition. The Elites might not have a uniform, but that trail of implant tats is as clear as a billboard.

"Really? That's some pretty cool tech." Gideon sounds genuinely interested in this guy. Hold up. Is he here to hit on me, or Travis? Now that would be an interesting turn of events.

"Yeah, sure is." Travis steps back again, swinging his arms a little before clasping his hands together. "Well, it was good to meet you both. I've got an early shift."

"Yeah, yeah for sure. Didn't mean to hold you up."

And just like that, Travis is gone, and I'm left alone with the sexiest man on the planet. The sexiest, and apparently the smoothest, because even I'm not completely sure if I just witnessed a pissing contest or the beginning of a beautiful friendship. I'm not even sure what to do at this point, so I just stare at him with what I hope isn't that doe-in-headlights expression so many girls seem to like.

Lucky for me, he doesn't leave me hanging for long. Stepping close enough for me to breath in the most expensive cologne I've ever smelled, he leans down until his breath is against my ear. I shiver at the closeness, the tension. My earlier confidence is shattered. I'm not the hunter anymore, I'm being hunted. And I love it.

"I hope I didn't interrupt anything important," he says as he runs a hand up my bare arm and I focus on remembering how to breath.

"No, I... He wasn't... I didn't..." What the hell is happening to me? This man is reducing me to a spineless puddle of girly clichés. I need to snap out of this. What would I do if this were anyone else? Shit.

I turn my head, our lips nearly touching as I look into green eyes that seem to be a shade darker than I remember. I take a fistful of his shirt in my left hand, pulling our bodies closer.

"Can I buy you a drink?" he asks, his voice an octave lower than the last time he spoke. His mouth is just millimeters from mine. Just a slight lean, and I could be tasting this god among men.

"I'd rather taste you." I release my hold on his shirt, moving down his rock-hard stomach to rest on the top of his jeans. And because I want to make sure he knows I'm not just talking about his mouth, I slide my hand under his shirt to pop the top button of his jeans.

Before I can even register his movement, my back is against his front. He has one arm around me, pinning my own arms to my sides and my body tight against his. Stim implant. This is going to be fun. I should probably be worried, or at least a little apprehensive... this man could break me if he wanted to. I'm way too turned on to give a shit.

I slowly move my hips from side to side. He sucks in a breath as I feel him growing hard against my back. Judging by what's obvious through our clothes, Elite Gideon is not going to disappoint. His grip relaxes just slightly, but instead of turning around I push out of his arms and walk away. I don't look back, because I have no doubt he's going to follow.

Through the crowd and out a side door, the cool night air washes over me just as his warm body crashes into mine. With speed that's faster than any normal man, he has me pinned against the rough side of the building. His big frame fills my vision, his arms braced against the wall on either side of my head. He hovers there, his face close to mine, a carnal heat in his eyes.

Just when I think he's going to tease me some more, his mouth claims mine. His kiss is intense, bruising. There's no slow burn, no exploration, just total dominance. I return every bit of what he gives, thoroughly acquainting myself with the texture and taste of his mouth.

His need is pressed against my belly, straining against his confining jeans. Reaching between us, I fumble with his zipper as my head spins from the ravenous kiss that shows no sign of slowing.

Just as I finally succeed in lowering the first barrier to what I want, he pushes away from the wall. I gasp as the cold air fills the void where his body was. The ghost of his kiss is still on my lips as I try to make sense of his sudden withdrawal.

He's standing a few feet away, just out of my reach. He's breathing heavy as he fixes his zipper and buttons his pants. His actions don't fit the heat in his eyes as they rake over me. I'm still struggling to catch my breath when he reaches out to cup my cheek, running the rough pad of his thumb over my lower lip.

"How about that drink?" he asks, his husky tone implying that he clearly meant to say *how about you come to my place so I can fuck you all night*.

But that's not what he said. And now he's staring at me like he actually wants an answer. What's going on? I didn't wear this skirt to make things complicated. We were literally seconds away from all my dreams coming true. Well, tonight's dreams anyway.

"Okay..." I'm still not entirely sure that wasn't a trick question.

He smiles. Actually smiles. Like he's happy with my answer. Then he pulls his hand away and heads back inside the bar.

As the dimly lit, yet always clean alley fades into view, I'm suddenly aware of a very pissed-off Golden Retriever.

Are you done? Damon's voice breaks through my thoughts.

He's wearing his cute doggy form while he waits outside the bar. It's much better for business than his brooding panther form. Or so we've been told on more than one occasion. Only downside is how many people want to pet him, or take him home, which explains why he's so pissed off right about now.

"Hell no." I turn and head back into the bar.

SURE ENOUGH, Gideon is waiting at the bar with two drinks. Something dark and neat in his glass, and what is no doubt my favorite whisky in another glass.

Thank you, Kelsey.

I slide onto the stool beside him, taking a slow sip of my Balvenie and watching his face as I try to figure out what the hell is happening.

Would it scare him away if I just told him straight up what I want? It's not drinks and friendly conversation, that's for damn sure. Then again, I'm pretty certain I made that abundantly clear on the floor, and in the alley. He's playing a game I don't know the rules for, and I'm not sure if that intrigues me or just pisses me off.

Maybe a little of both.

"You're an intense woman, Whisper." He's considering me with narrowed eyes as if trying to figure me out. "You're not at all what I was expecting."

"Are you saying I have a reputation?" I raise my eyebrows as if the idea surprises me.

He tilts his head to the side, pursing his lips as if choosing his words carefully. "Yes, you could say that. But as the only woman to graduate from the Academy, what can you expect? You didn't make many friends in the program, I'm guessing. Probably even some enemies given the way you consistently kick their asses in the stats every month."

Well. Now I'm starting to like this guy. It's not very often anyone acknowledges my efforts without some sort of insult tied in. I must look surprised by his comments, because he taps the fourth implant tattoo on his neck. It's the symbol for the ID implant, meaning he gets an instant neural upload of anyone's file, whenever he wants, just by looking at their face.

So jealous.

"Ah, I see. So, Gideon, why are you here? I'm sure there are much better bars up on the Solars." I don't actually mean that. I love this bar.

"Not really. It might look different up there, but people are still people, and rum is still rum." He punctuates that by taking a long drink. I watch the movement of his neck as he swallows, wishing I had gotten the chance to taste his skin, to run my tongue along his tattoos and down his chest. "I came here to find you. After I ran into you at Base, I just couldn't get you out of my mind."

I lick my lips, trying to push those mental images aside for later. "And you found me. So, what do you want to do with me?"

He pauses with his glass half-way to his mouth, a little of the heat returning to his eyes as he drops his gaze down to my mouth, to my chest. He wants me. It's so obvious, yet he's drawing it out. Making me doubt what I can feel simmering.

"I want to get to know you, Whisper. I want to take you out for dinner."

I nearly choke on my drink. I made it really freaking clear that I was a sure thing... and this guy wants to date me?

"I don't date." There's no beating around that one, so I might as well just spit it out. His eyes widen, as if he's not used to being turned down. Makes sense. Any girl would be crazy to turn him down. I'm not any girl. And I might be crazy. "Look. I respect you, and you seem like a decent guy. But you don't want to *get* to know *me*." I scoot forward on my seat until our thighs are touching, trailing my hand up his leg until it rests at his hip. "But I'd like to know you tonight. No complications, no dinner. Just two adults, finishing what you started out in that alley."

Black and white, buddy. Take it or leave.

He licks his lips, shifting in his seat as he adjusts his jeans. I try not to drool as I think about how close I was to getting my hands on that beautiful cock. I know it's beautiful, because the rest of him sure is. His eyes focus everywhere but on me, his jaw clenching and unclenching. What's up with this guy?

"I like you, Whisper. And I sure as hell want you. More than I've wanted anyone in a long time." That's a good start. "But I don't do one-night stands. Maybe I did in the past. In another life. But it's a rule I won't break."

Ouch.

"That's too bad, Gideon, because one night is all I do." And that's a rule I won't break.

He might think he likes me. He might think he's all noble and respectable, but he's a man. It wouldn't take long before he'd be bored with me and ready for a new toy. And even if he did stick around, I'd just get bored with him and be ready for a new toy. I like to fuck on occasion, but I don't need or want any of that emotional crap.

The only man I want to cuddle up and share I-love-you's with is big and furry. Damon is the only thing I've ever loved, and the only love I need.

Gideon nods, the open disappointment on his face almost making me sorry. He finishes his drink, sets his glass on the counter, and clears his throat. "Come work with me."

I laugh out loud, but quickly realize he's not laughing at all.

He's looking at me with a dead serious expression. I shake my head. This conversation is giving me whiplash.

"What do you want; a date or an Apprentice?"

"Both, preferably," he answers without hesitation.

I just stare at him dumbly, waiting for the punchline. Being taken as an Apprentice to an Elite is a big fucking deal. I'm not stupid enough to take him seriously.

After a long, awkward silence, he stands. The guy holds out his hand as if we just completed a business meeting. What the hell? Seriously, your tongue was down my throat less than ten minutes ago, and now we're going to shake hands?

Simply because I don't know what else to do, I take his hand and we shake. I'm not sure if I'm more attracted to him now that I know he's bat-shit crazy, or less.

Nah, pretty much the same. He's gorgeous.

"It was good to meet you, Whisper." His eyes flick briefly to my mouth. "I better get going before one of us breaks our own rules. If you change your mind, about either offer, give me a call."

He writes his number on a napkin, then gives me a wink. I'm fairly certain my chin hits my lap.

Just like that, he's gone.

Out of the corner of my eye I catch my drink being refilled. I turn my head to see Kelsey looking at me with a raised eyebrow. "Did I just see Whisper get turned down?"

"Worse. He wanted to *date* me."

She stares at me for a moment, as if waiting for a punch line. "Is that bad?"

I roll my eyes. "Have you ever seen me date anyone?"

"I would assume you don't bring your dates here. This is more of a place for finding a date, which it sounds like you did..." She's not appreciating my pain.

"Gideon isn't just everything I want in a fuckbuddy. He's everything I want to *be*, Kelsey." I'm whining because I know she'll listen whether she wants to or not. It's pretty much in her job description, both as my only female friend and as owner of the bar. "He's an Elite. There's no one above him. He answers directly to the Elders."

"Why do you want up there so bad? You're one of the top Agents. All your peers must either want to be you or be *with* you. How much more success do you need?"

I lower my eyes. When she puts it that way, I almost feel guilty for wanting more. I try to think of a witty comeback to lighten the conversation, but for some reason I just want to be honest. "I can't stay like this. What I've achieved might look like success, but I'm still the property of men. They tell me where to go and what to do. If I misstep or fail at a mission, they have the power to reduce me to nothing." The same nothing my parents and brothers always told me I was meant to be.

I nearly jump off my stool when she puts her hand on mine. She pulls back immediately, but the warmth of the gesture lingers on my skin. "You'll get there, if that's what you want. You've got the biggest balls in that place. I have no doubt about that."

We laugh together for a moment before she's called away by another customer.

"Text me if you feel like chatting," she calls back over her shoulder.

I almost want to stay and thank her for listening, for being a friend. The women I met at the Academy, the ones that worked staff positions or snuffed out of the Protector training program, they were far from friendly. Not that I put in the effort to build any bridges from my end. Kelsey's always been there, ever since I met her three years ago, on the night this place opened.

Fuck. I'm not going to get all sentimental just because I'm moping.

I down my drink in one pull. Suddenly, the only thing I want to do is go home and cuddle with my cat.

JOB OFFER

*a*pparently, that last drink did me in.

After leaving the bar to be greeted by an adorably pissed-off Retriever, I went straight home to crawl into bed with an equally pissed-off panther. I can literally change my clothes with just a thought, and yet I still passed out in my bar outfit. It takes a lot to get me drunk, thanks to my Medic. Lucky for me, it also has the handy side effect of making me immune to hangovers. And pregnancy... but that's not something I'm exactly at risk for with my current dry spell.

I push against the warm, furry body at my feet. Rolling onto my stomach, I groan as my face presses against a rough, thin napkin. I know without opening my eyes what it is.

"Can you believe that guy?" I say as I push myself off the bed, crumpling the napkin and chucking it into the garbage without bothering to look at the numbers. "He wanted to go on a *date*."

Didn't look like you were very opposed to that idea.

"Yeah right. I wanted to get laid. He wanted to have dinner."

I didn't like him.

I stretch my hands above my head, and my right shoulder adjusts with a satisfying pop.

"He's Gideon. One of the top Elites."

Damon just stares at me. His big, brown cat-eyes level with mine even though he's still laying down. His massive paws hang over the side of the bed, the end of his tail flicking from side to side. He clearly doesn't understand my problems, either.

"When I refused, he said he wanted to *work with me*. Can you imagine? Like I'd be so desperate to be his Apprentice that I'd go on a date with him just to get a shot."

But you do want to work with him.

"Sure. But making out at a bar isn't exactly official interview parameters. I'm not that naive."

Damon just huffs, clearly bored with the conversation.

I stand up from the bed, pausing to scratch him behind the ears for a bit before I head to the shower. As I start to walk away, one big paw hooks around my waist, pulling me back into a bear, er, cat-hug. I feel his teeth on my shoulder, biting down almost painfully, though I'd never let on it hurts.

It's something he's done since he was a kitten. I think it's a possessive thing, or a love thing. Maybe he just has to fight the urge to eat me now and again. I used to ask him why, but he's never given me a straight answer. Now, I just wait for him to let me go, then kiss him on the nose and walk away grateful I still have two arms.

Not that I think he would ever hurt me on purpose. I trust him with my life, one hundred percent. I just suspect that sometimes he struggles with his animal instincts more than others.

When he lets me go this time, I turn around and wrap my arms around his thick neck. We're the same height now, with him laying like a sphinx on my bed. I pull away and kiss the end of his nose, my hand trailing along the silvery scar that runs down his left front leg.

"I'm so glad you're not a man, Damon."

He growls, but it's not an angry sound. He knows what I mean.

I try again to make it to the shower, but my comm buzzes from its place on the bedside table. Heaving a sigh, I retrieve it. I'm only slightly worried it might be Gideon.

"It's Charles," I say as I smile and mentally high-five myself. "He has a job for us."

Damon immediately jumps from the bed, trotting out to the kitchen where he'll be waiting by the door. He likes the action almost as much as I do, even if he doesn't appreciate the kills.

"Let's eat before we check in!" I yell from the bedroom. If this job turns out to be a long one, I want a decent meal in my belly first.

"WHATCHA GOT FOR ME, CHARLES?" I ask as I push through the Commander's office door.

I'm in a great mood, despite my epic flop of a night. Nothing like the promise of a little action to make the world right again. It might not be exactly the kind of action I was searching for last night, but I'm pretty sure I like taking down bad guys just as much as I like sex.

He clears his throat. "Ah, Whisper..."

"Please let it be something interesting. I have some serious tension to work off-"

"Whisper, I believe you've met Elite Gideon." The Commander gestures past me, and I put two and two together to the sound of my least favorite feline laughing in my head.

I slow turn, standing a little straighter and plastering a smile on my face. "My apologies, Commander Jeffries. Elite Gideon."

I'm not sure what I interrupted, but I've never talked to

Charles so informally in front of anyone. Our personal relationship doesn't leave the privacy of his office. That's for both of our sakes. I don't need anyone assuming I'm getting special treatment, and he doesn't need anyone assuming he's giving it.

Because I'm not. And he's not.

It's because of him that I got my shot in the Academy, but it's my blood and sweat that got me through it. After I graduated, he wanted me on his team because I was good. Really good. Never once has he given me preferential treatment. He knows I'd be pissed if he even tried.

There's also the little issue of my future career with the Elites. Between this and the strange turn of events last night, I'm pretty sure Gideon isn't going to be singing my praises to the Elders. I basically threw myself at him... not that he was discouraging it in the beginning. And now he catches me being a little too friendly with my Commander. It's not the impression I imagined making if I ever found myself having an audience with an Elite.

"Good morning, Agent Whisper." Gideon's smile seems genuine as he reaches out a hand. I hesitate only a millisecond before taking it, and we shake hands like we just officially met. "It's refreshing to see a Commander having such a good rapport with his Agents."

Okay. That wasn't what I was expecting. "Commander Jeffries is an excellent Commander to work with, sir."

My eyes drop to his zipper when I say the word *sir*. I snap back at his face immediately, but it's clear my indiscretion didn't go unnoticed. He clears his throat, reaching a hand up to loosen his tie just a little.

"Elite Gideon arrived yesterday," Charles says, his voice back to normal after his obvious worry at the way I fumbled my way into this meeting. "He's looking to take on an Apprentice, and he was very impressed with your stats."

What the...

"I wanted to dig a little deeper into your jobs," Gideon adds, crossing his arms in front of his broad chest and keeping his eyes on mine. "Your stats are impressive, but that can just be the result of a lot of easy marks."

"I'm confident you'll find that's not the case." Very fucking confident. I'm also pretty confident that if he was seriously considering me, he won't be after last night. He's probably just here following through as a professional courtesy.

"Actually, I've finished my review. I was just in the middle of telling Commander Jeffries how impressed I am with what I saw. If you're interested, I'd like to start working together as soon as possible."

I clench my jaw to keep my chin from hitting the floor. My first instinct is that this is just some ploy; a game he's playing to get into my pants. But that's ridiculous, because we both know it was *me* who was trying to get into *his* pants.

Maybe he's setting me up... to embarrass me professionally as payback for last night. That doesn't make sense either. He's an Elite, not a Cadet with more spare time than brains.

What am I missing here, Damon?

I don't like him. He looks at you like you're food.

I don't know why I expected you to help.

I always help. We don't need him.

"Whisper has been looking for an opening with the Elite program," Jeffries speaks up, because it's clear I've lost my own ability to talk. He must notice how uncertain I am, because he quickly adds, "But I'm not sure this is the route she was searching for. Perhaps she can get back to you at a later date if she's interested?"

I'm still trying to find the hole, the catch, the hidden agenda that I'm clearly missing. Although I'm really good at ignoring him, Damon's warning isn't something I take lightly. He might not be a big talker, but when he voices his opinion it's usually for a good reason.

"I'd be interested in hearing the details," I blurt out, not entirely sure if I sound professional or terrified.

"Perfect." Gideon nods to Charles, reaching out to shake my hand yet again. He appears completely satisfied at the way this little meeting played out. "I'll pick you up at six. We can talk about the details over a meal."

He fails at hiding a grin as my eyes probably double in size. Did he just use a business proposal to get the date he wanted? Or was the date actually about the business proposal... *'I like you, Whisper. And I sure as hell want you. More than I've wanted anyone in a long time.'* No, that wasn't about business.

I don't know what this guy's real motives are, and that pisses me off.

Not that it matters now. The joke's on him if he thinks he's getting a date *or* a fuckbuddy out of this deal. I just want my ticket to the Solars.

NOT A DATE

he glowing display on my kitchen wall swaps over to 6:00 just as a dark green SUV pulls into my short driveway. I grab my bag of necessities and head out, not wanting to give him the chance to meet me at my door.

I skip down the few stairs, wearing a casual pair of black pants and a dark blue button-up blouse. It's business casual, which is what I'm hoping this little meeting will be. No one needs to know I spent the last few hours cycling through outfits to achieve that particular mixture of business and casual.

My hair is loose, hanging in thick waves. I've got a hair tie around my wrist, just in case the breeze picks up. A touch of mascara and some lip gloss, and I'm feeling more dressed-up than I have in a long time.

It's not a date.

I have no reason to be nervous.

The vehicle's windows are tinted so I can't see the person behind the wheel. Instinct has me putting a hand on the pistol at my hip, but any concern I have is short lived. The driver's door opens and Gideon steps out.

He's wearing a dark pair of jeans, fitted to his body as if they were tailored just for him. I stop in my tracks, helpless to prevent my eyes from travelling up his long legs, over the black button-up shirt that accentuates his gloriously ripped body, and directly to the smile that's playing across his lips. Lips I can vividly remember kissing mine like a fantasy come to life.

He is painfully sexy. He's also dressed much more casual than business. It doesn't matter. Tonight, I'm all business.

I've been thinking about it all day. If his offer is genuine, if he wants to give me a shot, I can't pass that up. I also won't be accused of sleeping my way up the ladder. That means even if he decides to take me up on last night's proposition, it has officially expired. That also means I need to stop looking at him like he's got the lead role in all my wildest fantasies.

"Hello, Elite Gideon." I greet him formally as I tear my gaze away from his body to look instead at his freshly washed truck. "I'll take my truck, so Damon doesn't shed on your seats."

"No need," he answers quickly. "Tarek's a bear by default. I'm used to the fur."

He opens the back door and I glance down at Damon, who's standing tight against my side. He looks up at me as he growls low in his chest, ears flattening briefly against his head.

"Don't worry, it's been cleaned. You won't smell like a bear when you get out."

I laugh because I know that's just what Damon was thinking. It's refreshing to be around someone who understands how Shifters think. They aren't exactly social butterflies.

"Come on," I say as I give him a rough pat on the head. He growls but follows my lead, jumping through the open door as I climb into the front.

Gideon slides in beside me, and I inhale a little deeper as his unique scent fills the space. A hint of expensive cologne mingles with a freshly showered, almost soapy smell. It's the same scent he was wearing last night, and the memories flood my mind. I squirm in the seat and wish that I had insisted on taking my own ride.

"Everything okay?"

"Fine," I answer a little too quickly, then clear my throat and remind myself that this is not a date. This is a job interview.

"Where's Tarek?"

"Probably above us. He likes his wings, and he doesn't like people. He's always close enough to communicate."

"Damon is pretty clingy. He doesn't let me too far from sight."

Maybe if you didn't take so many stupid risks. I ignore the voice in my head and the accompanying growl from the backseat.

"I can't say I blame him. You must have to watch your back more than most of us."

"I like to think I can hold my own."

"I have no doubt you can."

I look for the sarcasm that I assume is behind that comment, but his expression is neutral as he stares ahead at the road. I take a moment to appreciate the slight flex in his arm as he grips the wheel before averting my eyes safely back to my own side.

"Where are we going?"

"Nowhere special. Just a little diner I like with private booths so we can chat."

"Is that where you wanted to take me when you asked last night?" Holy shit. Did I seriously just bring that up? I sink a little lower in my seat and keep my eyes locked out my side window.

Of course, Gideon laughs, perfectly unfazed by my lapse. "No. I would have taken you somewhere much nicer than a diner. But you don't date."

It's safer if I just don't respond.

He seems to find that funny as well, and he laughs again. The sound is rich and deep as it fills the space around us. My embarrassment is fading, and it's quickly being replaced by just being pissed off at myself. I need to do a serious course correction here. Remind him why he's even considering me for his Apprentice.

I open my mouth to change the subject, but the vehicle slows as he turns into the parking lot of a local diner.

"Have you eaten here before?"

"No, I haven't gotten around to it yet."

I'm not about to tell him I despise fast food. It's kind of a hang-up from growing up eating nothing but take-out. After a while it all starts to taste the same; the subtle flavors of a shitty childhood.

"It's good. Tastes just like home cooking." He parks and slides out of his seat, opening the door for Damon. "Do you want to wait here? They won't let you inside, but if you have a form that blends in you can wait by the door."

Damon growls, baring his long, white fangs.

Come on buddy, just be polite to the guy.

I still don't like him.

He apparently decides to set his ego aside, because when his paws touch the ground he's in his Retriever form.

"Nice. Good choice."

"Only problem is that people tend to want to touch him when he's waiting alone."

"I suppose, but it's a breed that people are comfortable around, while still having the size to take down a human if something went south. It's a good choice."

Maybe he's a little smarter than I thought.

ONCE WE'RE SETTLED into our table, with burgers and fries on the way, it's even harder to keep my eyes off Gideon. It's one of those classic half-circle booths, and we're facing each other from opposite ends. I don't have any food to focus on yet, so I settle for inspecting the ice cubes in my glass as I stir them slowly with a straw.

I can feel him watching me, clearly not experiencing the same awkwardness I can't seem to shake. I suck in a breath, swallowing the ridiculous butterflies that seem intent on escaping my stomach.

"Why are you considering me for your Apprentice?"

I look him straight in the eyes. His lips part as he takes a deep breath. It seems I can affect him just as much as he affects me. I just need to take back the power that gives me, and then find a way to use it.

As he opens his mouth to respond, our food arrives. I have to admit it looks pretty good, and there's so much on the plate even Damon will get a good meal out of it. We both thank the young waitress, but she can't keep her eyes off Gideon. He smiles at her and I swear she actually melts into a puddle right in front of us.

Girl, I know how you feel.

"I already told you, your stats are impressive. You clearly have the skill and experience that this job requires."

"Sure, but you told me that back at Base. Why are we here, Elite Gideon?"

He nods, but instead of responding he takes a bite of his burger. I force myself not to watch him eat.

After a moment, he slides his plate across the table, moving along the booth until he's sitting so close I can feel the heat from his body. I know he's doing it for privacy, to be sure our conversation isn't overheard. Having him closer does nothing to help the war that's raging between my libido and my brain.

"I'm well aware that you're a woman, Whisper. I'm also well aware that nearly everyone in this organization thinks you shouldn't be where you are. I also know you have a superpower."

That statement takes me completely off guard. I stop mid-bite and set my burger down. I turn my body just enough to let him know he has my full attention. How does he know about my superpower?

"Any other Agent with your skill level can be seen coming a mile away. We all present the same. Same body type, same walk, same look in our eyes. It just comes with the job. But not you." He gives me an obvious once-over for the first time this evening. "Your marks must never see you coming, even when you're standing right in front of them."

"Are you suggesting I use my body to get at my marks?"

Yeah, I definitely do that. But my tone says I'm highly offended that he would suggest such a thing.

This is starting to play out like a trap. Like he's baiting me to admit to some unsavory thing; to cheating. There's nothing in the rulebook that says I can't use any means necessary to get what I'm after. Taking out the mark is the job. How I accomplish that is my business.

"It would be effective."

His tone isn't giving me any hints about what he wants to hear.

"I do whatever works. I study their files and figure out the perfect predator for my prey." Might as well spell it out for him. If he wants me to work with him, he's going to figure it out eventually. "If sniping or brute force is best, that's what I do. If they like vulnerable, innocent girls, I can do that, too. And if they like something a little more mature..."

I let my eyes drop to his mouth, as I slowly moisten my lips with the tip of my tongue. His eyes are drawn to the movement like a magnet, and in that moment, I make my shirt fade into a lacy, see through material. Right on cue, his eyes drop farther, down to the strappy, green bra that doesn't leave much to the imagination.

His lips part as his breathing becomes shallow. I gently rest my hand on his thigh, running my fingers up his leg as I lean almost imperceptibly closer. He mirrors the movement, leaning slightly toward me. I could kiss him so easily right now.

He reaches a hand toward my face, and in one quick movement I remove the gun from its holster at his hip. The barrel is pressed firmly into his ribs before he even has a chance to register what happened.

The look on his face is priceless.

Honestly, I will remember this moment for the rest of my life. It's a mixture of shock, embarrassment, confusion, fear... it's all there and I have all I can do not to laugh. I lay the weapon, safety still on, in the space between us. I return my shirt to its original fabric. I think I'll keep the bra for now.

I go back to eating, acting deliberately casual, as if nothing happened. He holsters his gun, still staring at me even though he's schooled his expression. I wish he would speak, but instead he follows my lead and goes back to eating. Even if that little demonstration lost me the job, I'd have to say it was well worth it.

We eat our fill, and although Gideon finishes his I've still got a good portion left for Damon. He insists on paying, since this was a business meeting, so I head out to get a few moments alone with Damon while he waits for the bill.

I lean against the truck as he eats my leftovers, still in his Retriever form. The air is still, and unusually warm for this time of evening. A little treat predicted for the next week or so, before the expected rain arrives.

Did you take the offer?

I'm not even sure if the offer's still on the table.

What did you do?

I showed him what I can do. Men don't like being overpowered by a woman. He's a nice guy, but I'm pretty sure he's not quite so eager to work with me now.

Nice guy?

"Hey, beautiful."

I turn my head toward the raspy voice that interrupted our silent conversation. A heavyset man is approaching us. He's about five-eight with full sleeve tattoos on either arm. Shoulder length blond hair and light eyes. No implant tats. He's walking toward me from the direction of a few parked cars and a group of about a dozen other men, all with the same unkempt hair and tattoos.

"You're looking a little lonely out here all by yourself." He stops beside me, leaning against the side of the truck as he reaches to touch the ends of my hair.

See, my problem is that I could take this guy easily. Just a little show of confidence and strength is usually all it takes to get an ass like him to back off. He'd call me a few choice words to shore up his ego, but ultimately go along his merry way. The problem comes if he doesn't take the cue. If he persists and I end up in an altercation with an unmarked civilian, who then gets injured, who then decides to complain to the Protectors. I can't afford to give them an excuse to suspend me.

Usually, I have a giant panther beside me to tip them off that I'm not such an easy target. Damon's still in his Retriever form, and he knows the situation as well as I do. If he shifts now and this guy pisses himself, he'll go crying to my bosses' boss just the same as if I broke his arm.

"I'm good, thanks," I say in a casual tone. "My date will be out any minute now."

"Ah, I see." A smile spreads across his face as if he's taken my statement as a challenge. "It looks to me like your date doesn't know how to show a woman like you a good time. How about you come with us, and I'll make you forget all about him."

He punctuates his offer by moving his hand up to tuck my hair behind my ear, then running his thick knuckles along my cheek.

"Made a new friend, Agent Whisper?" Gideon's voice is close, and I exhale the breath I've been holding since this dick put his hands on me.

I look up into his dull blue eyes, noticing that the whites have a faint yellow tint. I push my hair back over my shoulder, so he can see the implant tats now visible on my neck. A second later his eyes widen as I hear the unmistakable growl of my panther.

"How about you come with us, and we can talk about what exactly you like to do to lonely women after you lure them into your group?"

"I was just playing." He backs away, his hands raised in a gesture of surrender as his eyes dart between me, Damon, and Gideon. "We'd never hurt anyone."

I turn my back on him, opening the back door of the truck for Damon before letting myself into the front. Gideon is already behind the wheel when I close my door. His tires squeal on the concrete as we leave the diner.

"Why did you let him touch you like that?" He sounds genuinely pissed off, and for some reason that makes me a little happy.

"It's not a big deal."

"He could have hurt you."

"I heal." I tap my Medic tat for emphasis.

"Shit, Whisper. Do you like that kind of attention? Do you like putting yourself in danger?" Oh, he is really pissed.

"Gideon, seriously. What do you think would happen-"

"I think he would-"

"No. What do you think would happen if I gave that guy a broken bone, a black eye, or hell, even just wounded his pride? He'd go running to Base and report me for misconduct. We both know that my bosses would jump on any excuse to get me out of this program."

Gideon doesn't reply, but I can see his jaw flexing like he's grinding his teeth to keep from speaking. He's got both hands on the wheel, gripping it far tighter than necessary. It's pretty sexy, seeing him get all worked up. It's also a little sad, because I think this is honestly the first time he's realized how fucked up the system really is.

We pull into my driveway, and he jumps out to open Damon's door. I start toward the house, but my mind is spinning. I don't have a clue how to wrap up this interview, if it's even still an interview. I pretty much stomped all over his ego when I pulled that stunt in the diner... and then he saw me cower under the attention of that scumbag.

I keep walking until I have one hand on my door handle. When I turn around, Gideon's just a few feet away. He's also two steps down, making us about the same height. His forehead is creased, and he's looking off to the side. It gives me a chance to appreciate his features in the dim light from the bulb above my door.

When he turns his gaze on me, his eyes are shadowed with concern. It's kind of touching that this is bothering him so much.

With that inhuman speed of his, he's up the stairs before I even register he's moved. He plants his left hand on the door behind me, and his other hand tangles in my hair, cupping the back of my head. His lips are touching mine before I come to my senses and plant a firm hand on his chest.

A slight push is all it takes. He backs up immediately, running a nervous hand through his hair.

"I'm sorry, Whisper." It's as if he's apologizing on behalf of his gender. Or the entire system we live in. This guy needs to relax a little.

"I'm going to be an Elite. Maybe not now, through you, but someday. However flawed this system might be, it hasn't stopped me yet."

"It's not fair."

I can only laugh. "Goodnight, Gideon. Thank you for considering me for your Apprentice."

I hold out my hand, and he doesn't hesitate to shake it. I open my door, letting Damon in first before I follow, closing and locking it behind us.

I let out a long breath.

Damon's big head pushes against me until I finally clue in and start scratching his ears. He keeps pushing until I just give in and sit on the floor, granting him full access to rub his face against mine and bite at my shoulder. He's rougher than usual, wrapping a paw around my waist as his teeth and rough tongue claim my neck, shoulder and arms.

Jealous much.

"Buddy, easy, I get it. You own me."

You're mine.

I laugh at his display, even though it occurs to me that he might be a tad more possessive than the average Shifter.

BETRAYAL

$\mathcal{I}$ wake up late the next morning to find Damon stretched out alongside me. I don't remember having a nightmare, but I'm wrapped around him just the same.

I wonder what would've happened if I'd been more encouraging when Gideon tried to kiss me... if it would be his warm body against mine now, instead of this furry heat pad. I almost want him to officially take back his offer and pick another Apprentice. Maybe then... That's just my starving libido talking. I want that job more than I want a night with any man. Plus, Mr. Manners doesn't do casual sex. Even if it's obvious he wants it bad.

I roll out of bed, removing my clothes as I head to the bathroom. My comm buzzes, but I ignore it. I need a long, hot shower before I start another day of begging for work. I take a little extra time to think about Gideon while the steaming water runs over me, letting myself imagine him here. I picture the cascading water soaking his beautiful body as his hands slide across my skin.

It's a pale substitute for the real thing, but at least a little solo action will keep me from chasing after the first acceptable male I come across today.

After my shower, I grab my comm with fingers crossed. My hopes are up when I see there's a text message from Charles, but when I open it, I have to read it twice before I can process what it says.

Charles: Sounds like your meeting went well. Elite Gideon left word that your comm is registered at the Teleports. You can check in at Headquarters on Solar One tomorrow. If you're accepting the offer?

"Shit, Damon. We got the job."

What job?

He jumps down from the bed as I start to sift through my closet, trying to decide if I've got something to wear or if I should just convert some dirty laundry.

"With Gideon, dumbass." I read him the text from Charles, realizing I didn't actually message him back yet.

Me: Yes, of course! If you can spare me... I know I'm your best Agent ;)

He doesn't respond to that, but I'm too wired to even care. It's nearly 11:00 now, so I gather some leftovers from the fridge for Damon to eat.

"This is it, Damon. We're finally going up there."

Nothing wrong with down here.

"Buddy, I love you, but you're a pain in the ass." His eyes are narrow slits as he lowers his head, ears flattened, and begins to stalk toward me.

My comm buzzes with a new message. I dodge Damon's advance and scoot to the kitchen.

Charles: Can I buy you a drink to celebrate?

Me: Ok...

Charles: Don't worry, I won't make you hang out with the old folks for long. Meet me at that bar you like at 7?

Me: Sounds good!

He wants to say goodbye. When I go up there tomorrow, I'll

be working for Gideon. If I get a permanent position, I'll be working for the Elders directly. All this I knew, but the sudden reminder makes my head spin.

I brace myself against the small kitchen island, taking a deep breath to center myself. I've only ever worked for Commander Jeffries. He's supported me since day one and stepping out from under him is a little bit terrifying, to say the least.

Are you okay?

"I'm good. I just... it's a lot to process."

"ARE YOU SERIOUS?" Kelsey's voice jumps a couple octaves as she folds her hands in front of her chest, almost like a prayer.

"You bet. I head up there first thing in the morning."

She squeals and does a strange little wiggle, then reaches out to put a hand on mine. "I'm so proud of you. You're a good person, Whisper. You deserve this."

I don't get a chance to reply before she's summoned away by another customer. Her words make me all warm and tingly inside, and I haven't even started drinking yet. Can't say I agree about the 'good person' bit, but it's nice to hear it anyway.

"There's my girl!"

Charles's voice is warm and just a little thicker than usual. Guess I shouldn't have bothered saving the first drink of the evening for his arrival. He clearly started without me.

"Charles!" I say with equal enthusiasm, and he doesn't even blink at my use of his first name in public. A new era indeed.

He pats me roughly on the back as he takes the seat beside me, ordering up two imported beers that I've never tried. Kelsey slides the open bottles across the bar, and Charles taps his against mine with a satisfying *clink*.

"To you."

It seems like he might add more to the toast, but he thinks better of it and drinks. I laugh as I join him happily. I'm not a beer fan, but I have to admit this goes down smooth. Guess the price tag does make a difference. I might order this on a regular basis, once I'm earning the wages of an Elite.

We chat. We drink. I dance with anyone who looks like they know how to move.

The hours fly by and before I know it, I'm feeling more buzzed than I have in a long time. I'm way passed buzzed; I'm drunk. I laugh just thinking about it, and Charles laughs right along with me.

He's my new best friend.

"I gotta go home, buddy," I finally concede sometime after midnight. I'm hitting that wall where all I want to do is get home and snuggle my kitty.

"Yes, ma'am! You have to get up for work in the morning!" Charles slaps his hands on the table we migrated to. Come on, I'll call us a ride."

"No, my truck..."

He waves a hand, dismissing my concern. "I'll have our vehicles delivered before morning, no need to worry about it."

Sounds like a good plan to me. I step out into the warm night air, expecting it to straighten me up a little. Strangely enough, it has the opposite effect and I feel myself sway.

"Gotcha," Charles says, hooking his arm under mine and letting me lean on him. He's such a good man.

... one... okay?

Alcohol has never affected our Link before. I try to catch a glimpse of Damon, but Charles is the only thing keeping me upright. I didn't mean to overdo it, I was just... we were only...

I'm okay, just need to sleep it off.

I'm not even certain if he heard me, and as I'm looking around to spot him Charles guides me into the back seat of a car. I can't even think about resisting, I just want to be home in bed. I catch a quick glimpse of a golden dog as we pull away. He's going to be so pissed.

My head lands on Charles's shoulder. He smells like leather and beer and something smoky. I should apologize for my behavior, but the dim interior of the car is fading to a peaceful black.

We're walking again. His arm is around my waist now, and I'm barely contributing to the effort of walking up the stairs and into my own house.

He unlocks the door. I must have given him the key.

I'm sitting on the cool floor now, my back against the kitchen island. Charles is pacing in front of me. Back and forth, back and forth. Why is he so steady? Hell, I should be able to out-drink a man twice my age.

"This was never supposed to end this way, Jane."

I haven't heard that name since the ceremony that made me an Agent. It's the name my parents gave me. Whisper's my real name. Whisper in the Dark, my brothers called me. I was good at slipping around the house without a sound. That's the name I earned.

"Charles..."

My own voice is foreign to my ears. My arms are useless weights at my side.

"It's that assholes fault. Thinking he's being progressive, or clever, or maybe he just wants to get in your pants. Who the hell knows. Not like you'd play hard to get with him anyway."

He's pacing, running his hands through his hair. He looks over at me, as I'm looking back at him. His expression is pained, but I watch the emotion slowly melt into a deadly calm. He walks toward me, crouches down, and grips my chin with cold hands.

"Do you understand?"

I don't understand anything. Everything is wrong. I didn't drink that much, and drunk doesn't feel like this. I want to ask what's happening, but my mind is foggy and my body's dead weight.

"Jane." He says that name again, and I want to break his jaw. "You were never supposed to make it past the Academy. You sure as hell shouldn't have made it out of the Enforcers. A female Agent. Hell. What did you think would happen? Did you think you'd be allowed to continue? I tried. I really tried. Keep you busy, keep you on the ground. That was the condition. But you had to go and hook that... that Gideon."

Whisp... Damon's voice is in my head. He's close. I hear him scratch at the door, and I try to speak to him through our Link, but I don't think it's working. I've never left him behind. I've never locked him out.

"Dammit." Charles lets go of my face as he looks toward the door. "I'm going to kill you, Jane. I don't want to, but it's the price I have to pay for letting it get this far."

My heart's beating faster than it should, or possibly not at all. I hear him. Hear every fucking word, but it doesn't make sense. This is Commander Jeffries. Charles. He's always had my back. He's the one person I'd trust with my life...

"If I could've convinced you to stay on the ground, mind your business and do your job." He shakes his head, scrubbing a hand over his face. "But you won't, and now we've come to this."

The scratching at the door intensifies, joined by the heavy thuds of a body being thrown against it.

Charles stands, starts to walk away, then turns back to me as he levels a 9mm at my head. I can't believe this is how it ends. Betrayed in my own home. Without so much as a struggle.

I'm sorry, Damon. I love you. I pray he can hear me. My death will kill him. The loss of a bondmate triggers a Shifter's body to shut down. He'll be dead within a couple weeks, if his broken heart doesn't destroy him sooner. That thought makes my lungs contract, as my body starts to vibrate.

"Please..." I rasp out, as Charles's already pained expression crumbles even more. His hands shake as they grip his weapon of choice.

A bolt of pain slices through my eardrums as a shot splits the air. White-hot pain sears across my neck. Fuck. When's the last time this asshole fired his weapon?

The scratching at the door becomes frantic, though it's muffled and distant to my ears. He won't get through. He'll bloody himself trying, but the tech that kept us safe will seal our fate.

I close my eyes, waiting for the next shot. I summon my superpower, detaching from the pain and the fear, forcing my body to relax and take in air for as many breaths as I have left.

Something's happening. New sounds reach me through the fog. I struggle to bring my mind back to the present. Just as the room comes into focus, fresh pain detonates in my left side.

I grit my teeth against the pain, seeing the tile floor against my face. Its white surface is streaked with red. I see the door, open. Damon. Where's Damon? Please don't let him kill Damon before me.

Charles. He's on the floor, too. There's another man, standing over him. Naked. Makes sense. It makes sense that my brain would create a hallucination of the perfect male as it's last act. Fuck, why do my eyes have to be so blurry?

"Damon..." I feel the vibration of my words even though I can't hear them.

"I'm here, little one." I hear his voice. He's here, somewhere. Relief floods my veins, but I'm just so tired. I can't fight anymore.

DAMON

$\mathcal{I}$ am helpless to save her.

The thought only fuels my anger. This house was built to shelter us, coated in tech to protect us while we sleep. Now, it keeps me out like a fly against the window. Even my claws, sharpened to lethal points, are useless against the invisible barrier.

I keep trying. I claw and throw my weight against the door, then the window. Let my flesh tear and my body break if it means I have any hope of getting through.

If only I were bigger. Much bigger.

I picture the biggest creature I've ever laid eyes on. A massive, green dragon. The Elite's Shifter, Tarek. I saw him only from a distance, hovering in the air far above his bondmate. I try to picture the details of his form, try to make it my own.

I imagine wings sprouting from my back as scales replace my dense fur. I imagine my muscles stretching, expanding, growing until I can tear the roof off this tiny building. I try to harness the power and the strength that form would give me.

A gunshot sounds from inside my home. A strangled scream

reaches my ears, turning my anger into blinding rage. I can't grasp the dragon's form. I can't get through this cursed door.

I can't lose my Whisper.

If only... A thought strikes me, bringing with it a cold, clear determination. She hides a key to this door. A silly hang-up from her childhood, she says. From the years when keeping a key hidden was the only guarantee she had of being able to get inside her own home.

I pivot, leaping down the stairs and tearing up the lawn as I bolt around to the side of the house. A drainpipe. A patch of rocky turf. A few scrapes of my claws and a small, wooden box is unearthed.

Now my strength, my claws, my crushing jaws and deadly fangs... they are all useless for what I need to do. I imagine the form I need. It feels oddly familiar, almost welcoming, and I give myself over to the shift.

A rush of thoughts and emotions hit me like a physical blow to the head. My ears are ringing as my chest constricts with a wave of sheer panic. My body folds, falling to the ground on human hands and knees. Cold air rushes against vulnerable, hairless skin.

Sparks of white light cloud my vision. I blink and shake my head until I can see the small box on the ground in front of me. Reaching, I fumble again and again until I can finally control my long, awkward fingers. At last, I have it in my grasp, folding it open to reveal the shiny, metal key.

I stumble and trip over myself as I scramble to get back to the front door. With shaking hands, I fumble some more at the door handle before it mercifully clicks and the barrier between me and my Whisper is gone at last.

As the door swings open, I see a man. The Commander. He has a gun aimed at Whisp, who slouches like a doll against the island. Her limbs are slack, her head is tilted to reveal a red wound on her delicate neck.

I shift back to my panther form, growling my deadly intent as I leap at his body. The weapon fires before he attempts to turn it on me. He's too slow. He yells in fear as I plough into him, knocking him to the floor. The gun flies from his grip as his skull cracks against the hard floor. I close my jaws around his head, ready and willing to end this traitor permanently.

A soft whimper cuts through me like a knife. I turn toward Whisper to find her laying on her side. Red soaks through her shirt, and she gazes out at me with unfocused eyes. I forget the man on the floor, and I coax my body to take human form once again.

The headrush is slightly less painful this time. I force the onslaught of thoughts and emotions away, focusing on the only thing that matters.

"Damon..." Her voice is so frail.

"I'm here, little one," I say, speaking the words into the air between us.

She smiles softly, her face relaxing as her eyes close. I push the hair back from her neck. It's just a graze. Nothing her Medic can't handle. Holding my breath, I peel back the shirt from her abdomen. The wound looks painful, but it was another miss. Two splintered holes mark the places where the bullets struck the wooden island. I silently thank god, the universe, fate... whoever I should be thanking.

I glance behind me to make sure the Commander hasn't woken. He's right where I left him. Anger boils in my veins, but making Whisper comfortable is my first priority.

Sliding my arms gently under her small form, I lift her off the cold floor and cradle her against my body. She's warm and comfortable against me, and when I reach our bedroom, I'm almost reluctant to lay her down. It feels so good to be this close to her.

I put aside my selfishness and tuck her into the covers, leaving her for just a moment to fetch a warm, wet cloth from the bathroom. I clean her wounds as gently as I can. It's all I can do. Her heart beats strong, her breathing is steady, and her Medic will help her heal before any infection gets the chance to set in.

I stand by the bed and watch her, uncertain what to do next. I look down at my human form, then turn my head to catch my reflection in the tall mirror Whisp keeps in the corner of the room. It's strange, as any new form is, but it's also... comfortable.

I flex and stretch, intrigued at the way the muscles bunch and move under my skin. I touch every part I can reach, enjoying the sensations that ripple across my exposed flesh.

A sound comes from the direction of the kitchen. Movement. I shift to my panther form and head out to investigate. When I round the corner, the Commander is pulling himself up. The back of his head is matted with blood, but his legs are steady.

I lower my head, flattening my ears and baring my teeth in a growl that makes it clear his death is approaching.

He spins around, wobbling a bit before regaining his footing.

"Damon!" He shouts my name, holding up his hands in a gesture of surrender. "Please, Damon. I had no choice. If I didn't do it myself, they would have killed us both. I didn't want to do it. I never wanted to hurt her. But they would have done so much worse, I couldn't let them..."

I jump toward him, snarling as I swipe a clawed paw mere inches from his face. He cowers instantly, sniveling and mumbling and making more excuses.

"Please, if you kill me they will execute you and charge Whisp with my murder. I deserve it. I know that I deserve it. If you let me go, I'll do my best to slow them down."

I step back. He has a point, that I know, but without Whisper here to tell me what I should do, I'm torn. My instinct is to kill him for what he did, but there's also a part of me that wants to stand down and wait for her orders.

"Please, Damon." There's something satisfying about him begging for his life.

He inches backward. My hind legs are poised to leap as my jaws flex in anticipation. I've never wanted to kill a living thing as badly as I want to kill this man. I hold my ground. When the door shuts behind him, I shift to human form and lock it.

Returning to Whisper's side, I crawl carefully onto the bed. I stretch out beside her, as I always do when she has a nightmare. I touch her face, her hair, her arm. The feel of her skin against mine is like something out of a dream.

When sleep finally pulls my eyes closed, I'm confident that tomorrow she will wake up healthy and whole. And she will know exactly what we should do.

~

I'M IN MY BED. Alive.

The light streaming through the curtains says it's close to noon. Last night's clothes are blood stained and stinking, but a moment's concentration has them swapped out for clean sweat-pants and a t-shirt. It does nothing for the filth on my skin, but it's something.

Thanks to my Medic, there's no lingering effects of whatever drug took me out last night. There's some discomfort in my side, but a quick check confirms that no injury remains. The pain is just my brain struggling to process the unnatural healing. I'm back to full health. Full strength.

I turn from the window, expecting to see Damon beside me. My breath catches in my throat at the sight of a very naked man in his place. He's stretched out on his stomach, bare ass and long legs like a leftover figment of my delirium.

"Damon!" I call out, trying not to let the fear take over. He's fine. He has to be fine.

Naked Man jolts at my sudden outburst. He props himself up on his elbows and turns his face toward me. Shaggy, black hair cascades around his face. Dark eyes look into mine as a smile lights up his features. He's familiar... I can't quite place him. I should be terrified that he hurt Damon, but... his eyes. There's something so familiar.

"Who are you?"

Naked Man pushes himself up, sliding off the bed. He's moving deliberately slowly, which is smart because if he makes any sudden moves, I'll have the pistol out of it's headboard compartment before he can blink. He stands, turns to face me, and sweet fuck I must be dead.

This man is built out of my daydreams. He is seriously the most beautiful human I've ever laid eyes on. And he's hung like a porn star. He's not even hard, and that thing is huge. My mouth is watering, and my throat is dry; I'm not even sure if those two things can happen at the same time, but that's where I'm at.

"You know who I am."

His voice. It's as familiar as my own.

I force my eyes away from his cock and up to his ribs. A chill spreads through me as I see three scars, like claw marks. The left side of his neck; another scar that trails down over his shoulder. His right arm; an almost silvery line from shoulder to wrist.

I slide my legs off the bed, turning my back to him. My feet planted firmly on the floor, I brace my elbows on my knees and lean forward. I need to focus on breathing. I'm going insane. I force myself to think about last night, about every detail as hazy and muffled as it all is.

I'm fucked. Charles poisoned me and brought me home to kill

me. My only supporter, the closest thing I had to family, and he was just biding his time hoping I'd wash out or be killed? Nothing was real.

Damon... It can't be true. It can't be him.

It's okay, little one. We're okay.

No. No, please tell me that's not you. You can't take human form. It'll destroy you.

"They were wrong." Same voice, but not in my head.

I feel the bed dip, but I can't move. I can't look. I want so desperately to turn and see the familiar brown eyes, the big, furry body. Instead, a wide, warm hand slides against my back. I sit up straight and his breath is against my neck, his face in my hair as he inhales. Then, the gentle bite of teeth on my shoulder. It's too much. So familiar yet so fucked up.

I jump to my feet, turning to face him. He's already standing, inches from me, looking down at me with Damon's eyes. Damon's face. It might be the first time he's taken this form, but it's him as clear as day.

"What did you do with Charles?"

"He's alive. He convinced me that killing him would only bring you more trouble."

I nod. If I'd had any control over my own body, he'd be dead. But Damon's right, it would have only brought more trouble down on us.

"I need a shower, and you need to change back before you do some permanent damage."

I head for the bathroom, but his arm hooks my waist and pulls me back against him. The heat from his body soaks through me from head to toe. His wide hand is splayed across my stomach, and pressed against my back... I can't think about it. This is Damon, not a man. This is so wrong. I push away and he lets me go.

In the shower, my hands are shaking as I work the shampoo through my thick hair. I need to think.

I've been through shit before, I'm certainly not going to sit around and cry about my misfortune now. To hell with Commander Jeffries. He's got no say over the Elites, and I've already secured my offer from Gideon. I might be running late for my first day, but I'm going up there and you can be damn sure I'm going to prove I'm worthy of a permanent position.

I have a feeling I need to earn that title sooner, rather than later.

I'll come back to the coward another day, when I'm an Elite, and find out what the hell happened. For now, it doesn't matter. I just need to keep moving forward, like I always have.

Shake it off and show up.

I convert my sweats and t-shirt into dress pants and a crimson button-up before stepping back into my bedroom. My heart leaps at the sight of the big, black cat perched like a sphinx on my bed. I feel like I haven't seen him since we left yesterday. I walk up to him and put my hands on his face, rubbing him behind the ears and down his thick neck.

"Are you okay?"

Fuck, I hope he hasn't suffered some irreversible brain damage from that stupid stunt. I can't even imagine-

Look at me, Whisp.

His voice has a different tone, a new edge that wasn't there before. I do as he asks, looking into soft, chocolate eyes that are the same as they have always been, yet different somehow.

"Please tell me you're okay. I can't lose you, Damon."

They were wrong.

He wraps his big paws around me as his form reshapes into the man. I try to push away, but he holds me tight. He's sitting on the edge of the bed, looking up at me as his hands move to grip my hips, preventing me from putting some distance between us.

I can't look at him. I just have to close my eyes.

"They were wrong. It was strange at first; the thoughts... the emotions. It was like I suddenly had answers to questions I hadn't even considered asking. The world got a lot bigger and a lot more complicated. I remembered things I've heard in the past, things that didn't seem important, but now make sense. The animal brain is simple, basic. But the thoughts I have in this form, I don't even know how to describe them."

"Damon, what if it's hurting you? What if it's causing damage you can't sense yet? Everyone knows Shifters can't take human form. It's too much. It will drive you insane. That's why it's illegal for you to even try. They will put you down if they find out. I can't lose you."

"Look at me!"

"Fuck, Damon!" I snap at him, and he finally lets me pull out of his grip. I immediately feel bad for yelling at him, but shit, this is just beyond reality. I grab a towel and chuck it in his general direction. "Just wrap that around your waist at least."

He laughs. Fuck, it's a sexy sound. I've heard him laugh in my head, but through the air it's like I can feel the vibration on my skin. This is not good. I might have entertained some dark fantasies in the past, but this is much too real. I can not be attracted to Damon.

"Look at me," he demands again, and I do as he wants.

He's wrapped the towel low around his waist, tucked in the same way I tuck my own. It's almost worse than seeing him naked. His long, strong legs disappear under the terrycloth that ends mid-thigh. Narrow hips, a long waist and broad chest, framed on either side by impressively muscular arms. He's ripped like he's been spending his free time at a gym instead of taking every spare moment for naps. I work my ass off for just a hint of abs, and this guy is shredded from napping.

My inspection reaches his face, and I can barely breath. He's perfect. It's as if he listened to every comment I ever made about what I like in a man, then put it all together into this utterly perfect package. Yet it's distinctly him, too. I should have known it was him the moment I laid eyes on him.

I have to go. I'm already late, and I need that position as Gideon's apprentice more than ever. I obviously can't go back to my old job, even if taking this new position is guaranteed to paint an even bigger target on my head. Better to fight my way forward than do nothing.

"What exactly happened with Jeffries?"

Damon's eyes drop, his forehead creasing just slightly. "He locked me out. He was going to kill you. The only way I could get through the door was with human hands. He said if he didn't do it, someone else was going to do worse."

"You did this to save me."

"I would do anything for you. You know that."

I swallow the lump in my throat. "I know."

He steps toward me and reaches out to cup the side of my neck. His fingers thread into my hair as his thumb brushes across my cheek. I'm frozen to the spot, barely breathing. This is Damon. My Shifter. He's bitten me, scratched me, slept in my bed for years... but he is not a man. I can't let my mind go there.

"I can't lose you Damon. You're my partner. My best friend. My..."

His grip tightens on the side of my face, as he leans down and presses his mouth against the opposite side of my neck. He bites me. The wet heat of his tongue slides across my skin. My legs go weak as he alternates between biting me and licking me, working his way slowly up my neck. I let him do it, as I always have when he gets in the mood for his strange displays of affection or possession. It's no different now. It's just Damon doing what Damon does.

His attentions reach the top of my neck, and he begins to work his way along my jaw as a low growl rumbles in his chest. His mouth reaches mine, our lips just barely touching.

"I can give you what you need now, Whisper."

His meaning hits me like a jolt of electricity. I push myself away from him, but he grabs my ass with his free hand and pulls me tight against him. Sweet fuck, he's hard as steel. He's spent his entire life as an asexual animal, and suddenly he's grinding his cock against my belly like he knows exactly what to do with it. There's no way he does, but a few choice images of me showing him flash through my mind.

"Stop!"

I shove against him and he lets me go. I immediately turn around. I can't look at him. Not until I've purged those images from my mind... maybe not even then.

"What I need is you. My Shifter. I can't..."

His warm, furry head presses against my side, tucking under my hand. On instinct, I start scratching him behind his ears. It's suddenly so ordinary. Yet it's nothing like before. Everything is different now, and I'm not sure I know what to do with it all.

SOLAR ONE

We walk across the glossy, white tile of a lobby that's an exact replica of the ground level base. The Headquarters of the United Army of Terran Protectors: Aerial Division. Or, as the locals like to call it, HQ.

I'm walking with my chin up, with all the confidence of an Agent who is right where they're meant to be. I can't say the same for Damon, though. He's stalking beside me with his head on a swivel, sure that an assassin waits around every corner.

I understand his worry, but knowing he has my back lets me focus on where I need to go. And it's keeping him busy enough that he hasn't brought up last night, or this morning. I still don't have my head on straight about the whole mess, but I've got my game face on and I'm confident no one will know anything is out of order.

Hiding my emotions is something I'm pretty good at. Sucking it up and moving on after some asshole thinks they broke me; I'm a pro.

We're getting all the usual stares and whispers from the civilians and Agents we pass, but I couldn't care less. I could have worn street clothes; blended in a little better. But I work here. I'm dressed in my tactical gear, my pistol on my hip and blades secured to the outside of my thighs.

Two Agents are walking toward me, one with a cougar at his side and the other with a grizzly lumbering behind. I try not to look star-struck when I recognize their faces. Elites. As they draw near, the taller one gives me a quick once-over. I wait for the customary insults or propositions, but he only nods and continues on his way.

I near the wide, curved reception desk and stop to wait my turn. The attendant behind the counter is chatting quietly with a woman who looks like she's never had to work a day in her life. She's tall and slim, the delicate heels of her strappy shoes making it clear she never has to worry about moving too quickly. She's wearing a long, form-fitting dress that covers her from neck to ankles yet hugs her slight curves. It's like she couldn't decide between modest or sexy, so opted for both. Her ginger hair is gathered into a twist at the nape of her neck, and when she finishes her hushed conversation and turns to leave, I catch a glimpse of honey-brown eyes and thick lashes.

The woman turns her gaze on me as she passes, surprise flashing briefly as she parts her crimson lips.

"Forgive me," she says as she reaches out and touches my arm. "Do I know you?"

"No ma'am. I just arrived."

Her eyebrows are perfectly symmetrical. Her makeup is as flawless as her hair. I can't imagine such a level of personal care is enjoyable. I like to be clean, don't get me wrong... but my 2-in-1 shampoo is as fancy as I get.

"I don't mean to be rude, but are you an Agent?"

I stifle a laugh, creating a sort of choking sound that makes her matching eyebrows raise. I'm pretty sure this lady doesn't know what rude means. I wonder what her eyebrows would do if

I told her a few of the 'rude' things I've been asked in the past. Hell, in the last week.

"Yes, I'm an Agent. I've been offered a position as an Apprentice."

She bites her lower lip, and I swear her eyes glisten like she's on the verge of tears. She holds out a slender hand, fingers tipped with evenly manicured nails. I take it cautiously, and she shakes my hand with a firm grip.

"My name is Tanikka Durant. It's an honor to meet you Agent..." her voice trails off and it takes me a few breaths to realize I haven't given her my name.

"Whisper."

"Agent Whisper. It's very good to meet you."

She gives my hand another squeeze as I stare at her awkwardly, then she continues on her way.

I step up to the woman behind the reception desk, and she flashes me a wide smile. She's a couple years younger than me, with big blue eyes and hair dyed to match.

"Welcome!" She greets me as if she's been waiting for me. "You must be Agent Whisper!"

"That's me."

"It's so great to meet you." She stands, offering her hand over the counter separating us, but then thinks better of it and withdraws. "I hope your trip up was comfortable?"

Comfortable. Sure. If you call being stuffed into a microwave and vibrated until your teeth feel like they're about to shatter *comfortable*. As curious as I was about experiencing the teleports for the first time, I'll be perfectly content if I never step foot in one again.

"Yes, thank you." I return her gesture by offering my own hand, and she beams as she shakes it.

"I just have to say, you are such an inspiration."

What is wrong with this place?

"Thank you. That's very kind of you. I'm just here as an Apprentice though, I'm not hired yet."

She laughs, covering her bright smile with a hand as she shakes her head. "Don't be so modest! You made it through the Academy. You're an Agent!"

"Yes, I am."

I know my tone is less than enthusiastic. After last night, I'm not exactly sure I'm still an Agent. If Gideon doesn't sign off on my advancement, I'm not sure I'm anything at all.

"You're a hero. An inspiration to any girl that has a little badass on the inside." She winks, and I feel a surge of gratitude for her efforts. It might be her job to make the newbs feel valued, but even so, it's pretty nice for a change.

"Thank you. I needed to hear that today. What's your name?"

"Anytime. I'm Dawn. I'm happy to provide your daily dose of fangirl. Or be your best friend. Whichever."

I laugh as she keeps a totally straight face. "Okay." I force my own expression to match hers. "Nice to meet you, Dawn."

She claps her hands together and beams.

"Oh! I do believe the person you're waiting for is just arriving. And you can definitely color me jealous..."

She points behind me. The front of the building is clear glass, providing an unobstructed view of a wide courtyard and the glimmering city beyond. I can hardly believe my eyes as a big, emerald dragon touches down. It's like nothing I've ever seen before. Its back is as tall as a bus. It's long, and lean, with big, round eyes.

Even more impressive is the man on its back. Gideon unstraps his legs from the saddle, slides to the ground, and starts toward the entrance with the casual manner of someone who treats riding a dragon like an everyday occurrence. Which it is, I suppose.

"That man is the reason I bring extra panties to work."

Where has this girl been all my life? I hold up a fist, and she bumps it. That's all there is to it. He's impossibly good looking. Every woman feels this way when he walks toward them, staring into her eyes as if she's the only person in the room. He stops just an arm's length away, and I feel... less affected by him than I expected I would.

After seeing Damon's human form, up close and in detail, I'm not sure I can appreciate mortal men quite the same anymore.

Shit, I'm in trouble.

"Beautiful," I say after a silence that stretches just a little too long. He raises an eyebrow, and I find myself fumbling to recover my dignity. "Tarek, I meant Tarek. He's really incredible."

Damon growls beside me, and I rest my hand on his shoulder.

"Yes, he definitely is," Gideon agrees. "Don't be in any rush to try that out, Damon. Most Shifters never get there. Get the hang of something easier, like an eagle. Then try for something from myth, like a phoenix. It's a strong form; tough and resilient. Don't let the whole fire mythology throw you off, it's just a big bird, however you imagine it to be, with skin so tough you're practically bulletproof."

Hearing him talking to Damon like a person makes me nearly giddy. I wonder briefly what he would think if he met Damon in human form... but I push that thought right away. No one can ever know about that.

"Elite Gideon..."

"Just call me Gideon."

I nod. I want to thank him, to let him know what an honor it is to be here. But first impressions are everything, right? We might not actually be meeting for the first time, but it's the first moments of this new work relationship. He's clearly opting for a fresh start, with his casual yet professional tone.

"I'm just Whisper. It's been my name since long before the Academy."

My mind flashes to images of last night, of the way Charles

called me 'Jane'. Gideon probably knows that name. I suspect he's the kind of person who digs to the bottom of every file he pulls up.

"Fair enough, Whisper."

"Are we going up to see the Elders?"

He laughs, motioning for me to follow him back toward the door. I turn and catch Dawn's eye, giving her a little wave before I go. She flashes me a smile, and a thumbs up.

"You're not an Elite yet. You'll get to stand in the Atrium when that day comes. For now, you'll just have to trust your orders through me."

"How long will that be?"

"Depends on how things go, and what positions open up while you're with me. I'll send back reports every day, and when the Elders think you're ready, they'll tell us."

Makes sense, I suppose. I just need a few good marks, and I'll show them why they need me. I'm definitely itching for some action. I haven't had a job since that pretty thing in the bunker. I need to secure that title, whatever it takes, as soon as possible. Before someone finds out about last night. Before Charles or someone else decides to finish the job.

EASY TARGET

"*Y*ou're going to knock on the front door?"

"Of course." Gideon looks at me like he doesn't understand my confusion.

"Don't you have a mark? A file? If we knock on the door, he's not going to be stupid enough to answer."

"This isn't the job you're used to, Whisper. You've been a glorified bounty hunter, but that's not what I do."

We're parked in the suburbs, a strip of residential zoning that makes up the outside edge of the circular city. It looks like any other neighborhood, if you squint just enough. There's no rock up here, and very little wood. Most everything is made of metal or some kind of composite, either from Earth or shipped in from off-world. The technology used to keep these things in the air is most definitely from off-world.

From where we are, I can see the tall, glimmering structures of the city looming over the houses on one side, and nothing but sky on the other. There's a small part of my brain that wants to take a moment to appreciate where I am; to stare out the window and marvel at the city I'd only previously dreamed of visiting.

I'll make time for sight-seeing when I'm a permanent resident.

"What exactly do you do, then?"

"An Elite's job is to protect and serve the Elders. We're not at war, and the crime rate up here is far lower than on the ground. That means most of the time, my job is to fly around, keep watch, and make sure anyone who thinks about causing trouble knows what they'll be up against."

"Sounds like fun."

"It's better than killing people for credits."

Guess that depends on your point of view. I get the impression that mentioning I actually like my job won't go over so well. I'm not seeking a promotion because I don't like what I do.

"Who do you think is in this house?"

"All I know is there's been some reports from neighbors about 'strange activity'. They indicate this address might be involved in a smuggling operation. What they're moving or where they're moving it to, I can't guess. This visit is just to get a closer look, see if we can figure out another piece of the puzzle."

In other words, this is my second chance to show him what I can do.

"Put ears on me. I'll go."

"You're not going up there alone."

"Seriously, Gideon. I'm here because of my superpower, remember? Those were your words, right before I nearly offed you with your own gun."

He looks wounded when I bring up that little emasculating exchange at the diner. I had no doubt I'd be using it against him at least once.

"That's not-"

"You know I'm right. If you knock on their door, you won't see anything they don't want you to see."

"I don't like the idea of you going alone. If the intel's correct, you could be walking into anything from drug smuggling to human trafficking."

I wave my hand, brushing off his concerns like the pointless waste of time they are. "I'll have two Shifters and an Elite nearby for backup. I think I'll be fine."

I'll come with you as a dog.

No. I'll go alone. It's a simple task, but I don't want to take any chances. Having you with me might tip them off.

I don't like you going alone.

You don't like me going to the bathroom alone.

I look back at Damon, but the moment our eyes meet I turn toward the house again. Moving on from what Charles did is simple. I've got plenty of practice. I'm having a lot more trouble getting back to business-as-usual with Damon. Just when I start to feel like everything is normal, I catch his eye and see a man where my sweet, simple, loyal panther used to be.

"I'm guessing by the way he's growling that he agrees with me?"

"It doesn't matter. Look, can we agree that I'm a competent Agent, and that I'm here because of my skillset and not because you want a girlfriend?"

"Of course."

"Then let me do my job."

He breathes in through his nose, his chest expanding as his jaw flexes. I'm actually a little worried that I took that too far... he is my superior during this arrangement, after all. My concerns are short-lived, as he reaches into a compartment on the dash and pulls out a little box.

"Put this on." He takes out a tiny, black clip and hands it to me.

He tucks a little earbud into his own ear, watching me as I fasten the discreet mic to the fabric of my bra.

"Hold still." He reaches over and presses his thumb against my neck. "A screen. It will hide your implant tats."

I pull down the visor, checking out my neck in the warped mirror. Sure enough, it looks bare. I reach up and touch the spot where my tattoos are, feeling the slight bumps.

"You get much better toys up here."

I flip the visor back into place before slipping out of the truck. I unclasp the holsters from my thighs, laying my knives on the seat. My belt with its heavy pistol follows.

"Whisper..."

"Yes?" I hesitate before closing the door, taking just a moment to appreciate the concern on that pretty face of his. He's worried I'll be killed in action by ringing a doorbell.

"What's your plan?"

"I'm going to ring the doorbell and ask if they're smugglers." I give him a big smile and close the door. It's definitely a perk that he can hear me, but I can't hear him.

Be careful.

Always am, kitty cat.

Time to get my game face on. My pants morph into low-rise, distressed jeans that cling to me like body paint. My shirt gives way to a midriff baring corset-style top. It's sleeveless, shows off my navel jewelry and gives a good view of the girls. All to ensure no one remembers my face.

I walk up the sidewalk, two houses down from Gideon's green truck, then turn to face a cute, quaint little bungalow. It's a silvery color, with big windows and solar panels on the roof. It's the same as every other house I've seen up here, except for the fact that all the curtains are drawn closed. There's no flowers either, in the little beds along the front.

I walk up to the door and knock. Fuck, I hope I'm greeted by something I can work with. If this turns out to be the home of a proper little suburban housewife, I'm going to feel like a dick.

The door opens a few inches, and I'm not disappointed. A man in his mid-late twenties opens the door. He's shirtless, showing off a very slim body and a lot of colorful tattoos. He's sprouting a few day's growth and a few piercings on his face. His hair is clipped even shorter than his fledgling beard.

I suck in a breath, wide-eyed as my gaze travels over his torso. His tattoos are interesting, but I'm looking at them like I've never seen such incredible ink.

"Can I help you?" He opens the door farther.

"I'm sorry, I..." I lower my eyes and chew on my lower lip, wrapping my arms around myself. "This is really stupid, but, ah, my friends dared me to come over here."

He looks over my shoulder, finding that I'm alone, then returns his attention to me. He leans against the door jamb, hooking a thumb into the waist of his jeans.

"And so, you did."

"Yes." I giggle nervously, rocking a little on my feet. "I'm just going to say it. Um, we heard that you were dealers. That you were selling drugs."

I slowly bring my eyes up to his face, but his expression is guarded, giving nothing away. He's also not closing the door in my face.

"And if that were true?"

"Well, I, we don't need much. Just enough for a few friends. I don't have any credits, but I-"

"Little lady, I'm no drug dealer. But I'm pretty sure I can hook you up. Why don't you come inside so we can talk about it?"

"Yeah? I mean, I know it's probably stupid for me to go into a stranger's house... but my friend just lives down the street."

"It's fine. Come in."

He moves out of the doorway, just enough for me to squeeze by. Then he closes the door behind me, putting a calloused hand on my hip as he leads me around a corner and into a sitting room.

A second man sits on a sofa, also shirtless but lacking the tattoos and scruff. He's built a little heavier, but I wouldn't guess he spends much time in the gym.

Two girls are sitting beside him, one under each arm. They are young and a little too thin, but what catches my attention most is the clothes they're wearing. Gauzy slips, identical to each other to the one I saw on the girl at my last job. I don't have to think about it for more than a second to know what that means.

"I'm sorry. This was a bad idea. I shouldn't be here."

"Don't worry, sweetheart," my guide reassures me, putting a hand on my chin to tip my face up. "My buddy won't bother us. He's got his own company. We can go somewhere quiet."

His hand moves from my chin, trailing down my neck to cup my left breast. Smooth, buddy.

"No, please. I changed my mind." My chin quivers, my eyes wide and pleading.

I'm seriously hating that Gideon is hearing this. He better stay the hell away.

I'm fine, just making my exit. Try to keep Mr. Manners from barging in here to defend my virtue. Hopefully Damon can keep him in check.

"Don't be scared, beautiful. You're going to get exactly what you came for."

I already did.

I pull away from him, heading for the door that's just a few strides away. Of course, he grabs my arm, which earns him a direct kick to the junk. He drops to the floor with a pitiful howl, and his buddy jumps from the sofa. I waste no time letting myself out the door to run down the driveway and up the street. I keep jogging at a steady clip past Gideon's truck.

A few blocks down he pulls up beside me, and I gratefully jump in.

"What the fuck?"

I laugh, even though I'm just a little bit out of breath. I reach into the back and scratch Damon's head.

"That's not very good manners, Elite Gideon."

"You do know I could hear you, right?"

"That was the point of the mic."

I remove the little black clip from my bra and hand it back. I realize I'm still wearing my easy-target clothes, so I quickly swap back to my tactical.

"What were you thinking?"

I look over at him fully for the first time since getting back into the truck. He looks intense. I think exasperated is an accurate description. And he's got some fresh scratches on his arm, so clearly Damon had to intervene, as I suspected.

"I was thinking the best way to have a look inside would be to get myself invited in. Which I did."

He's still pissed, and it's definitely a sexy look on him. The way he's gripping the wheel, jaw flexing...

"On my last job, there was a girl. Mid-to-late teens. She wasn't supposed to be there. None of the intel suggested my mark would be travelling with a girl. She was thin, her hair was messy, and she was wearing this little gauzy slip..."

"I saw the file for your last job."

Of course he did.

"There were two girls in this house. Same age, same physical condition, same clothes. All three of them had the same tattoo; inner left wrist, two circles."

He's silent, watching the road as he drives along the wide highway that separates the suburbs from the city center. I launch into a detailed account of everything I saw in the house;

describing the people, decor, smells, anything I can recall. When I finish and my eyes focus again on the real world instead of the images from my memory, I realize we've stopped.

"Why..."

"You'll see."

WINGS

e're at what looks like a dock or a pier, only instead of ocean there's nothing but sky. Just meters away from where we stand, a simple rope separates us from a deadly drop. It surprises me at first that there aren't safety precautions, barriers, or even warning signs. It's just another example of how different life is up here.

Everyone that lives on the Solars has a clear purpose. There are no prisons, no untreated mental illness, no homeless or unwanted. All of that is sent back to the ground. There's not even a high population of children, and certainly none that would be running unsupervised on the outskirts of the city. There aren't even any public schools. The Solars are elevated cities for an elevated population.

I walk closer to the edge, and my knees start to weaken before I even look over. A guttural roar and a blast of wind nearly knock me on my ass, as a green wall of scales rushes up from below. I catch my footing as Tarek circles once before landing gracefully beside Gideon.

Damon is already at my side, but he sidles a little closer until his shoulder touches my thigh. I absently stroke his head, but I can't take my eyes off the dragon in front of me. He's magnificent. Iridescent green scales catch the light as he moves. He holds his head high, scanning the horizon with emerald eyes.

"Ready to fly?"

"Hell yes."

I'm not even going to pretend I wasn't waiting for that offer.

I look down at Damon, who hardly seems to be sharing my enthusiasm.

Wait for me here?

I hate to leave him behind. I know how much it will bother him that he can't follow, but I can't refuse the chance to ride a dragon.

He flattens his ears as he sits, curling his long tail around his feet.

Just a few strides, and I'm within arm's reach of a dragon. I want so much to reach out and touch his smooth scales, but I know Shifters enough to respect the fact that he won't like anyone but Gideon touching him. I'm certain it took some creative bargaining to convince him to let me ride, and I certainly don't want to push my luck.

Gideon is already strapped into the saddle with his legs bound. There are straps circling the base of Tarek's wings, front legs and neck. It all looks well engineered and sturdy, but there is definitely no passenger seat. Gideon scoots his ass back, a clear invitation for me to sit in front of him. Tarek settles low to the ground, his forearm creating a step for me to hoist myself up.

Gideon reaches a hand down, but I ignore it and climb up on my own. As I swing my leg over, he grips my hips and guides me to settle into the tight squeeze between him and the front rise of the saddle. There's a modified pommel, like curved handles, and he grips it tightly with his left hand while his right snakes around my waist, holding me tightly against him.

I'm trying very hard to focus on the dragon between my legs.

The wall of hard, warm male against my back is making that a lot more difficult than it should be. And because I have zero self-control, I move my hips just a little. His breath hisses as he grips me a little tighter, and the unmistakable ridge against my ass grows a whole lot firmer.

"Are you ready?" he says it with a voice as husky as a daydream, and I can only nod.

A few jarring steps later, and Tarek walks off the edge. My stomach is in my throat as we drop, but he quickly levels out into a smooth glide. A faint chill ripples across my skin as we pass through the invisible bubble of the Solar's atmosphere.

I'm currently, at this very moment, riding a dragon.

The pure exhilaration of it nearly blows my mind. Then I'm hit with the realization that Gideon's arms are the only thing keeping me attached to said Dragon, and I'm pretty sure my heart has forgotten how to beat.

"Are you okay?"

His mouth is close to my ear, his lips nearly brushing my skin. My entire body is electrified. I don't even know if I'm terrified or just having the best thrill of my life. Maybe it's both.

"I'm good."

I hope I sound more confident than I feel.

I squint my eyes against the wind, taking in the view of Moridian sprawled about thirty thousand feet below us. Mismatched buildings and an overlapping gridwork of roads stretch out until they meet the ocean. Shining, modern offices and decaying slums alternate with comfy suburbs and packed downtown districts. It's a city that started small, and grew beyond capacity until it spilled out over its own borders to overtake the landscape.

Tarek banks to the right, and I grip the saddle tightly even though Gideon still holds me firmly in place. In this direction, Moridian tapers off until it ends at the feet of Morwood Forest.

The vast, protected woodlands stretch out beyond the curved horizon. They shelter wildlife and more than a few criminals hoping to lose the law without losing themselves.

Tarek banks again, and we're coasting on the wind back to Solar One. The floating city stands out in stark contrast to the ground city below and the natural simplicity of the forest. A flash of light in the distance catches my eye; a shuttle is taking off, bound for one of the dozens of other worlds Earth does business with.

It's beautiful, I suppose. All of it. I just find it hard to accept that the technology exists to keep the rich and powerful in such opulent surroundings, while the majority of humanity still struggles with poverty, overcrowding and disease.

"Beautiful, isn't it?" Gideon speaks against my ear.

WAIT FOR ME HERE?

That just might be my least favorite sentence. She makes it sound like a question, but what choice do I have other than to do as she asks?

The limits of my self-control are tested as I watch her climb the body of that ugly dragon. Then Gideon puts his hands on her. He guides her into the saddle and tight against his own body. The fact that she's enjoying being in his arms is written all over her face, and she confirms that by flashing a playful grin as she moves her hips against his.

When he leans in to speak for only her to hear, I nearly shift. Let him see my human form. Let him know that Whisper doesn't need his attention or his body. I have everything she needs to keep her safe and happy.

They walk off the edge without a backward glance. I snarl and growl and claw at the hard ground, furious at how helpless I am to follow.

But that's not true. I've never taken a winged form, but that doesn't mean I can't.

I try to focus on the form I want. I cycle through the birds I've seen up close, but none of them seem quite right. I remember the creature Gideon described. The phoenix. I've never taken an imaginary form before, and my attempt at summoning a dragon was a clear failure. This one feels different. I can picture the black feathers, the strong beak and tapered talons. I can feel the way the air enters my lungs, and the way my weight balances on two legs.

I start to reshape, gritting my teeth against the discomfort. A sudden stab of pain accompanies the sound of cracking bones, fading away almost immediately as I stretch my wings. I move and test my muscles and joints. I twist my neck from side to side and try my weight on first one leg, then the other.

When I look toward the distant shape of Tarek and my Whisper, my eyes focus in with such detail I can see the smile on her face. I wobble to the edge, expecting to feel a rush of fear at the prospect of jumping into thin air. The avian instincts kick in, and I take to the sky as if I were born to fly.

The wind around my body feels like freedom. I can't imagine why I've never tried this before. I dip and circle, learning the limits of my ability. Movement from below catches my attention, and the urge to hunt pulls at me.

I push it aside, focusing on my reason for taking this form. Tarek has begun to turn, making a lazy circle back toward the Solar. A few strong pushes with my wings, and I'm well above them. Twisting in the air, I swoop down to fly level at their left.

Tarek doesn't acknowledge my presence, not that I would expect him to. I'm bigger than any other bird, but still small next to a dragon. Gideon spots me first, and the surprise on his face is almost as satisfying as the shock that lights up my Whisper's eyes.

I open my beak, letting out a predatory shriek.

Well, I guess we don't have to take the teleport home tonight.

TAREK LANDS in my front yard, his big body taking up most of it. Lights pop on at some of the neighbor's houses, and a few of them even venture out onto their doorsteps to get a better view. Gideon unstraps his legs before hoisting himself off. He slides to the ground with practiced ease before he reaches up to offer me a hand, and I don't even consider playing it tough. I'm not sure if I'll ever walk again.

"It's normal," he reassures me, his tone almost clinical as he grips my waist to help me stay upright. "It took me a couple weeks before I stopped falling on my ass after every flight."

I laugh at the image of him being so awkward. I probably laugh a bit more than the situation calls for, but I'm still high on the adrenaline and pure wonder of what I just did.

Tarek settles down to rest on his belly. His green scales capture the last slivers of evening light, giving his hide a metallic, rainbow hue.

When the giddiness wears off, I glance around for any sign of Damon. He was incredible. When that huge, black raptor joined us... I don't think I've ever felt such pride. How could he have mastered a *phoenix* so quickly? It blows my mind.

We're almost at my door, and my legs are starting to behave more like my own limbs again. Gideon still has a hand on my arm, but he removes it when he sees I've gotten the hang of walking again. I stop, turn to face him, and can't for the life of me form any words. I open my mouth to try, but then his lips are on mine. Soft. Gentle.

Damon's face appears behind my eyelids. His human face that I've been trying all day not to think of. I didn't hear him arrive, but I know he's watching. He's always near, always watching me. It just feels different now.

I push just lightly against Gideon's chest, knowing that's all it will take. He immediately backs away enough to give me room to take him in. His pale green eyes are a shade darker. His lips are parted, chest rising and falling with heavy breaths.

"I need this job, Gideon. I need it fair and square."

He steps back farther, biting his lower lip as he shoves his hands into his pockets. He's adorably awkward, and ridiculously sexy. I should be climbing this man like a tree and begging him to come into my bed.

But I can't stop thinking about Damon. I've been fighting the thoughts all day. Now I'm home and we're about to settle in for the night. In *our* bed. The same as we've done every night for years.

"I'm sorry. That was out of line."

I feel a stab of guilt. I'm not just helplessly attracted to this man; I also actually like him. That's a rare combination.

"No, it's fine. Really." I tuck back the hair that's fallen out of my elastic. "I... you know I..." Fuck, I'm so awkward at this. Whatever this is.

It's not like I can tell him about Damon. Or about the fact that my Commander just tried to murder me, and I need this position so he can't get at me to finish the job. I might like the guy, but I don't know him well enough to trust him with information that could put an even bigger target on my head.

"You don't need to explain," he says, rescuing me from my brain-mouth glitching. "You did good today. Even if I don't particularly enjoy your methods. You got the job done."

"Thank you."

He looks back at Tarek, who has possibly fallen asleep on my front lawn.

"I'll pick you up in the morning?"

I can't stop my grin at the thought of riding Tarek again. "Sounds good."

I stay on my front step, watching until Gideon and Tarek have flown out of sight. It's only then that I catch a flicker of movement in the shadows, a flash of red eyeshine in the porch light as Damon's panther materializes out of the darkness.

UNDERSTANDING

"*S*o, how did it feel to fly?"

I'm doing my best to act normal, casual, like there's nothing different about this night. Digging through the fridge for some inspiration serves as a good excuse to avoid looking at Damon. It's not quite distracting enough to keep my mind off the two bullet holes clearly visible in my white kitchen island. It's definitely not distracting enough to keep the memories of last night from replaying on loop in my head.

I'm perfectly safe in this house. With the door locked and Damon by my side, there is nothing and no one that could get to me. Knowing that's a fact doesn't stop my stomach from twisting and turning painfully in my gut.

"I'll be able to take dragon form one day soon. You can fly with me then."

"Well, don't rush it..." I close the fridge and lean my forehead against the cool exterior. "Damon, you can't do this. You can't take human form."

"I don't like it when he puts his mouth on you."

My jealous panther. Oh, hell.

"Damon..." I turn around, ready to explain to him in no uncertain terms why he can't do this again.

He's standing just a few feet away, hip against the island, thick arms crossed over his broad, bare chest. I can't breathe. I'm a sexual person. I have a strong libido and a dirty mind. However you want to describe it, I admit it. No arguments here. But I can not, I will not, be attracted to my Shifter. Damon. My *cat*.

"Thank you for finding pants, at least."

He looks down at the loose, black pants that sit low on his hips and do nothing to conceal the fact that he is very well endowed. Not that I'm looking, or care, it's just impossible not to notice. Plus, last time he was naked and... I am not looking at, nor am I thinking about Damon's penis.

"I shifted a saddle once for a horse form. That night we got stranded up in Fentondale. Same concept with clothes, I guess."

"That's good."

I've lost my interest in cooking, it seems. Times like this I wish I liked take-out. I pull my hair free of the elastic, shaking it out into messy waves. What I want more than anything right now is to be asleep. It's been a long twenty-four hours.

I check my comm for the millionth time today. I don't know why I think Charles might send me a message. The only message I'll be getting from him or whoever he works for will be one I don't see coming.

I'm safe in this house. I'll be safer once I'm an Elite.

I glance at Damon, but look away when I realize he's still staring at me. His usual indifferent, even aloof observations are replaced by a mask of concentration. He's thinking thoughts and feeling emotions he's never experienced. He's thinking about me, figuring me out. I can sense his curiosity. His judgement.

Maybe I'm the one overthinking this.

He's still my Damon, same as always. Changing his form doesn't change who he is. It's me that's projecting my issues onto him. Just because his current form seems like it might just be inspired by all the physical traits I drool over in a man. Just because I can't stop the primal side of my brain from responding to his appearance. That doesn't mean I should suddenly change the way I treat him.

"Are you okay, little one?"

He's been calling me that familiar endearment ever since he first took his panther form, but like everything else, it feels very different when he's in that body.

"Yeah, of course. I'm just tired. And I'm worried about you. What if this is hurting you?"

"It's not."

He takes a step forward, but I quickly retreat toward the hallway.

"I'm going to bed." I'm already halfway to the bedroom. "Now that you have thumbs, you can cook for yourself." I laugh at my own joke, but it sounds forced.

I don't wait for his response, just hurry into my bedroom and close the door behind me. I've never closed him out. He sleeps every night in my bed. It's never felt weird.

I look around the room, and all I see is me. My clothes, my books, my favorite shade of deep purple on the walls. There's nothing here that's Damon's, and yet this is just as much his bedroom as mine.

A scratching at the door brings me out of my thoughts, and I open it without hesitation. Damon saunters by on four legs, brushing against me as he goes. With an effortless leap he's on the bed, stretching out along the bottom as he does every night.

This feels perfectly normal. He's the same creature I left in the kitchen, yet just because he has this form, I can't even imagine being uncomfortable around him.

"I'm sorry, Damon," I say on a sigh as I stash my weapons in the bedside table and convert my clothes into flannel sleep pants and a tank-top. "I just can't wrap my head around you looking like a human. I'm worried that it's hurting you. You're supposed to go crazy trying to adapt to a human brain. And even if they're wrong, it's still completely against the law... if you get caught... I just don't want to lose you."

Instead of answering, he starts to purr. If I wasn't already bone tired, that sound would still knock me out. I crawl under the covers and welcome the gentle wave of sleep that washes over me. My blissful departure is cut short, as I'm pulled back to alertness by the press of teeth on my shoulder. Human teeth.

"I can't stop thinking about the way he touches you. The way he kisses you."

Damon's words send a shiver down my spine. His hand slides over my waist, pushing the thin material of my shirt out of the way until the heat of his palm covers my stomach. I'm trying not to react, but I can hear the unsteadiness in my own breathing. He pulls me back against him, grinding a thick erection against my ass. I can't control the moan that slips through my lips, though I immediately wish I could take it back.

The sound seems to encourage him, and he presses against me even harder. His face is buried in my neck, his hot breath against my skin as his breathing becomes just as unsteady as mine. His hand moves from my stomach, sliding under the waist of my pants.

"Damon, no..."

My protest is weak, and he ignores it as his hand slides lower. His fingertips quickly find the sensitive nub that makes me reflexively buck against him. He moves his finger in firm, fast circles, and I can't even process what's happening before I'm on the brink of climax. He bites my shoulder as I bite my pillow, muffling my cries as I shatter under an intense orgasm.

As I come back down from the high, my entire body is hypersensitive. His wide hand is back on my stomach, keeping my ass pressed firmly against the hardest cock I've ever felt. His face is buried in my hair, his breathing rough, almost growling with every exhale.

How the fuck did he know how to do that? I've rarely met a man who knows where to find my clit, let alone what to do with it. I can't even...

"Whisper." His ragged voice is filled with need, and I suddenly realize what should have been obvious.

He knows what I like, because he's always here. I make him wait outside the room when I bring someone home, sure, but how many nights have I been on my own, giving myself a quick release? He's never paid much attention other than to express mild annoyance. But he's never felt it before, never been able to relate. He knows what I need, but he doesn't know his own body at all.

He grinds against me again, slow and firm.

I am so going to hell for this.

I reach behind me, sliding my hand between us and under his thin pants. When I close around the base of his thick shaft, he sucks in a breath and the hand on my stomach grips me almost painfully tight. I stroke along the smooth length of him as his entire body trembles.

Quickening the pace, I'm rewarded by his guttural, deliciously masculine moan.

I think I'm shaking, too. His heavy length in my hand and the sounds he makes are bringing me back to the edge. I squirm just a little, trying without success not to think about how incredible it would be to ride him while he has his first orgasm. His first sexual experience.

I keep up the quick, steady rhythm, turning just enough so I can see his face. His eyes are closed, teeth bared. His body tenses, every muscle flexing as the hand on my belly curls into a tight fist. In the next breath, his cock bucks and pulses in my grip. He buries his face in the pillow to stifle the feral roar that rips from his lungs.

I keep stroking him as I feel hot cum soaking through my shirt. When the tension in his body starts to relax, I release my grip. He stays unmoving, breathing heavily. When he lifts his face out of the pillow, his dark eyes meet mine and he holds my gaze.

Holy Fuck.

What did I just do? What did *we* just do?

SEX.

It's not like I didn't know what it was. It's not like I hadn't heard Whisper talk about it often enough. There was no particular point when I learned about it; it just was. Just like plenty of other things. My accelerated growth meant that I didn't experience a lot for myself... I just sort of absorbed it from Whisper's mind and memories. It was just something that existed, irrelevant in my daily life.

Now, I understand.

I had only intended to help her relax. I could tell by the way she was acting that she was stressed. The events of last evening were no doubt playing through her mind, and she would have tossed and turned for a sleepless night. When she's feeling that way, she touches herself. I've been aware of her doing so many times, her soft moans signaling the moment the tension leaves her body and sleep can take over.

I wanted to help her. I wanted to show her that I can be useful in this form. Certainly more useful than Gideon.

She stirs in her sleep, and I stroke her soft hair until she stills again. I pull her body closer, wrapping around her so that as much of me is touching as much of her as possible.

Touching her makes my skin feel like it's electrified.

Touching her while she found her release... that was like a bolt of lightning to every inch of my being. I've never felt such... need. I didn't know what to do with it. I was considering leaving her side, putting some distance between us until I figured out how to get control over my own body.

Then she touched me. I hadn't known such wholly consuming sensations, such pleasure, could even exist.

I nuzzle my face in her neck. I nip at her shoulder and run my fingers along her ribs, her side, her hip. I want to do that again. I want to do that and more. I want her to wake up now, turn toward me and touch me with those soft, skilled hands.

She moans encouragingly in her sleep, then slaps me away like a pest. I shouldn't disturb her. She deserves the rest. I know what this body needs now. Just like Whisper's done many times before, I can find my own release.

My hand isn't nearly as satisfying as hers, but I find a pressure and rhythm that feels good. I let my mind wonder to thoughts of Whisper. The fresh, floral scent of her hair. The sweet, salty taste of her skin. The way her warm hand gripped me, stroking me from base to tip with such care and skill.

It doesn't take long for the pressure to build. Every muscle in my body tightens until a wave of pleasure courses through me. I growl through clenched teeth as my release erupts across my stomach and chest. It's far less intense than when Whisper helped, but the aftermath is total relaxation.

I make a quick trip to the bathroom to clean up the evidence of my experiment. Then I'm back at Whisper's side, pulling her against me and surrounding myself in her scent and warmth. Sleep takes me quickly this time, and brings with it vivid dreams of us.

MOTIVES

"**W**hat is this?"

"It's a bar." Gideon shifts in his seat, his hands flexing on the steering wheel. His tone is a little too forced for this to be a casual stop after a long day.

He arrived at my house at the butt-crack of dawn, which would have normally pissed me off, but for some reason I'd rather not think about, I got a great night's sleep. Besides, the promise of a dragon ride in the morning is a sure way to get the blood flowing.

That was all the excitement on the menu though, as the rest of the day since has been what he calls 'patrolling'. What that amounts to is Tarek and Damon taking to the air, watching for anything suspicious or out of the ordinary, while Gideon and I drive around in his truck doing the same. When the entire population of a city is upper class, there isn't much suspicious activity to speak of.

This was not a good day for my mind to be idle. There might not have been much happening outside the tinted windows, but inside my head has been a shit show. I'm still trying to think my way through this mess with Charles. And then there's Damon...

I can't even believe what happened. It was so out of line, so unnatural, so wrong. But it didn't feel wrong. Not last night, and not this morning when I woke up still held tight in Damon's human arms. His thick bicep for a pillow, my fingers intertwined with his. It was anything but wrong. It felt... real.

But it's not real. He's a Shifter, not a human. I'm playing a dangerous game with him, and he's the one who will end up getting hurt. If he gets caught, they'll put him down. He shouldn't be able to do what he's doing. It's not possible, or at least it's not supposed to be. I can't make a bit of sense out of it.

"Why are we at a bar?"

I hope he doesn't pick up on the irritated edge to my tone. It's definitely not him that's got me bent out of shape. Not even a little. He's been nothing but polite and professional all day, and I haven't even pictured him naked once, which might mean I'm dying.

"I thought you could use a drink."

Okay. I'll play along. Maybe this is some kind of test. He tried to bore me all day, but I went along with it without complaint. Now he wants to see if I'll get drunk and sully the good name of the Elites. Or maybe he's planning an ambush, to test my reflexes after I let my guard down.

"Sounds good to me." I flash him an overly cheery smile.

He just nods. I start to open the door, but he touches my arm and I jump.

"I need you to do something, but I can't explain why. Can you do that?"

"Sure, boss. Whatever you need."

He cringes at my use of the word 'boss'. Guess he doesn't like being reminded we've crossed a bit of a professional line. Thank fuck he doesn't know that barely making out with him is the least inappropriate thing I've done.

He's still working his hands on the steering wheel. "Put on the same outfit you used yesterday. Not the exact same, but same idea. Cover your tats and leave your weapons."

His voice has an edge I've never heard in it before. I'm not sure if this is a test, but it's clear he's taking it pretty seriously. I do as he says, removing my weapons before digging into the glove box to find the screen that will hide my implant tats. After placing the tiny device and checking it in the visor mirror, I convert my clothes into the same low-rise jeans, and a deep purple halter top that leaves my back exposed.

"How's this?"

He nods, but his eyes say plenty considering he can't seem to tear them away from my bare shoulders. By his expression, I'm not sure if he's about to bitch at me for baring too much or come across the seat and remove the rest. Hopefully neither.

"Good," he says at last, looking away as if he just realized he's been staring. "Just go in and get a drink. Something fruity. Then sit alone by the front window. Keep your eyes down and don't interact with anyone who doesn't approach you first. Like you've run away from home or fell out with friends."

I wait for more, but it seems that's all the info he wants me to have.

"Okay. How long do I stay there?"

"Not long. Just finish your drink slowly, maybe glance out the window like you're nervous. When you leave, walk south. I'll pick you up when I'm sure you haven't been tailed."

Okay then. This isn't creepy at all.

I slide out of the truck, and the moment the door closes behind me I feel it. The thrill of being on a job. I might not have an actual mark, but the anticipation of the hunt is just the same. The mystery of not knowing the purpose of this exercise is a new kind of thrill, and I can't say I'm not enjoying it. I slip into the character Gideon described.

I'm young, about 18. I've run away from home, tired of living a cozy life of luxury and eager for some excitement. I tried to get my hands on some drugs yesterday to impress the new friends I've been hanging out with, but I chickened out when the tattooed guy got a little too personal. Now I'm second guessing my choices, but I still have a little rebel in me as I use my fake ID to get myself the weakest drink possible without stooping to beer. I'm terrified my parents will find me, even though they would never think to search for me in this part of town.

Once inside, I look around for a few minutes, getting acquainted with the layout and people. Down on the ground, this place would be a high-end spot. Up here, the chrome countertops and glass tables probably aren't impressing anyone. The majority of the patrons are middle-aged men, wearing suits and looking like their desk jobs might just be the death of them. There's a table of younger people celebrating something in a back booth. A few couples scattered around, knees touching under the tables.

I approach the counter, keeping my arms crossed in front of me as I order a vodka and cranberry. This character of mine probably doesn't know what any of the drinks on the menu are, but she's heard her mother order 'vodka and cranberry' at restaurants, so she can order that here with a measure of confidence in her voice.

Drink in hand, I make my way to a small table beside the front window. I glance at the street outside before settling my gaze on the drink in front of me. I'm looking around the room, too. I've never been in a bar, so it's all a curiosity to me.

There's a booth near me that catches my attention, though I don't let on as my eyes continue to sweep the room, check the street, and watch my ice cubes swirl ahead of my straw. The booth that's piqued my interest is near the window, just close enough that its occupants can see outside without being seen by anyone passing by.

There are three men sitting there. Two are facing away from

me, but the third I can see clearly. Close cropped, dark hair and a handsome face. He's clean shaven, lean but fit judging from the arm and thigh I can see around the side of the booth. I'm not sure at first what it is about these men that's caught my attention, but after sipping delicately for the first half of my drink, it clicks.

They're doing the same thing I am. Watching the other patrons and the street, only talking amongst themselves occasionally while slowly nursing their drafts. I don't know what that means, but I have a suspicion this is the reason I'm here.

I let my eyes drift to the man facing me, and I'm not surprised to find he's already looking my way. Our eyes connect for just a moment before I smile shyly and drop my gaze back to my glass.

I don't look his way again, though I keep him in my peripheral.

My drink is almost gone, down to the watery mouthful at the end, when a blue t-shirt slides into the chair opposite mine. Hello, handsome. I look up with a startled expression, glancing quickly around the bar and out the window as if afraid this stranger has somehow brought my parents with him.

"Hello, pretty lady," he greets me with a friendly smile and deep blue eyes that hold mine in a practiced, steady gaze.

"Hi, um, thank you." I dip my eyes, then look back up at him as if incapable of keeping my gaze away.

"I've been watching you, sitting here alone. I wanted to join you, but I couldn't imagine that a woman like you wouldn't have a date arriving at any moment."

"Oh, no, I... I was just about to head home." My voice cracks at the mention of home, and the corner of his mouth twitches subtly.

"Don't go yet." He reaches across the table and places a warm hand lightly on mine. I jump at the contact, but don't pull away. "I know we've only just met, but I feel a connection with you. I can see how just the thought of going home hurts you, and I can't bear the idea of you hurting."

I bite my trembling lower lip, turning my eyes to the window as I pull my hand from his to wrap my arms around myself. I try to think of a good response to his nauseating little speech, but nothing convincing comes to mind. Silence is probably the best option, anyway. I doubt he's targeting me for the conversation.

"I know a safe place you can stay," he continues, his baby blues full of concern.

"Thank you." I slide out of the booth as if suddenly spooked. "I have to go, but thank you."

I don't look back as I make my way quickly to the door and out into the cool evening. My instructions were to leave when I finished my drink. Hopefully my abrupt exit took him by surprise enough that he won't follow, but as I head south along the empty sidewalk, I get the feeling that's not the case.

He's following you. Damon confirms my suspicions. *Take your next right. Gideon's waiting.*

I do as Damon suggests, imagining him watching over me from above. Just as he said, Gideon's truck is waiting. I slide into the passenger seat and he rolls ahead, accelerating as quickly as he can without revving the engine.

"Who was he?"

It's obvious that wasn't a test. Gideon knew that man would be there, or at least suspected he would. I'm not sure why he felt the need to keep me in the dark, but I get the impression I've just been used as bait.

"Fuck!" Gideon's fist slams into the steering wheel as he curses, and I nearly jump out of my skin at the sudden outburst.

I snap my eyes from the deserted road ahead to the nearly empty sidewalks, but I can't see any reason for his sudden alarm.

"What the hell?"

He pulls over to the side of the street and throws it into park, then scrubs both hands through his hair as he mutters a few more curses under his breath. I'm not entirely sure if I should question his behavior, or just sit quietly while he works through his problem.

He turns in his seat, bracing an arm against the wheel as his eyes lock on mine. The intensity of the emotion there takes my breath away, and all I can do is wait.

"I hoped it wouldn't come to this, Whisper. Honestly. You were the only one who could get in there; get their attention. But I like you. I didn't expect that to happen. I tried to find another way, but I can't... I just can't miss this opportunity."

"What the hell are you talking about, Gideon? You're not making any fucking sense."

Holy shit, he's having a mental breakdown.

Damon, are you close?

I'm here, little one. Are you okay?

I'm fine. Stay close.

"My sister was murdered almost a year ago. Her daughter, my niece, was taken." He pauses, his jaw flexing as his chest rises and falls rapidly. He's fighting to keep his composure, but his grief, his pain, is written all over his face. My own chest constricts, and I have to grip the edge of the seat to stop myself from reaching out to offer him comfort. "I know where they're keeping her, but I can't get close enough."

"You're an Elite. Surely the Elders would..."

"They won't help."

"Why wouldn't-"

"They don't believe me. Officially, Claire committed suicide. Camilla ran away. They said I was too close to the situation. That I wasn't thinking clearly. They said I wasn't looking at the facts, but I was the only one who knew the facts. Claire wouldn't kill herself. Camilla wouldn't run away. It's just not possible."

"If you're so sure, the other Elites could help. If you proved what you're saying..."

"It's been almost a year. I begged and I fought for them to help me, until they threatened to strip me of my title. Without that, I'd have no hope of finding Camilla. They couldn't see past the conflict of interest. The other Elites won't disobey the Elders. It's what we are. Puppets with the illusion of freedom."

"Gideon, I'm sorry you've been through this, but why are you telling me now?"

He takes a deep breath as he looks at me. He seems older, the fine lines around his eyes deeper than I remember. His pale green eyes are dark, and there's an almost visible weight in the slump of his shoulders.

How have I not noticed this before? The grief and pain he's obviously been keeping just under the surface. Why did he feel the need to hide it so well?

"I've exhausted all my leads, all my contacts, and all my options. Horizon Zero is more than just a massive organization; it's an empire. I don't know how high their reach goes, but it's high enough that I know better than to shine a light on it. I just want my niece back. Safe."

"What makes you think I can help you? If you haven't been able to get near them..."

"Think about it, Whisper. You knocked on their front door, and they invited you in. You sat in plain sight, and they approached you. You're probably the only Agent who can do this."

So, it was a test. The house and the bar. Only he wasn't testing me, he was testing them. Horizon Zero. He was testing to see if they liked what they saw. A sour taste rises in the back of my throat as the pieces come together.

"You want me to be taken."

His eyes drop from mine even as his head nods in agreement.

"Did you even look at my file, or just my photo?"

"You deserve to be up here. You have more skill than most of your peers, or even most of the Elites I know."

I scoff at that, though I do feel a twinge of guilt. He's in a shitty place, and I sympathize with him, but there's no way in hell I'm going against the Elder's orders to help him. I need this promotion, and I need it fast. Going against the Elders to help an Elite who's apparently on shaky ground as it is... that's not the way to get what I'm after.

"I'm sorry for your loss, Gideon. But I'm here to earn my promotion. I can't go against the Elders to help you, or anyone.... It would be suicide for my career."

"They would never know. You just need to let them take you to their holding house, find Camilla when you get there, and help her escape. You have the skills. You can do this, and no one will ever know."

"If you want my help, we go to the Elders first."

"No. They can't know about this. Not until she's safe."

I take a deep breath and close my eyes for a moment, attempting to calm myself before I say or do something I'll regret. The fucking poster boy for the Elites sets his sights on me, wanting to take me under his wing, and I actually buy his bullshit. Of course it wasn't real. Of course it was never about me or my abilities. It was always about him and how he could use me to get what he needed.

Typical fucking man.

"I won't throw away my chance at becoming an Elite. I feel for you and I want to help, but I won't risk it."

"Fuck, Whisper!" His fist connects with the dash, making the entire console shake. "You're my only chance at getting her out of there. It needs to happen now. There are dozens of holding houses, in dozens of cities, but that guy back there works at Camilla's. I need to get her out before they ship her off somewhere I can't follow. She's already been kept there longer than most."

"No. Getting into the Elite program-"

"You're never going to be an Elite."

His words hit me like a blow to the gut. My body turns to ice as I fully grasp what's happening.

"What are you saying?" I ask the question, but I already know what's coming. I'm about to be blackmailed.

"I didn't want to do this. I swear I didn't. But you're not giving me any choice. If you won't help me, I will make sure you never step foot on the Solars again." He's looking right at me, a wild expression on his face. I can see a tremble in the hand that still grips the wheel. "I will speak to the Elders, and make sure they never look twice at you again. Your career will be over."

I want to break his fucking nose. My right hand closes into a fist, and I can almost hear that satisfying crunch of bone and cartilage. Who the fuck does he think he is? But even as the rage brings searing heat back to my veins, I know damn well he can do exactly what he is threatening. He can ruin me, just like that.

"Fuck you."

"Just do what I'm asking. Just do it. When she's safe, I swear on her life I'll sign off on your promotion. You'll be an Elite, and no one will ever know about this. I swear."

"You expect me to believe anything you say?" I bite my tongue, literally. He's got me by the balls, and there's not a damn thing I can do about it. I want to talk to Damon, but I already know what he would say. He would only want me to stay safe. He'd tell me to walk away now and forget about our plans. My plans.

Go home, Damon. I'll meet you there as soon as I can.

I'm not leaving you. What's going on?

I'll talk to you later. Everything is fine. There's nothing more you can do, just meet me at home.

Lying to him makes me feel like shit. There's nothing he could say or do to help this mess, and putting him in danger would only make it worse. I can't go back. Charles made sure of that. Without the Protectors, I'm nothing. No one. What was the point of surviving my childhood, what was the point of fighting through the Academy, if it all falls apart now?

One job. Go undercover and get pushed around a little. Nothing I haven't been through before. I save the girl, which is a pretty decent goal, and then Gideon goes to bat for me. Simple. Win-win. When the papers are signed and the deal's done, I'll break his fucking nose.

That thought makes me smile, as the panic fades away. I look at Gideon, and he jumps a little at what I'm sure is not a sane expression on my face.

"It's a deal."

His eyes widen in surprise as his body stiffens. If he expected me to argue and whine about it, he doesn't know a damn thing about me.

I make sure the screen is still in place on my neck before I slip out of the truck. Heading back the way I came, I let the cluster-fuck of emotions I just went through bubble to the surface until it shows on my face. Tears would be handy right about now, but I ran out of those a lifetime ago.

The rebellious girl that ran out of the bar is having second thoughts, and she's heading back to the arms of the last person who showed her some kindness.

RESCUE

*F*lying away from Whisper's location is like tearing off a limb. It's not right. I shouldn't go. But she made her request crystal clear; there's nothing more I can do. I could ignore her orders and stay anyway. It's a tempting thought, but I don't adjust my course as I fly toward our home on my own.

Landing at my destination, I have to shift to my human form to work the door. Once inside, I start the easy shift back to my panther. It's the body I'm most comfortable in, yet I don't feel like shifting now. I stay in my human form, even though there's no reason for it without Whisper nearby. I do a partial shift instead, changing my simple pants into jeans and a black t-shirt, just because I can.

A heavy emotion settles in my gut. She wanted me gone. She wanted me to go home without her, while she stayed out on her own with Gideon. I know my Whisper. I know she likes to play with certain men and women that she finds attractive. I also know she finds Gideon particularly attractive, though I don't see what's so special about him.

I thought she would have no need for that anymore. I thought I would be enough for her now.

I feel... angry. Angry at Whisper. Angry at myself for thinking what happened last night meant something more.

I don't have to stay here and wait for her. I don't have to do everything she asks as if she holds some physical power over my body. The thought is almost frightening, but it's also very, very empowering.

I head out into the drizzly night, lock the door behind me, and shove the key into my pocket.

As I walk down the street of our neighborhood, I'm not at all bothered by the frail rain beginning to soak through my clothes. The dark of the evening allows me a glimpse into the lives of the people Whisp calls neighbors. I've never really paid any attention to them. Through open curtains, the lights from their houses show me young couples and busy families. There's also the occasional older pair, nearing the end of their expected lifespan.

I'm not thinking about anything in particular, just walking and taking it in. My life has been very different from the years these people have lived and grown. I've never given it much thought, or even had any opinions about it one way or another.

Nearly five years ago, I was born at BioSol Labs. A genetically modified animal created to bond with a human and use their experiences and education to shape my own personality. I grew fast, matching my Whisper, my bondmate, in biological age after about six months. I don't have my own past. I've never considered what my future might be. I've only ever cared about her.

I'm lost in thought and my legs are growing tired when I find myself deep inside the commercial zone that sits north of our house. It's bright and busy with vehicles and people on foot. The wet night isn't stopping them either, though they take cover under hoods and umbrellas. All of them have somewhere to be. All of them have some important task that needs their attention.

I slide away from the endless trickle of bodies, stepping into the dark mouth of a narrow alley. The scent of human waste and rotting food is unpleasant even with this weak nose, but I ignore it. My skin is beginning to prickle with the cold, but it's not enough to make me want to shift to a more weatherproof form.

I want to observe, unseen. I want to see the expressions on their faces as they walk alone. I want to see their body language as they move together in pairs. It's fascinating. Like I'm seeing people for the first time, even though I've spent my life among them.

A shuffle of paper and the clink of glass draws my attention from the street to the darkness behind me. I step farther into it, letting my eyes adjust. The brick walls of the buildings lead to a dead end, barricaded with more brick. Garbage dumpsters account for the smell in the air, as even more trash litters the cracking pavement and gathers in sopping heaps at the edges.

It's disgusting. I turn to leave, but the faint sound of movement catches my attention again. I turn to my right, my eyes focusing on a pile of paper and cloth tucked in a corner where dumpster meets cold brick. A pair of eyes stare back at me from the heap. Small, human eyes.

I crouch low, attempting to appear smaller so I don't threaten whatever this is.

"Please," a small voice drifts out from the heap. "Don't tell them I'm here."

Something in my chest pinches as I stare back at the pleading, blue eyes. It takes me a few breaths before I remember that I can talk to this human, this child. I can talk to it and be understood. I've never talked to anyone but Whisper.

"Who are you hiding from?" I speak in a voice that is as soft and low as I can make it.

"Nobody." The immediate reply is firm and confident, and I smile at the way his small voice takes on a slightly deeper tone. "I'm not afraid of nobody. I just don't want the Enforcers to find me here. I searched all day for this spot."

"Where do you live?"

"Nowhere."

Homeless people. It's a common enough sight here on the ground. So common, they blend into the background like stray cats and hookers. Just another thing I never gave any thought to. I search my memories, trying to find a thread of something that I can use.

Fentondale. Whisp and I were there on a job. A pimp that liked to get a little too rough. I cringe now, as I realize a little more fully what that might have meant. He took us on quite a chase around the city. Including a detour through the yard of a huge, white-sided home for orphaned children.

"Fenton House," I say the name I recall from the sign over the door. "Do you know that place?"

The boy's eyes light up, and he leans out from under his flimsy, protective pile of other peoples trash. "Sure!" He crawls out a little farther, and I'm taken aback by just how small he really is. "Dustin said he was going there. His aunt was taking him when she couldn't keep him no more. He said it was so big, everyone got their own bed!"

"Why don't you go there?"

"Oh, I don't have an aunt."

"You could take a bus or a train."

He shakes his head. His mop of dark, wet hair spraying water like a wet dog. "They don't let kids like me ride."

I should go find Whisper. I can't leave this child, but I also don't know what to do with him. She would be able to tell me... I don't need her to tell me what to do. I can help this boy on my own.

"Have you ever met an Agent?"

His eyes widen to saucers at the mention of Whisper's rank. "No, sir." He answers, as if I might be referring to myself as the Agent.

"What about a Shifter?"

He shakes his head again, his eyes narrowing slightly as he tries to work out what I'm getting around to.

"Can you keep a secret?" I wonder if he even has the ability to understand the importance of the secret I'm referring to.

He nods, but his eyes are growing wary now. I don't want to think this through enough to start worrying about the danger I'm putting myself in by exposing what I've done. I just shift.

The boy gasps with surprise, scurrying back to the safety of his corner just for a moment. His curiosity wins out, and he creeps forward inch by inch until he can reach out and run his hands over the yellow fur of my retriever. His grin is infectious, and my tongue lolls out in a dog's laugh.

I step back from him, returning to my human form slowly so he can see the transition in detail.

"That was awesome!" His voice pitches so high he almost squeaks. Any fear he felt is gone. He looks around and out toward the road. "I thought Shifter's couldn't copy humans?"

"We aren't allowed. I want to help you, but I'll need you to keep this a secret. Just between us. Can you do that?"

He's nodding before I've even finished asking the question. "Yes. I won't tell anyone. Ever." He makes a crossing motion over his chest as if that might prove his sincerity. It's good enough for me.

"I can take you to Fenton House. Would you like that?"

His eyes light up. "I would, sir."

"Okay. I'm going to shift into something bigger, so you can ride. Are you afraid of heights?"

He shakes his head. I hope this isn't going to scare him off. My phoenix is big, but not built for carrying even a small passenger. But if I can create one form from my imagination, there's no reason I can't create another.

I concentrate on the image I have in mind. A hybrid of sorts.

The perfect solution for getting him to the next city. My body obeys, and I start twisting into a larger version of my panther. My head and neck form out of the image of my phoenix, as thick, feathered wings stretch out from behind my shoulder blades. I move my tail, confirming it's avian and not feline. This combo should be able to fly, I hope.

When it's done, I look down at the boy. He's standing now, with nothing but awe plastered on his smiling face. I crouch down, offering him my back, and he climbs right on. I lope out of the alley, needing more space to spread my wings. Our appearance causes more than a few startled screams and slammed breaks, but I don't linger to draw any more attention.

I take off as gently as I can, staying level and steady just above the city lights. It's going to be a long flight, but his small body is tucked securely into my fur and feathers. He's safe and warm for what might be the first time in his short life.

For the first time in my life, which I realize has probably been even shorter than his, I feel like I might be doing something truly meaningful.

A DULL PAIN sears behind my eyes as light filters through my lids. This is the second time I've been unconscious in the last week, but this time there's no naked Damon to pick me up from the ground. There's no one at all, as I pull myself up and take stock of the six by six room, empty save for the dirty mattress that I've been deposited on.

The chloroform was serious overkill, considering I was planning to go with him willingly. Not that I got the chance to tell him that. His buddy jumped me from behind the moment I fell into his arms with my sad story about not being allowed to return home. It took a lot of self-control not to defend myself, and to breathe deep to ensure the drug worked despite my Medic. At least the only injury I seem to have sustained is a splitting headache that will pass in a moment.

This better be the same place Camilla is being held. I'm still not clear on the details of how Gideon could be so sure. The fact remains that I need to do this job if I'm going to get promoted. That's all that matters right now. If I have to get a little dirty, so be it.

I'm okay, Damon, I'll be home as soon as I can.

I don't know where I am or how long I've been here, but I know he can't hear me. I can't describe it, but I can feel when he's out of range of our Link implants. It's kind of like how silence is too loud sometimes. Not exactly like that, but almost.

There's no sign of surveillance in the room. Good thing, because I'm most likely awake long before they would have expected the drug to wear off. I sit, focusing on breathing and keeping calm. Without windows or a clock, time is abstract and irrelevant. I sink inside myself.

The door swings open, and I nearly lunge at the man who enters before I catch myself and cower in the corner instead. He's about 5'7", stocky and a little soft around the middle. His head is shaved, though he has a well-kept coppery beard that rests against his chest. He brings the distinct scent of bacon with him, and my stomach reacts with a growl.

"Good morning, little mouse," he says with a friendly voice and a hint of laughter. "Are you hungry?"

I flash him a hopeful look before dropping my eyes back to the floor and tucking a little tighter into the corner. He laughs, but it's not a sinister sound. I don't get the feeling he means me any harm. Other than holding me captive, of course.

"Come on, breakfast is in the kitchen."

With that statement he turns and walks back through the door, leaving it open in a clear invitation for me to follow. My curiosity about this place is starting to peak, but I have to stay in character. I'm just a pampered runaway regretting my recent life choices.

I stand, finding my legs to be a bit unsteady at first. I go with it and hold the door frame for support as I timidly follow him through.

Outside my little room is a narrow hallway, leading past a dirty little bathroom and into a sitting room. It's sparsely furnished, and the walls look like they've been needing a fresh coat of paint for more than a few years. Dust covers the odd shelf or painting that hangs on the walls. Dirt and garbage collect in the corners, while the center of the floor is worn through the finish. Thick curtains are drawn across the single window, and the door is locked with a heavy metal bar. This house is clearly not anyone's home.

The room is empty, but low voices guide me around a corner and into a dimly lit kitchen. The age and misuse of the place is even more obvious in here, as the countertops have a visible sag and the stove looks like it hasn't cooked a meal in months. I'm pretty sure I see a long tail flick out from beneath it before disappearing again. I turn my attention to the oval table at the far end of the room, where the man who opened my door sits with two other men and three young women.

The girls are looking at me, each of their faces telling a different story. One, a thin little thing with long pale hair and crystal blue eyes only catches my gaze for a moment before lowering her eyes to the plate of bacon in front of her. Another, with short-cropped chestnut curls and eyes to match holds my gaze for a little longer, but she too looks down at her food without a word.

The third sits tall with her shoulders squared. She looks back at me with obvious challenge in her pale green eyes. Even if I hadn't just committed her face to memory, I would know she was Gideon's family with one glance. Her auburn hair is shoulder length, and it's clean and tidy compared to the other two girls. She's even wearing a pair of jeans and a worn t-shirt, while the others are dressed in those gauzy slips I'd be happy never seeing again.

"Welcome." The friendly greeting comes from the tallest of the three men. He's built lean, with hair falling in greasy tendrils past his shoulders.

"Cam, show your new roommate around." The third man speaks with more authority in his voice, and definitely no hint of friendliness.

"Yes, Archer." Camilla's voice is firm but soft. She seems confident and comfortable even as she jumps to obey the order.

She keeps her eyes on mine as she rounds the table. Archer gives her ass a firm squeeze as she passes, not earning so much as a flinch. She walks past me, her shoulder bumping mine with a clear message. She's showing me where she fits in the chain of command, and where I fit.

"Follow me," she says without bothering to check if I do.

She stops outside the bathroom, planting her hands on her hips.

"This is the ladies' room. There's a shelf with your name on it that has the basics; hairbrush, toothbrush, soap and so on. Use it wisely, you won't get replacements while you're here."

"No one's asked me my name," I say in a quiet voice, wrapping my arms around my waist.

She looks at me with a blank expression, then rolls her eyes. "I take it Darrel didn't bother to tell you anything."

"I don't know..."

"Whatever. Look, whoever you were yesterday, forget about it. Why they chose you doesn't matter, and there's no going back. Just accept that and skip the part where you whine and cry about how unfair it is. Okay? Your name is..." She pauses to lean into the bathroom, squinting at the masking tape labels on four narrow shelves. "... Hanna. Don't bother telling me the name you had yesterday, because it's dead. Your bedroom is in there." She points up the hall to the room I woke up in. "Behave yourself, and you'll get more comforts. Be a little bitch, and you'll lose what you have. Got it? Rules are simple. Do what you're told, when you're told, and don't ever ask questions."

"Why am I here?"

She glares at me, and I'm expecting a lecture about how I was just told not to ask questions. Instead, she takes a deep breath and rolls her eyes again.

"I don't know you, and I don't plan to get to know you. You're here because you're weak, alone, and sufficiently fuck-able. You're not a person anymore, you're property. A pet at best. Prove you're compliant, trainable and smart enough to keep your mouth shut unless you're told otherwise, and maybe you'll get yourself purchased by a kind, rich old man who just wants something pretty to look at. Be difficult, and you'll be broken by less humane methods and sold to someone who knows how to keep you on your knees. Understand?"

Holy shit. I don't need to fake my expression as I feel the blood drain from my face. I'm not really here. I'm not this victim she's describing. I'm undercover and I'll be leaving very soon. I have to remind myself of that, because her speech has left me feeling pretty damn bleak. How many girls have gone through here? How many have heard these words and gone on to live through that fate?

"Is Cam your real name?"

"I kept my name, because they knew it when they took me. I was chosen, not picked up because I had nowhere else to go."

"Why are you helping them?"

"That mouth is going to get you into a heap of trouble, *Hanna*."

"Yours seems to be serving you just fine."

A smile cracks her stern features for just a moment before she turns to retrieve a folded cloth from a bathroom drawer.

"Put this on before you come back to the kitchen."

It's the same gauzy material I've seen on the other girls. I stand in place, reviewing everything she's told me and finding it hard to take my eyes off the dusty shelf with my new name on it. The label is wilted around the edges, the soap far from new. I'm not the first Hanna, and I won't be the last.

"Is it just the seven of us here?"

"What?"

"Is there anyone else in or around this house, Camilla?"

Her eyes fly open as she sucks in a breath. She's smart. Smart enough to get herself under the protection of the house leader, and I can only imagine what that took. She did what she had to do to survive. I would bet she did it knowing that her best chance was to stay as close as possible to where she was taken from. Most of these girls would have no one looking for them, but she had her uncle Gideon.

"No, it's just us."

"Tell Archer I'm refusing the dress." I snatch it out of her hands as she gets dangerously close to hyperventilating. I grab my toothbrush. "You waited here for him, right? Because you knew he would come for you?"

Her eyes well up with tears, but she nods her head.

"Don't fuck it up then, okay?"

She nods again, wiping her eyes before heading back to the kitchen.

I step into my room and slam the door behind me. With the toothbrush gripped firmly in my right hand, I stand facing away from the door. I took the abuse and bullshit from my brothers for years, because I didn't know another way. I did what I had to do to survive, and it made me who I am today. If I could go back and give myself some advice, I'd tell that scared little girl to kill the fuckers in their sleep and burn it to the ground.

I'm not a little girl anymore. I don't have to wait for them to be asleep.

The door swings open and a baritone laugh fills the small space. "Sounds like someone needs to learn their place."

One hand grabs a fistful of my hair as the other grips the waist of my pants. It doesn't give me a lot of maneuverability, but the element of surprise and the wall to boost off of are just enough that I can kick off, twist, and plant the toothbrush through his eye and half-way to the back of his skull.

His death is quicker than he deserved.

I struggle to guide his heavy carcass quietly down to the mattress without getting any blood on myself. One down, two to go. I'm high on the adrenaline rush. Fuck, I love this feeling.

I give him a bit of a pat down, and damn if I don't find a sweet little pistol tucked in the back of his jeans. Thank you very much. A quick check confirms it seems to be in working order with three rounds to play with.

When I enter the kitchen, tall and greasy is leaning into the fridge. Copper beard is still sitting at the table, eating what's left of his bacon. Camilla is back in her seat at the table, her expression mostly neutral as her wide eyes look past me. The other two girls have moved to the sitting room.

I'll only get one of them by surprise, and if it comes down to a struggle, I have better chances against greasy. I walk past where he's now prying the top off a beer, and he's momentarily confused as he turns his head to the side, looking for Archer, I assume.

On second thought, he's a little too alert for comfort. I pull the pistol from behind my back and put a bullet in his face.

"What the fuck!" Copper beard knocks his chair over as he jumps to his feet.

"Don't move, asshole."

Camilla is pressed against the wall, tears streaking down her face. She inches her way along the cupboards, heading for a safer position off to my side. The initial screaming that came from the sitting room has stopped, thankfully. I just hope those girls have the sense to keep back.

I could squeeze the trigger now, but I can't resist drawing it out just a little.

"You're a bit pale, *little mouse.*"

"Who are you?" he stammers, and I delight in the last of the color draining from his face as I peel the tiny screen off my neck.

"My name is Agent Whisper. Now, how about you tell me where I can find your boss?"

"Archer, he's..."

"Not the corpse in my room. Who do you work for?"

"I... I can't. They'll kill me."

"I was hoping you'd say that." I pull the trigger to the sound of a new chorus of screams. "Ready to go home, Camilla?"

PROMOTION

The massive, domed Atrium at the top of HQ is, in my opinion, a bit on the theatrical side. It's kind of what I pictured the Elder's chamber looking like, though part of me thought it would just be an ordinary office once I finally got here.

Damon stands at my right, his shoulder touching my hip. He's been attached to me since I got back, though he's barely said a word. I have a feeling it'll be hard to convince him to let me out of his sight ever again.

When the dust settled and the paperwork was done, I returned home to find him asleep on the couch in his human form. I was too tired to think straight, and thankfully he didn't pressure me for details. He simply switched to his panther form and kept me warm while I slept.

The next morning, I woke to Gideon pounding on my door. A hasty dragon flight and a whirlwind of last-minute debriefing... and here we all are.

Gideon stands at my left now. He's back to his usual confident, controlled self. It's a far stretch from the blackmailing traitor I got acquainted with just twenty-four hours ago. And an even farther stretch from the loving, emotional uncle I watched fall to pieces as he was reunited with his niece.

Whatever he did, however he used me, I can't fault him one bit. I just can't. Such love and devotion in a family isn't something I understood, but I think I get it now. He would have done anything for her; sacrificed anything and anyone.

"And do you, Elite Gideon, vouch for Agent Jane "Whisper" Anderson's fitness and suitability for a place as your equal?" As Elder Marcus speaks, all in attendance look to Gideon.

The room is filled with people I don't know. Politicians, military, reporters, and residents of Solar One; all gathered to watch the first woman ever to be granted the title of Elite. It's a bit intimidating, to say the least. It all happened so fast that I really didn't expect so much fuss. I kind of figured they'd go out of their way to draw as little attention as possible to the whole thing.

I look up at Gideon, and his pale green eyes meet mine. He holds my future in his grasp at this very moment, his next words sealing my fate. Maybe that's the catch. Get me here, as visible and public as possible, just to have him announce that I'll never be good enough.

Charles's words echo through my mind; *What did you think would happen? Did you think you'd be allowed to continue?*

I hold my breath, imagining all the things Gideon could say now that would send me back to the ground. Back to nothing.

"I would be honored to have Agent Whisper at my side as I defend this administration. I would consider myself fortunate if she were to have my back should we go to war. I vouch for her fitness and suitability for the role of Elite. I accept full responsibility should my words prove false."

Holy fuck. That was it. Those were the words I've heard recited at every Elite's induction I've ever watched onscreen. I look away from him, up at the clear sky beyond the glass dome of the Atrium. The Elders are all watching me now, dressed in identical black robes as they sit on thier high-backed oak chairs.

"Welcome, Elite Whisper. It is an honor to be the first to congratulate you on this occasion."

I dip my head, crossing my right arm over my chest to make a fist over my heart. "Thank you, Elders. The honor is mine."

Holy fuck, Damon, we did it!

He starts to purr, a sound I rarely hear him make outside of our bed. It's all so surreal, like a dream. Just too good to be...

"Of course, there are no open active positions at the moment," Elder Marcus adds, and a few of the other Elders nod their agreement.

I look up at Gideon, but his expression is unchanged. What the hell?

"I don't understand," I say, to him or to the Elders. Whoever will fill me in.

"We can grant you the title today, Elite Whisper," Elder... I can't remember which one he is... fills me in, a bit of color rising in his cheeks as he makes up the lie as he goes. "But we are not in need of another active Elite at this time, so you will return to your previous post until we have need of your services."

What. The. Fuck.

Easy, little one.

I reach to bury my fingers in Damon's fur, grounding myself to keep from saying something that will make this worse. I can't go back to my previous post. Title or no title, I have nothing to go back to.

"I have need of an Elite." A female voice cuts through the charged silence, and I catch the flash of irritation on Elder Marcus's face before I turn toward the source.

Tanya. No, Tanikka. The wealthy woman I met briefly when I first came to HQ.

"My name is Tanikka Durant. Wife of Isaac Durant. Daughter-in-Law of Elder Marcus. I have been in need of a personal guard for some time, but I have yet to find an Elite who suits me. Elite Whisper has the qualities I am searching for, and I would be pleased to hire her. Effective immediately."

My eyes must be ten times their usual size as I struggle to keep my jaw from hitting the floor. The man beside her grasps her arm, tight enough to make her flinch, and whispers something in her ear.

"Very well." Elder Tobias nods his head in approval, though I'm almost certain he receives a bit of a salty side-eye from Elder Marcus. "Elite Whisper, you have your posting."

With that, the ten Elders stand as one and begin to file out of the room. The crowd, which seems to have doubled in size during the proceedings, hums with conversation.

Warm breath caresses my ear, as Gideon's low voice speaks just for me, "Congratulations, Whisper. You deserve this."

I turn to thank him, but he's already making his way through the crowd. A gentle hand on my arm makes me jump, and I turn to see Tanikka's honey-brown eyes and crimson smile.

"Tanikka, I... thank you."

"I'm sorry to spring that on you. I didn't get a chance to pull you aside earlier, but when they said they were sending you back, well, I just couldn't let that happen. I hope I didn't overstep. You can certainly decline the job offer, if you would prefer."

"No, I'm... thank you. I would be happy to work for you."

"Oh, wonderful!"

She loops an arm through mine and leads me through the crowd. Questions are being thrown at me from all directions; about my past, my time at the Academy, my work as an Agent, and even my sex life. Tanikka's a pro at dodging them all, and I'm more than happy to avoid the spotlight. My goal was to get to the top, not to be any sort of celebrity or public figure.

We pass out of the glass dome and into an elevator. Although there is plenty of room, no one steps forward to join us. The doors slide closed and Tanikka lets out a soft chuckle.

I look at her, and she blushes.

"I'm sorry. Your Shifter is quite intimidating. I can see why people give you a wide berth." Her expression grows a shade more serious. "I can see by the way he clings to your side that you have a strong bond. His eyes never stray from you for long. It's the second reason I wanted you so badly for this job."

I laugh at the way Damon stiffens at her words. He moves a few inches away, as if he's embarrassed by her observation.

"And what was the first reason?"

She smiles, her red lip stain framing brilliantly white teeth, "That you don't have a penis, of course."

I choke on my laugh, which produces a ridiculous snorting sound.

"I'm sorry," she bites her lower lip, fighting her smile. "That was a bit crude. I'm just tired of being surrounded by these alpha-male types. And the women up here; like pampered pure-bred lapdogs, devoted to their husbands as long as they get to keep spending their credits while contributing nothing to society." She blushes again, as if she's embarrassed by her own rant. "I'm no better, I suppose, but you... you are a woman I want to get to know."

I consider her descriptions, and her confessions. What a roller coaster of a day. I went from being held captive by human smugglers, to being promoted to Elite, to being sent back to ground. Now here I am, hired to guard someone I could actually give a shit about.

"Of course, as an Elite you don't really work for anyone in particular. You answer to the Elders directly, and no one else can control your actions. If you agree to this contract with me, it would be honorable to give me sufficient notice should you choose to move on to another post. However, you are in no way bound or obligated to follow anyone's orders, save for the Elders themselves. You do understand that?"

"Yes, thank you." I understand that perfectly clearly. Charles and whoever he really works for can't touch me here. "Do you even need a personal guard?" I'm almost afraid to hear her answer. I can't refuse the job, but the thought of it being a fake post just to satisfy her own curiosity...

"Yes, I do." Her answer is immediate, her gaze dropping to the floor. "My husband's job calls him away a lot, and when he is home there are strangers in and out at all hours. It's not that there has been any specific threat, but I just haven't felt safe. You know? It's not going to be a taxing position for you, but I would feel more comfortable knowing that someone like you, with your skill, were nearby should anything happen. Does that seem silly?"

"No, not at all," I assure her. Though, really, it kind of does. How much danger could possibly lurk in her mansion in the Solars? She has no idea what it's like to live under constant threat, knowing that falling asleep in your own bed is a dangerous prospect. "Damon and I have seen plenty of excitement. We'd be happy with a quiet post for a change."

"Lovely! Oh, and you must tell me some of your stories. I bet you have some good ones!"

Luckily the elevator doors open at the main lobby, and I don't get the chance to regale her with any of those stories.

I don't even feel the pressure of the usual stares as we cross the lobby, though I do crane my neck to get a glimpse of the blue-haired Dawn. She's already looking my way, from her post behind the reception desk. She throws me two thumbs-up and a smile that lights up the room.

Tanikka's chattiness takes an intermission as we leave HQ and slip into the backseat of a pristine white car.

I'll be above.

Okay. Thanks.

I feel a little tug of regret that Damon has to leave my side, but I don't show it. He steps back from the car as the driver closes our door, and I'm treated to a rare sight. His feline form ripples and twists, lush fur turning into glistening feathers. In the space of a few heartbeats, my panther spreads his wings and takes to the air in phoenix form. Incredible.

"That was incredible," Tanikka echoes my own thoughts. "I've never seen one shift."

"He doesn't usually do it in front of anyone. I'm not sure why, but he seems self-conscious about it."

"Do you talk with him? I know you communicate," she taps her slim neck, void of any tattoos, "But is it like actual conversation? Does he have that level of awareness?"

"Yes. He's very much his own person." I force the image of Damon in human form out of my head. That's not something I can ever tell, not to anyone. My new status as an Elite would do nothing to save him if that indiscretion were to be discovered.

"Incredible," she repeats, but doesn't question me farther.

NEW HOME

I close the heavy door behind me, appreciating the first moment alone I've had all day. It came as no surprise when Tanikka's home turned out to be a penthouse mansion, adorning the top of one of the tallest buildings in the center of Solar One. She gave me a brief tour of the opulent home, making sure I could easily find the kitchen, gym, swimming pool, library... yeah, this place is pretty ridiculous.

She actually apologized for giving me the 'small' guest suite, but holy hell this room is bigger than my entire house. No exaggeration.

It's a simple, open concept decorated in shades of beige with splashes of blue. There's chairs, cushions, books, a huge bed tucked into a sheltered nook, and a bathroom with a massive Jacuzzi. Best of all, there's a big balcony overlooking the city, making the perfect place for Damon to come and go with his new wings.

He came with us in panther form through the downstairs entrance. Now that we're alone in this room he's on the balcony, front paws up on the railing as he scans the breathtaking view. The gleaming, metal city surrounds us. The cool, evening air barely stirs the light curtains, even though the clouds look a bit angry outside the protection of the Solar's artificial atmosphere.

Tanikka was chatty, though mostly about her routines and how the household works. No prying questions about me or my past, thankfully. I'm sure that will come.

I quietly lock the door, just because I can. I'll have my things brought up tomorrow, and I suppose I might as well sell the house... or maybe just rent it out for now. If this doesn't work out long term...

I turn away from the door and reflexively unholster my pistol when I see a man standing in the middle of the room.

"Fuck, Damon!" I put my gun away. His smile is full of mischief as he stalks toward me. His bare chest and abs are impossible to tear my eyes away from, and he's formed a snug pair of faded jeans that sit low on his hips. "You can't..."

He plows into me, his mouth crushing against mine as his body presses me against the door. His hand tangles in my hair at the back of my head, his other arm wrapping around my waist.

I should stop him.

His kiss is awkward... his first. Our first. I relax into him, letting my lips part as his mouth explores mine, his tongue delving deep.

I should stop him, but the nagging thought gives way to the heat of the moment. Instead, I meet his tongue with mine. He growls, and when I kiss him back, nipping at his full, soft lips, his entire body trembles against me. His arousal is hard against my belly, straining against the confining fabric of his jeans. I can't even think straight.

He grips my thighs, lifting me off the ground to carry me across the room. He drops me on the bed, and I bounce slightly when I land on a plush comforter over a soft mattress. He's standing beside the bed, looking down at me with hunger in his eyes, chest heaving, fists clenched and that thick cock straining against his jeans. Fuck. He looks like every fantasy I've ever had, rolled into one perfect man.

"I want you, Whisper," he speaks at last, and his words are halting. Unsure. "I don't fully know what that means, and I don't want to hurt you. Ever. But I need to be closer to you, I want to... I want all of you."

He looks down at me with raw desire, but there's pain there two. And shame. He has this body, and these emotions, but he doesn't know what to do with them.

Oh fuck. I can't. We can't...

But why not? He might not be human, but his body sure as hell is. And if he doesn't explore this with me, would our bond stop him from finding someone else? Slipping away while I sleep for some casual sex... just the thought of another woman touching him, showing him.

Fuck it.

I slide to the edge of the bed, my knees on either side of his legs, and grip the waist of his jeans. I pull the zipper down with shaking fingers, watching his eyes blaze with lust. I push the pants down over his thick thighs, his cock springs free, and I forget how to breathe.

He is pure perfection. I want nothing more than to taste his flesh. I want him to have it all; everything he doesn't know how to ask for. I grip his thick erection, holding him steady as my tongue draws a long, lazy path from the base to the sweet, silky tip.

His breath hisses through his teeth, turning into a deep moan that rumbles through his entire body.

I scoot back onto the bed, pulling my clothes off as I go. He stays in place, only his eyes giving away the fierce emotions raging as he watches me. In a moment, I'm naked in front of him. He still hasn't moved, but his gaze has gone from hungry to deliriously feral. I hold out my hand in silent invitation, and he climbs onto the bed.

He moves to crawl over me, but I push him until he rolls onto his back. Confusion clouds his features for a brief moment before I straddle his hips. I lean forward, kissing his lips and the familiar scar on his neck. I lift myself up and lower my body down onto him.

We gasp in unison as he stretches me. A hint of pain mingles with the intense pleasure until my body adjusts to his size, and when I've taken the length of him in, it's like nothing I've ever experienced. I'm lightheaded, intoxicated with just the feel of him filling me.

His lips are parted, his forehead creased as his eyes travel up and down my body, always returning to the place where we are now joined. His hands grip my thighs, then move up my waist until he cups my breasts. The sensation of his hands on my skin while his hardness fills my core sends a wave a pleasure through me, and I start to move my hips in slow circles.

Grinding against him, the pleasure builds fast. I desperately want to make it last. But I can hear his breath coming faster. His hands are gripping my waist firmly as his hips rise and fall to meet the tempo I've set. He's just as close as I am, and the mere thought sends me flying over the edge. As waves of pleasure cascade over my body, I hear him climax along with me. He pulses inside me, as he moves his hips at an even faster pace, sending me crashing into another orgasm right on the heels of the first.

The world fades away, and there is only his body and mine and an unquantifiable pleasure that my mind can barely comprehend. We were made for this. We were made to fit together.

I melt onto the blankets beside him, and I'm vaguely aware of him shuffling us around until I'm wrapped tightly in his arms with

a velvety sheet over us. As the aftershocks fade, I'm left utterly
spent and thoroughly, completely, happy.

THE ROOM IS bright when my Whisper finally begins to stir in my
arms. I've spent the night watching her sleep, savoring the feel of
her skin against mine, and replaying our mating in my mind's eye.

I have always loved this woman. As a partner, as a friend, as a
piece of my heart. But now that I truly understand the depth of
our connection, the extent that a human heart can entwine itself
with another, I can never go back.

But I know my Whisper. I know what she fears. While the rest
of the world keeps their distance from my panther form, my
Whisper fears this form more than anything. She is brave, strong,
intelligent... but delicate in ways only I can see.

As her brown eyes flutter open, her peaceful expression is
interrupted by a flash of fear. It makes my heart ache, that I could
be the cause of her distress.

She showed me what our bodies can do. After a night of
imagining all the possibilities, I have so much more I'm desperate
to try. Already my body is responding to her, to the thoughts of
what I want to do with her. She notices, and the glimmer of heat
in her eyes is all the encouragement I need.

I cover her mouth with mine, and she opens for me to taste
her. It's not enough. I want so much more.

I abandon the sweetness of her mouth to taste the skin of her
neck. She whimpers when I bite her flesh, arching her back as I
nip and kiss my way down over her collarbone.

When I reach the pebbled peaks of her breasts, she moans and
squirms beneath me. I devour each in turn; licking, sucking and
biting the peaks as I knead the soft flesh with my hands. She loves

it as much as I do, judging by the way she claws at my back, urging me closer.

Her need is clear. Her desire to join with me is all I could have imagined and more. My cock is painfully hard, begging to be buried deep inside her, but I'm far from done worshipping every inch of my mate.

I pull away from her chest, dragging the rough stubble that grows on my face down over her flat stomach. Her skin is so soft and sweet as she trembles delicately beneath my touch. She gasps as I reach my destination and I push her legs apart, savoring the sight of her open beneath me for just a moment before I lower my head to taste her.

The sweetness of her core explodes across my tongue as her hips buck against me. I hold her thighs in place, delving my tongue deep with long, slow laps. The whimpers and moans that escape her are enough to make me lose control, but I'm not ready to stop yet.

I kiss her, pulling that delicious nub into my mouth and sucking it firmly. She cries out with pleasure, and I alternate sucking, licking and nipping her until she's nearly thrashing beneath me.

She stifles a scream.

I pull away, but her hands grab fistfuls of my hair, locking me in place between her legs. Her scream is a sound of pleasure. Pleasure caused by me. By my touch and my tongue. The realization pushes me over the edge of sanity, and I pull out of her grasp, climb up her body, and bury myself completely inside her with one strong thrust.

She cries out again, but I cover her mouth with mine as I ride the waves of her pleasure. She urges me faster and harder as her sharp nails dig into my skin. Bracing my arms on either side of her shoulders, I pull away from her slick heat, only to bury myself again. Over and over, I pound my hips against hers, holding nothing back. I can't get enough of her. My body was made for this.

She grips my wrists, anchoring herself as her legs wrap around my waist. Her eyes are wild, her hair splayed in tangles over the bed. She's the most beautiful thing I've ever laid eyes on. I lean down to taste her mouth, her throat, her shoulder.

I want this to last forever, but as her tight core clenches around me and she cries my name, I'm plummeting over the edge right with her. My own release slams into me with a force beyond anything I've ever felt. It radiates through me, consuming me with its intensity as I empty myself inside her.

I feel her relax as she comes down from her own orgasm, and as suddenly as it hit me the intensity fades until I'm left boneless and spent.

I collapse onto the bed beside her, using the last of my strength to pull her tightly against me.

"Holy shit, Damon," she says against my chest. The breathless awe in her voice mirrors my own emotions, and I'm the luckiest creature that ever lived.

I run my hand over her flawless skin, from shoulder to hip and back again, savoring the feel of her in my arms as my body hums with the afterglow of our mating. Her hand brushes lightly over me with the same lazy fascination, tracing the contours of my chest and stomach, and following the veins along my arm.

We stay wrapped up in each other, enjoying the simple pleasure of touch, until I follow her into dreamless sleep.

The next thing I'm aware of is a stinging slap against my stomach. I force my eyes open, reluctantly emerging from the best sleep of my life. I don't know if it's been minutes or hours, but as my surroundings come into focus, I see Whisper land another solid slap to my gut. I growl, and she slaps me again for no good reason.

"Wake up, sleeping beauty. Tanikka's at the door, you gotta shift."

She starts to move away, but I loop an arm around her waist and pull her back for a slow kiss. I want to pull her closer, but she pushes out of my grip as she slips off the bed and heads for the door.

I shift into my panther with barely a second to spare. My heightened sense of smell is bombarded with the heavy scent of our mating, and I can't resist burying my face in the soft blankets to inhale the delicious reminder of last night and this morning.

"Damon!"

Whisper's stern call commands my attention, and I jump off the bed and lope toward her. Beside her, my shoulder resting against her hip, I feel the calmness that only comes when I'm touching her. She scratches my head in that way that sends tingles down my spine.

"I'm going to go with Tanikka. Meet the staff, learn the routines, figure out how I can be of help; boring stuff."

I'll go with you, my mate.

She stiffens at my words, and I look up at her to make sure she's alright. Her brow is creased, her lips pressed tightly together.

I won't be leaving the house. You won't be needed.

I growl at the thought of any distance between us. This is the second time she has ordered me away from her side, claiming she doesn't need me. I bite her thigh to remind her who she belongs to. As much as I don't want to, I obey. Shaking my head, I lope back to the comfort of the soft bed. I burrow myself into the blankets, finding the place that smells most like my Whisper, then drift off back to sleep.

SAME SHIT

I pause just outside the door to my suite, rocking on my heels as I chew the inside of my cheek. It's been a long day shadowing Tanikka. She reviewed the staff schedules and her own itinerary for the next month. She had me study the layout of the house and learn the names and faces of all the important political personalities that might show up for meetings with her husband.

It's been exhausting, in a watching paint dry kind of way.

There's not a lot for me to do on a day-to-day basis when Tanikka is at home. Walk the halls now and then. Have Damon fly the exterior just as often. Her main need is for me to be at her side when she goes out. Certainly nothing like the risk and thrill of the kind of jobs I'm used to.

It didn't happen how I thought it would. Being used and blackmailed by Gideon makes my stomach turn when I think about it. But that's on me. I knew better than to trust a man. Charles. Gideon. In the end, they will all just do what they need to do to get what they want for themselves. Not that I can blame Gideon for wanting to save Camilla... it actually makes me like the guy even more. But trust him? Not making that mistake again.

Freeing those girls and ending the assholes that held them captive; that felt damn good. It was a pretty great finale to my time as an Agent. No regrets there. But the thought that's stuck in the back of my mind, the nagging feeling that's haunting me, is that those weren't the only girls suffering that fate. Not by a long shot. I want to ignore it, push it away and enjoy the luxury I've earned... but it's not as easy as I thought it would be.

It's not my problem. The human smuggling organizations have been around forever. Opening trade routes off-planet simply increased the demand. These are facts I've known. I've just never had such clear faces to put to the problem.

I'll talk to Gideon about it. He knows more than most, and I'm sure he's just as bothered as I am by the victims still trapped. Not today, though. He's had less than twenty-four hours with his niece. I'm sure he's not ready to jump back into the action just yet. I've got plenty to occupy myself with for now.

I reach for the door handle with an unsteady hand. It seems I've found an entirely different kind of risk and thrill. I'm pretty confident that what I'm doing with Damon is wrong on a bunch of levels. But I just can't resist.

I showed him how to fuck last night. This morning, he returned the favor by taking me to a level of carnal bliss I never knew existed. Was that three orgasms, or four? By that point, I barely knew my own name let alone how to count.

The rational side of my brain tells me I'm playing a dangerous game, and I need to stop before it gets out of control. But the rest of me is just debating what to show him next. He apparently has some serious natural talent in the oral department, and the idea of returning that favor makes my mouth water.

The thought that we can work and live in this beautiful place, and explore this... whatever this is... every night; it's just too good to be true. As long as no one suspects, what harm could it be? The way it felt to be with him... I've never experienced anything even close to that before.

But that's selfish. He would do anything for me. It's just the way he was made. He's not human. Taking advantage of his self-less nature so that I can have mind-blowing sex whenever I want... that just sounds so wrong.

I'm such a coward. I'm standing here outside my door fanta-sizing and worrying about what will happen when I go in, but too chicken to actually turn the handle.

Which reminds me, Tanikka mentioned she made arrange-ments for me to get my Stim implant. All Elites get it, for an increase in strength and speed. I hate the thought of going under for the procedure, but I'm certainly looking forward to the payoff after. I reach for my comm, I could text her and ask, but I could also just walk back to her office and avoid Damon a little longer.

Yep, option B.

I turn on my heels and retreat back through the hardwood hallways. When I reach her door, I lift a hand to knock. She told me to come and go as I please. I lower my arm and just call a *hello* as I open the door.

The scene inside the room doesn't make sense, but my instincts take over and I draw my weapon, pointing it at Isaac Durant's chest as I walk slowly forward.

"Whisper, stop!" Tanikka's voice is shaky as she picks herself up off the floor. Up from where she landed after his fist knocked her off her feet. Tears have streaked her flawless makeup, black mascara running down her cheeks. "This isn't any of your concern."

"I told you having her here was a bad idea," her husband hisses through clenched teeth, balling his fist as if he would strike her again with me right here.

"Tanikka, come with me." I motion with a tilt of my head for her to retreat through the door, my gun still aimed at her husband.

I would very much love to pull the trigger.

"Put that fucking gun away." He starts to walk toward me. There's no hint of fear in his eyes, which only makes me want to kill him slower.

"Stop it! Both of you!" Tanikka puts herself between us, one hand on her husband's chest and the other waving me away. "Just go, Whisper."

Her voice is steady now, commanding. But her eyes are pleading, begging me to listen. I'm powerless. I can't injure the son of an Elder and heir to that title without ensuring I never see the light of day again. And she would defend him, both physically and legally, of that I have no doubt. She might be up here, at the top of the world and in the highest position a woman can occupy, but her eyes right now are that of every abused woman I've ever encountered.

"I can help you," I offer as I holster my weapon. I know it's a pointless gesture.

"I'm fine. It was a misunderstanding. Between all of us. It won't happen again." She looks from me to Isaac as she speaks, but he only grins in my direction. He knows exactly where things stand. Exactly how safe he is as a man in a man's world.

"Yes, ma'am."

She flinches as I deliberately use the formal term even though we've been on a first-name basis since we met.

"Go back to your suite. I have no need of your services until nine tomorrow morning, when we leave for your appointment."

Well, I got my question answered at least. With no choice but to obey, for now, I nod and turn back the way I came. The muffled sound of their arguing follows me for just a little while, until I'm too far away to hear.

This time, I don't hesitate to open my own door.

My beautiful panther hops down from the bed, his body reforming into the shape of a man that makes me instantly heat up by a few degrees. His playful expression turns to concern as he gets closer, and my heart melts as he pulls me into his strong embrace. I wrap my arms around his waist, resting my cheek against the hard comfort of his bare chest.

What's wrong, little one?

I tell him everything that just happened. In the past, he would listen and give brief opinions, never seeming to put much thought into any of the decisions I was faced with. He was there for muscle and protection, not so much for heavy debates. In human form, he seems to think more, feel more, understand more. All the reasons we were told a Shifter brain couldn't handle human form. He should have gone insane with the overload of information and yet he has adapted almost seamlessly.

Is he unique? Or was it always a lie? I'll probably never know, because I'll never risk his safety by asking the questions.

"You can't help her if she doesn't want to be helped. You would only be risking your own safety. You've dealt with people in this situation before."

"I know. I do. But I just..." He waits patiently for me to find the words, one arm holding me tight while the other strokes softly through my hair. He's petting me. Just like I do for him when he's agitated. "If someone like Tanikka can't even be above such things, what hope is there for any female? What's the point of any of this? I fought to get to the top, and here I am working for a woman who is nothing more than a man's possession. I'll never be free of it. No one will. What's the point of even trying?"

I hate the sound of my own voice. I hate the words I'm saying. But no matter how I look at it, they're true. This world is broken, and I was naïve to think I could ever be free of the bullshit.

"Whisper," he says against my ear, and I can't miss the hint of heat in his voice. "I think I know what would make you feel better."

My body responds instantly to his suggestive tone. Just the hint of sex in his voice and I'm ready to ignore my problems and forget the world.

"Damon..."

He pushes away from me and I catch the mischievous grin on his face before he turns and walks toward the balcony. Once outside, he swings his long legs up and over the railing before pushing off into thin air. My heart lurches as he disappears, even though I know he can sprout wings in an instant.

I shake off the pointless whining, heading for the balcony to get a glimpse of his glossy feathers. Maybe I'll get a good, close look at him this time.

The moment I step out into the cool air, a huge winged form swoops up from below. The creature is as black as pitch and has a wingspan of at least fifteen feet. I instinctively reach for my weapon, but relax an instant later as recognition dawns.

Damon lands on the balcony with the soft paws of his panther form. His body's a much larger version of his panther. He has the head of his phoenix form with big, saucer eyes and a hooked beak that shines like ebony in the light from my suite. He tucks thickly feathered wings into his body.

I'm speechless for a moment as I take in the sight of him, and I can't stop the embarrassingly girly squeal that comes out of me.

"You're a *griffon*! Holy shit, Damon! When did you learn this?"

He shakes his head, his big eyes darting away from me to look out over the city.

Wow. I'm simply in awe of him. I reach out to touch his thick neck, but his head jerks backward. I stay still, with my hand extended, until he leans forward into my touch. His new forms always come with their own quirks and instincts that he has to learn to overcome, so I don't take it personally that his griffon is a little skittish.

"Are you good?"

He shakes his head as if clearing his thoughts, then fluffs his wings before tucking them back to his sides.

I'm good. Climb on.

He lowers himself down, but I hesitate. It's a little too soon to trust the new form quite that much.

"Maybe not yet... I'll give you a bit more time to get the hang of it."

Climb on. I know what will make you feel better.

BROKEN

*T*his is exactly what I needed.

I welcome the familiar, sour scent that carries notes of sweat and bleach. It's a Friday night and Kelseys is crowded as usual. The tables are filled with couples and groups of co-workers enjoying some down time at the end of their work week. The dance floor, though not large, teems with young people enjoying the modern, up-beat tunes that vibrate through the floorboards.

Flying with Damon was insanely fun and more than a little terrifying. Landing in the bar's parking lot had attracted a flow of curious onlookers, and I suspect he hadn't minded the attention one bit. He had flared his wings and posed with an air of vanity I've never seen in him before. I guess his griffon comes with a bit of an ego.

I was more than happy to leave the attention for him.

I slipped away from the crowd, swapping out my clothes for something more casual and untying my hair. Damon was right. I need a drink or four to unwind and get my mind off Tanikka and all the new bullshit I've stepped in.

I slide onto my favorite seat, in my favorite bar, and wait for my favorite bartender. She doesn't disappoint, and within minutes a glass of my Balvenie slides toward me.

"I didn't think I'd see you down here again so soon."

It's so good to see her again. A pang of guilt hits me as I realize I haven't even texted her once since I went up to work as Gideon's Apprentice.

"I wanted to see a familiar face." My smile doesn't convince her for a moment.

"Oh girl, what's up? Grass isn't so green up there after all?"

My face must answer for me, because she immediately gestures with a finger for me to wait a moment. She talks in the ear of the other two bartenders on duty, before shucking her apron and making her way around the bar to slide onto the stool beside me.

"You're busy tonight, there's no need..."

"Don't be silly." She reaches to put a warm hand on my thigh, and I cover it with my own. "I always have time for you."

"You're a good friend." That's more than I can say about myself.

"Yes, I am." I look up expecting to see her sassy grin, but she's all serious. "I mean it, Whisp. We've been friends for a long time, but you've always held back. You're strong and independent, and I respect that, but everyone needs a friend. Talk to me."

And I do. I tell her everything, almost. Jeffries betrayal and Damon's human form... though I skip the part about us hooking up. I tell her about Gideon's ulterior motives, his niece and the girls being sold. I tell her about Tanikka and her husband. It all comes out, in hushed tones as we lean toward each other on our stools. At some point her hands grab mine, and then I'm finished and we're sitting in silence as I wait for her to respond.

Was it too much? I shouldn't have put all that on her. The relief I feel at having unloaded my shit is immediately replaced by a fresh wave of guilt and some regret to boot. I didn't just tell her my problems as if she should give a shit, I also told her things no one should know. Things that could get me and Damon into some serious trouble. How stupid could I be?

"Thank you."

Her words are barely audible over the noise of the bar, but they bring me out of my thoughts and back to the woman sitting in front of me.

"I shouldn't have told you all that."

"No. Don't say that. I want you to trust me."

We sit in silence as I finish my drink. I'm not really sure how to proceed after all that, and I start to fidget as my eyes scan across the other patrons. Some are having a great time celebrating or just enjoying their companions. Some look to be drowning their problems in a glass. One face grabs my attention and makes my breath catch in my lungs.

Damon.

He's standing near the door, wearing jeans and a plain black shirt. Two girls, barely twenty-one if you add them together, hover a little too close for comfort. They're chatting him up as they talk with their hands, taking every opportunity to touch his arms.

I grit my teeth. What the hell would possess him to come in here? He hates the crowds and the attention. He definitely hates being touched by anyone other than me.

"Who's *that*?" Kelsey asks with a lilt in her voice that makes my temper rise even more. "He's been looking at you like a cat with a mouse."

I don't answer. I just sit there staring, possibly with actual smoke coming out of my ears.

"Oh shit. Is that *him*?"

"Yeah."

"Wow. I have to say..."

"No, you don't."

"... He's pretty damn sexy. You definitely skipped over that part of the story, and I know you noticed. If I were even a little bit straight..."

"Kelsey, stop. He's a Shifter."

"So?"

I want to argue with her, but I'm too distracted by the sight of him and those little tramps. One of them grabs his hand in both of hers, leading him to the dance floor. In a moment, he's sand-wiched between them as they grind to the beat, letting their dirty little hands wander over him.

He doesn't resist, not even for a second. And he doesn't glance my way. I take a deep breath and turn away from the scene, forcing my attention back to Kelsey.

"Are you okay?" She looks at me with raised eyebrows as I exhale the breath I've apparently been holding. "I'm not going to have a cat fight in my bar tonight, am I? No pun intended."

"No. Of course not. He's doing what he wants to do. There's no harm in that. It's not like he's going to shift in plain sight. He's an adult. It's none of my business."

"Wow. Okay. Defensive much?" She tips her head back and forth as if she's weighing her next words. "You like him. And I don't mean the way most people like their cats. You *like* him."

"Kelsey, seriously. I'm a grown woman and he's a Shifter. He's my best friend. I'm just worried about him."

"Right." She leans closer to me, her voice dropping even farther. "You know he's kind of perfect for you, don't you?"

"What?"

"He's Damon! He's your partner. Your best friend. You trust him with your life. You've told me these things many times." She pauses as a smile spreads across her face, then alters the tone of her voice for an unflattering impersonation of my own. "*If only he had a cock, he'd be the perfect man.*"

She bursts into a giddy laugh, and I swivel on my stool so I can lean my elbows on the counter and bury my face in my hands.

Her laugh stops abruptly, and I look up from my wallowing. I follow her gaze to see Damon, still sandwiched between the sorority twins. The blond has a hand snaked around the back of his neck as she stretches up on the tips of her gaudy red shoes. Her lips are planted firmly on his.

It looks like a one-sided thing, like she just planted one on him and he doesn't know what to do. I stiffen, ready to go to his aid, but then he puts an arm around her waist.

He's fucking kissing her back.

"See?"

I turn my back to him and his new plaything. Kelsey's face has fallen with a look of disappointment, and that sure as hell better not be pity in her eyes.

It's not like this is unexpected. I was just too blind to see it coming. He took the body of a man, and he's been learning what it means to be a man. It was only a matter of time before his affection for me took a back seat to the seduction of a new piece of ass.

It shouldn't bother me. We had fun while it lasted. But a man's a man, no matter how selfless and noble they think they are. They're all the same in the end.

"Maybe he just doesn't know any better. You've kept him hidden away, and he's got all these new... urges."

"Stop, Kelsey."

"I'm sorry."

I wave her off, pulling my comm out of my pocket. I've got bigger things to be thinking about than my twisted sex life. I pull up Gideon's number and send off a quick message.

Me: Hey. We need to talk. You free in the morning?

Gideon: *Can do. Where?*

Me: Meet me at the edge.

Gideon: I'll be there at seven.

Damn, he's an early riser. I guess I am now, too, with this gig. Tanikka's day starts at eight, so meeting Gideon at seven works just perfect.

"I've gotta go. Early start tomorrow."

I down the drink that was evidently refilled at some point during our conversation, then slip off my stool. Kelsey grabs my arm and pulls me into a hug before I can get away. I give in without protest, enjoying the chance to breath in her sweet, vanilla scent.

"It's not all bad, you know?" She says.

I roll my eyes as I shuffle backwards out of her grip, but she takes my face in her hands to coax me to look at her.

"I mean it. The world's not all bad. You came from a shitty place and your job has you involved with truly awful people. But that doesn't mean the whole world is like that. People are mostly good. Mostly happy. Not all women are oppressed and living under men's thumbs. I own this bar, it's my name on the door, and no man tells me what to do. You've got to let yourself see the good stuff, too. Don't get yourself killed trying to save the world."

I nod, giving her another quick hug as I blink away the sting in my eyes. I kiss her quickly, but there's no spark there. We've had some great times in the past. She's a good friend, and a crazy fun lover, but it was never quite enough. I'm hopelessly attracted to the opposite sex, even though I don't particularly like any I've met so far.

To be perfectly honest, I liked it just fine that way. Always hunting, always looking for my next plaything. Never quite satisfied. Then Damon had to go and ruin everything. Him and his perfect body, and his apparently natural ability to deliver earth shattering orgasms. Why can't it just be fun and casual, without all this moral, emotional crap mixed in?

No, I can't save the world. But I can kill some of the assholes that make life hell for innocent people. I just need to stop acting like the weak, whiny girl I'm starting to turn into. I don't need a lover. I need my Shifter to watch my back.

I turn my attention to my man-panther, and steel myself to haul his ass home.

~

I'VE NEVER CARED much for interacting with humans. They've never cared much for interacting with me, either. That's always suited me just fine. I've never felt the need to communicate with anyone other than my Whisper.

Until I met the boy in the alley. Eric. I earned his trust and took him to safety. I spoke with the owners of the orphanage as if I were just another human. They thanked me. They told me I had done a good thing, and that Eric's life would be forever changed.

He hugged my neck and told me he would never forget me... and never tell my secret to anyone.

Now, I'm curious about the people around me.

I brought Whisper to her favorite bar because it always cheers her up. I hadn't considered that it would be any different than any other visit, with me waiting outside while she does whatever it is she does. But I see things differently now. I hear things I've never paid attention to before.

The people outside the bar wanted to get close to me. They wanted to take photos of me and touch me. It was a little odd, but I couldn't really blame them. I saw my griffon form in my reflection over the water and it was an impressive sight.

I was enjoying the attention when the thought struck me. Whisper's words came back to me from memory, from all the times she talked about coming here. All the times she talked about needing to find a male to satisfy her.

I brought her here to relax and feel happy, not to find another male.

As anger spread through me, a new thought came to mind; I could follow her inside. She wouldn't need to find a new male if I were there with her. No one would know what I really was. My human form would blend in perfectly.

It was a great idea.

I flew out of sight, shifted to my panther form so I could slink along with the shadows until I found a safe spot to take my human form. When I returned to the bar, no one looked twice at me. I was just another human.

Now, I'm standing inside the bar that Whisper loves. Some people look at me with curious expressions, but no one seems afraid or angry with my presence. I spot my mate right away. At first, I'm relieved to see her deep in conversation with another female. The relief quickly fades to jealousy again as I recognize the other woman. Kelsey.

Whisper never brought men home. She liked to play with them, but she never trusted one enough to bring home. Kelsey was different. When Kelsey came home with Whisper, they locked me out of the bedroom. Now, it makes me question everything I thought I knew.

Is this female more than just a friend? Is she Whisper's mate? I force my eyes away from her to scan around the room. There are dimly lit tables full of people talking, eating, and drinking. There's a wide section, lit with colorful, flashing lights where people stand against each other, moving their bodies in time with the beating music.

I look at the people around me, and I see that the couples are not only male and female. There are female pairs, male pairs, and pairs where I can't even guess their gender. It seems humans don't only bond with the opposite sex. They must choose their mates for some other reason.

I take a closer look at a few males, but don't feel any particular attraction. I look closer at a few females, and though I do find them slightly more enjoyable to watch, there's still no spark of attraction.

I look back at Whisper, and just the sight of her across the room makes my heart race. I've felt this connection with her since the moment I first laid eyes on her. It's only grown stronger, and I can't imagine wanting to be close to anyone but her. I've never thought about it, but it makes perfect sense. I would love Whisper regardless of her form, of that I am certain. Though I am very grateful she happens to have this particular form.

She is my mate. She may not be ready to admit it yet, but I'm going to make damn sure no one comes between us. Not even her Kelsey.

I move toward her, but two young females block my path.

"Hey, I'm Malorie." The first one practically purrs as she touches my arm.

"I'm Sonya." The second one bites her lower lip as she peers up at me through thick eyelashes.

I feel my hackles rise, even though I technically don't have hackles in this form. These girls are acting exactly the way Whisp does when she's luring in a mark. Do they suspect what I am? Can they tell?

"Hello."

I'm suddenly not sure if my voice sounds human enough. Whisp's warnings about the danger of being caught taking human form are echoing in my mind.

The females continue to talk, chattering on about boyfriends and work and things I can't quite make sense of. They keep touching me. I want to back out of their reach, but I know this behavior too well. They want something from me.

When Whisp acts like this, her marks never suspect a thing. They fall for it every time. So, I let them talk, and touch me, and pull me toward the flashing lights and thick crowd. The girls surround me, pressing their bodies against mine and urging me to move with them.

It's not unpleasant; the vibration of the pounding music and the bodies pressed against mine. My cock stirs as they move in ways that remind me of mating with Whisper, but I can easily ignore it.

I move with them, dance with them, giving them no reason to suspect I have anything to hide. It's easy, fun even, until one of them presses her mouth to mine. I don't want to taste anyone but Whisper, but if this is a test I won't fail. I kiss her back, even though she tastes like rotten berries.

I pull away from her when I can stand it no longer. The second girl immediately slides in, urging me to kiss her, too. She's even bolder than the first. She reaches her hand between us and finds the ridge of my semi-hard cock. Apparently, my body is willing even when my mind is far from interested. She seems pleased with her discovery as her tongue finds mine and she moans a sound of pleasure.

A fist grabs the front of my shirt, and I'm lurched away from the dance floor. The girls begin to protest, but one glare from Whisper has them tucking their tails and retreating. She keeps hold of my shirt as she nearly drags me out of the bar, though I would obviously follow her willingly.

"What the fuck?" She shouts at me as soon as we're away from the building.

I can't help but grin when I realize that she's jealous. Very jealous. I close the distance between us, needing to have her in my arms and erase the memory of those other women from my body.

She blocks me, shoving both hands against my chest as she backs away. I've clearly pissed her off.

"What the fuck do you think you were doing with those girls?"

"They wanted something from me."

"Obviously they wanted something from you! They wanted your cock. From what I saw, you seemed pretty fucking happy to give it to them."

"I didn't-"

"Whatever. I don't care who you fuck, I just don't want to see you get caught and put down!"

She's jealous. She's jealous, but she has no reason to be. I could never want another woman.

"I wouldn't *fuck* anyone. You're the only-"

"Just stop, Damon. You don't have to explain yourself. What you do is your business, it's not like we're really... a thing. I just need to get home."

I don't know what to say to her. We're not a thing? We're everything.

I step away from her, even though I desperately want to get closer. I step back and will my body to reform into my griffon. It's a painful shift, but quick. As soon as I stand before her in my new form, her features soften. She looks at me with pride and affection once again.

I wish she would look at me like this when I'm in human form. When I can hold her and kiss her and make her mine. Maybe she never will.

I crouch low to the ground and she doesn't waste a moment climbing on. The thick feathers on my neck make solid hand-holds, and a perfect spot to bury her face when the wind gets too strong. She grips me tight, and I put all my focus into flying steady and even.

When I land on the balcony after our unhurried flight, I wait impatiently for her to slide off and open the glass doors. As soon as she steps inside, her clothes fade into a soft sleeping outfit. I can hardly wait to have her in my arms.

I shift, concentrating on the loose, black pants and t-shirt that will cover me. Clothes take a bit of effort, but sticking to the same ones is making it easier each time. I pad toward her on human feet until I can finally slide my arms around her waist and pull her tight against me.

She feels like home. All I can think about is stripping her down and savoring every inch of her skin. I want to make her scream my name again. I want to bury myself inside her and show her how much I love her.

"Damon," she says on a sigh, and my heart swells when there's no trace of anger in her voice. "I'm sorry. I shouldn't have let this go so far. You're a Shifter, not a human. I let your appearance fuck with my head, and it went too far."

She pushes out of my arms. Her words don't make sense.

"You loved me long before I could take this form. We spent every moment together, and I was always loyal to you..."

"Yes, but you're a Shifter. A modified animal. And I'm your bondmate; you were made to be loyal to me. This form just makes it seem like something more, but it's... it's just fucked up."

A heat boils inside my chest, making my limbs turn cold. I don't feel like holding her. I don't even want to be close to her. I grit my teeth, trying to stop the words that are forming. Or maybe I want her to hear them.

"I'm not human, but I'm not an animal, either. I don't know what I am. All I know is that since the moment I first saw you, you're all I've cared about. I thought you felt the same. You wanted me in your bed. You wanted me close every moment. I thought that was because you loved me, but maybe you just needed me. Loving you was just another job you needed me to do."

"No, Damon." Her eyes are glassy as she wraps her arms around herself.

My words are hurting her, but I ignore the urge to comfort her. I want her to hurt. I want her to feel what I feel when she pushes me away and tells me how wrong it is for us to be together.

"After all this time, you still don't trust me. You still don't love me. Maybe you are too broken, Whisper. Maybe you just like it in the dark."

It's too far. She recoils as if I've struck her, and the pain on her face cuts me to my core. Too many emotions are at war inside me, I can't think straight. I have to get away from her, from all of this. I take my panther form, feeling immediate relief as the pressure that was building fades away. I lope to the balcony, and leap into my phoenix.

CHOICES

I lean my elbows on a cold, metal post as I strain my eyes against the glaring morning sun. Moridian is sprawled out below, hazy blue skies above. I reach my hand out, stretching my fingers as far as I can over the edge. I keep thinking I'll see him flying along the horizon. Flying toward me.

He didn't return last night. I can't remember the last time I slept alone, and just the thought makes me cringe. I hate these feelings of guilt and worry. If he just hadn't taken human form. If things could just be the way they were before. Our relationship was simple, comfortable, safe. Now it feels more like a *relationship*. Like we had a lover's spat.

I guess we kind of did.

Fuck.

I keep replaying the words he said. He was right; I'm selfish and I'm broken. But I knew that already... I just don't know how he didn't. Now he's pissed off and gone who knows where, and I'm left as an Elite without a Shifter.

Maybe I should get a new one.

"Fuck," I say to no one. I tap my boot against the post in a steady rhythm, just to hear something other than my own thoughts.

Even the idea of replacing him feels completely wrong. He's not my property. He's not a *pet*. And I honestly don't care about the job right now. I just want him here and safe, with me.

That thought makes my blood run cold. I've never cared about anything or anyone more than my place in the Protectors. But Damon... the thought of having any of this without him by my side is just... it's just not possible.

I need to see him. I need to look him in the eyes and tell him exactly how much he means to me, because I sure as hell didn't show him any affection last night. I was awful to him.

A door thumps behind me, and familiar boots approach.

"Where does Tarek sleep?"

"What? Wherever the fuck he wants, why?"

"Does he sleep with you?"

"No. Why would I... what do you want, Whisper? Why am I here?"

Damon was right. We always had something different. But it wasn't because I didn't want to sleep alone. It just always felt right to have him close. I never questioned it.

I turn around, hoping Gideon can't see the emotions hiding under my fake smile. I take one look at him, and my breath catches in my throat. He looks like shit. He's got bags under his eyes and three days growth on his face. I think he slept in his clothes.

"What happened to you? What's wrong."

He looks away from me, clenching his jaw and fighting to keep his composure. I don't know what to do, what to say. He looks like he's lost...

"Camilla. Is she okay?"

His composure cracks for a moment, but he steels his expression. His voice is strained when he speaks. "She's gone. She couldn't live with it. The shit they did to her. The shit they made her do. I couldn't help her."

His words hit me like a punch in the gut.

"No, I... I saved her. I killed those assholes and got her out of there."

A sickening laugh bursts out of him, and he turns to leave.

"She was dead long before that."

I'm frozen to the spot for a moment, but then I rush to block his path. "We have to get the rest of them out. We have to stop them, all of them... We can't let more girls be taken."

"We can't do anything. We can't make any difference. I tried for months and accomplished nothing."

"Until you found me. Right?"

He laughs, shaking his head as he shoulders past me. I block his path again.

"Fuck off, Whisper."

"Just give me a name."

He tries again to push past me, but I'm not backing down. He might have lost his will to fight, but I've got plenty to spare. I'll take the fuckers down alone.

"Durant. How's that for a name?" He spits the words, then sighs as he hangs his head.

It takes me a second to realize what he's saying. "Tanikka's husband? Isaac?"

"Tanikka, Isaac, Elder Marcus. They're all fucking corrupt. Probably half the Elders. It's money, Whisper. Open your eyes. It's what keeps us up here, what keeps us relevant off-world. We're a small, overpopulated, polluted planet. But we have drugs and we have women. What do you think paid for all the tech we have? The Solars, the Aquatics, teleports, Shifters, implants... none of our tech came from earth, and none of it was cheap."

Bile rises in the back of my throat, and I step aside to let him pass. He doesn't hesitate, and in a moment, I hear his engine rev as he spins out of the lot. I wish Damon were here. I wish he had heard that. I need to talk to him, and I need to bury my fingers in his fur and feel grounded again.

Most of all, I need to kick some ass.

I PUSH through Tanikka's office door, both relieved and disappointed to find her alone. I'm itching to confront her husband. I can feel it like a prickle across my skin. It's a level of anger that makes me want to smile as I picture the ways I could hurt him and anyone else who thinks they can treat women like currency.

Tanikka looks up from her desk, loose strands of hair falling delicately around her face. Her eyes are heavy, dark circles beneath them and not a trace of the crimson that usually paints her lips.

"Whisper, oh!" She startles as she looks from me to the ornate, wooden clock on the wall. "I apologize, I lost track of the time."

She stands, smoothing her hair with her hands. She's wearing the same clothes she had on yesterday. This regal, wife-of-a-future-Elder looks like nothing more than a frail housewife too scared to sleep in her own bed. A twinge of sympathy cuts through my rage, but I force it away.

I like being angry. It gets shit done.

"What do you know about your husband's involvement with Horizon Zero?" My voice is deliberately neutral. I could just as easily be asking her what's on the agenda for the day.

Her eyes go wide, the whites visible around her iris's. She looks like she would flee, if I weren't blocking her only exit. I wait quietly, hands at my sides. She grips the edge of her desk, leaning into it as she lets out a long breath.

"I know nothing."

"Bullshit."

She snaps her eyes up to mine. Finally, there's a hint of fight in her.

"Do you think so? Because when I went to the Elders, when I told them what I heard and what I thought... they were confident that I *knew nothing*. No facts, no proof. No reason to poison the reputation of a *respectable public figure and philanthropist.*"

Well, that takes me back a step. She went to the Elders about her husband? I close the door behind me and walk cautiously up to her desk. Across the wide surface she stands straight, crossing her arms in front of her slim chest.

"You told the Elders your husband was involved with a company that abducts and sells human girls?"

She cringes, tilting her head away and closing her eyes. "I told them what I heard; That girls were being taken. I told them they were being shipped off-world and that my husband knew about it. But they were right, I had no proof. Nothing but the ramblings of a disgruntled wife attempting to get even with her husband."

That's not what I expected to hear when I came to confront her.

I need you here. I reach out to Damon, but I know he's not close enough to hear me. I ignore the tendrils of fear creeping through me, refusing to consider that he might not come back.

"Where's Isaac now?"

I need to follow this through. I'm not entirely confident that I should do it alone, but who else would back me up? I can't wait for Damon, assuming he plans to return at all. Fuck knows I'd deserve it if he left me, after how I treated him. I took down that holding house alone, and I can damn well take down this house, too.

Tanikka closes her eyes. She nods. "He's in our kitchen, finishing his coffee before he begins his day. He's a predictable man."

"Is he alone?"

She holds my gaze for a while before she speaks.

"Yes," she answers, her voice barely more than a breath. I don't miss the way her head moves almost imperceptibly from side to side; an unconscious *no* even as her words say otherwise. She's torn between helping me and protecting herself. Maybe she knows he's not so alone after all.

Doesn't matter.

I leave her to her thoughts, walking the halls with a casual stride. I pass a few staff, returning the occasional nod or quick greeting. Outside the wide, double doors that lead to the Durant's private living quarters, I stop and listen. No sound comes from behind them, and no trace of steps from the direction I came. I withdraw my pistol, sliding the safety, and enter.

Isaac sits alone at a high, white table. He's holding a steaming coffee mug in one hand and swiping a tablet screen with his other. He looks comfortable, relaxed, unaware.

The open concept kitchen, dining and living room is a picture of minimalism and brightly lit from the floor to ceiling windows. Tanikka gave me a brief tour yesterday, so I know the two open doors on the opposite side of the room lead to the large, equally bright bedroom and bathroom.

I level my gun with his torso and take a step forward. When I'm halfway across the room, he turns toward me with a casual smile. Sipping from his mug, he looks at me with a comfortable ease that makes it clear he is not surprised by my presence.

"Hello, Elite Whisper," he greets me with a confident tone,

like he's not at all affected by the weapon pointed at him. It makes me want to squeeze the trigger. Just once.

"Tell me about the girls that are being taken. Tell me about Horizon Zero."

With a deep breath, he leans back in his chair, cracking his knuckles as he appears to consider my question. He's not at all surprised by my presence, nor my inquiry. I can't accept that Tanikka warned him. He must have her office monitored. Possibly my suite, as well. Heat rises up my neck as I think of the things he would have heard or seen over the last couple days.

"Is this worth your job, Elite Whisper? Do you plan to sacrifice your title for something you can't possibly comprehend, let along stop?"

I hate that I hesitate to answer. Exposing him as a criminal won't hurt my career. If anything, it will give me some serious points. No more filler positions. They might actually see me as a valuable part of the Elite program.

"What do you know about the girls?"

"Well, let me think now. Are you referring to the Companions?" He looks at me as if needing clarification, but I don't play along. "If so, I'm aware of a company that connects unfortunate young women with individuals, or families, in need of their services. They're called Companions, and serve many purposes including childcare, companionship for the elderly, and housekeeping. Great care is taken to ensure the right fit is found for all parties involved."

That's how he sells it. How he keeps the Elders satisfied and the books above the table. But I don't think for a second I've conveniently found myself living in the home of the man behind it all. This prick is a politician through and through. I doubt he's ever even seen one of those girls in person.

"Sounds like a perfectly respectable business, Isaac. How

about you give me an address and a couple names, so I can look into hiring someone for my grandmother?"

"How about you put that gun down first?" He slowly picks up his mug and takes a sip, keeping his eyes on me. He sets it down again, then shows me his palms in a gesture of surrender. "I can assure you I value my life over my loyalty to but one of the many companies I work with. I'll give you what you want, if we can talk about it like adults."

"You can talk just fine like this."

I lower my aim to his thigh. I don't plan to be up for any murder charges, but I'll gladly give him a nice, clean wound to the leg and a limp to remember me by.

"Fine. Have it your way. Hunter."

The moment he speaks, there's a blur of movement to my left. A massive form erupts from behind the kitchen counter. I squeeze the trigger, hearing a roar of pain just as the body of a fucking tiger hits me like a bus. I go down hard, the sound of my head hitting the tile resonating like an explosion behind my eyes.

I see nothing but black as I slide my knife from its holster on my thigh and swing. The fucker must dodge me, because I hit nothing but air. Jaws close around my arm as a heavy paw pins me to the floor. I grit my teeth to keep from screaming as teeth sink through the skin and threaten to break bone.

I claw at the beast's eyes with my free hand as I kick upward with my legs. He shifts his stance, one paw pinning my other arm as he settles his weight down on top of me.

I stop struggling. It's futile, and giving in to panic won't get me anywhere. Pain sears in my arm where his teeth are still buried in my flesh, but it's not broken. As I relax, my vision begins to clear.

The vibrant orange, black and white strips of a tiger Shifter come into focus. He's four, maybe even five hundred pounds. His massive head is next to mine as he maintains his grip on my arm and his thick, lush fur is absolutely stunning. I have the sudden urge to run my hands over him; find out if he's as soft as he looks. He's fucking beautiful, even if he is holding my life in his jaws.

I turn my head carefully to see Isaac leaning against the counter, his face twisted in pain as he ties a belt around his bloody thigh. He'll survive.

I will myself to stay relaxed, breathing deep and denying the instinct to fight back or escape. The pressure on my arm eases, though doesn't release fully. I'll heal. My Medic will see to that. I won't panic. It's not over yet.

I know Shifters enough to know this one has no desire to kill me. He could have ended this in an instant if that were his goal, but he's only following orders. He's talking through his Link, I can see it in his big, golden eyes. But there's no Agent here. Only Isaac with no trace of implant tats on his neck.

"What's a politician doing with a Shifter?" My voice sounds pathetically weak from the weight on my chest. "You're an impressive creature," I add, because it's true and because it can't hurt to carn some favor from the one sitting on me.

I feel the vibration through my body as he growls low in his chest, a satisfied sound that tells me he doesn't mind being complimented in the least.

Fucking cats.

A menacing growl fills the room as a mass of black fur collides with the tiger. He releases his grip on my arm, answering with an earsplitting snarl that's thick with fury. The moment the weight is off me, I gulp in greedy breaths and scramble out of the path of the clashing felines.

Damon. Any relief at having him back is immediately shattered by the scene in front of me. The tiger is almost double Damon's size, though my deadly panther is far more agile. He succeeds in opening some serious wounds with his initial attack, but it's not long before the bigger cat has him pinned. Massive jaws crush down on that silky black neck as blood pools on the white tile.

"Damon!" I scream his name as if it will make any difference at all, scrabbling for the gun that is nowhere to be found. I retrieve my knife, hurling myself toward the tiger with no coherent thoughts, only sheer desperation.

Run, little one, his voice fills my head as pain erupts against the back of my skull and my world fades to black.

PURPOSE

I reach my hand across the empty bed, stretching my fingers in search of thick fur or soft skin. Memory hits me like a knife to the heart. I sit up, throwing the covers off as I stumble to my feet. Stars swim across my vision as my lungs struggle to take in enough oxygen to keep me conscious.

"Whoa lady, take it easy!" A man jumps up from an armchair at my bedside. He's tall, thickly muscled. "Call the boss," he instructs a second man standing by the door.

Damon! I call through our Link, putting as much force into the word as I can. "Damon!" I yell out loud, desperate to get any response at all from him. *Just tell me you're okay. Please.*

"Good morning, Elite Whisper."

Isaac's voice is smooth as silk as he strides into my suite. His gait is steady, without so much as a limp to remind him of the bullet I put in his thigh. It shouldn't surprise me. He had no tat to indicate he was paired with a Shifter. There's no telling what other modifications he's concealing. To carry an implant without the corresponding tattoo on your neck is a serious crime. This asshole clearly thinks he's above the law, and I would love nothing more than to show him how wrong he is.

My own arm feels fine. Just a bit of soreness and probably some fresh, pink skin where the wounds had been.

"Where's Damon?"

That final image plays on loop in my mind. My beautiful panther being crushed under the jaws of a tiger. My stomach lurches. He's hurt. He's injured somewhere needing my help.

"Your Shifter's dead. Such a waste of a magnificent creature. I offer you my sincere condolences."

The knife in my heart twists, and the floor sways. Asshole. Fucking asshole. If he thinks he can break me, he's going to think again.

"Bullshit," I spit at him, satisfied with the way he steps back as I start toward him.

His meat shields move to block me, and I know I've got zero chance of reaching him. But it's that look on his face that I want to see. That look that says he knows damn well if it were down to just me and him, I'd have him by the balls in an instant.

"It's true. You saw for yourself. He was no match for my Hunter."

Damon! Answer me!

It's not true. It can't be because I'd know it if he were dead. I'd feel it. Fuck, why did I have to pick a fight with him at Kelseys? If I hadn't been such an asshole, he would have been by my side like always. He would have smelled the tiger. He would have talked me out of this entire shitshow.

"Bullshit," I say again.

Isaac holds out his hand, palm up, and time stops.

My body goes cold, the rhythm of my heart beating in my ears the only sound I hear. He's still talking, I can see his lips moving, but my whole world has been reduced to the tiny, oval object in his hand.

He passes it to one of the men between us, who drops it in my outstretched palm. A microchip. The number 6423 is etched plainly in its casing. It's the chip they put in Damon the day he received his first implant. Deep in the muscle under his shoulder. Permanent.

"No," I say, as if my words can make this all go away.

"I thought of bringing you an ear or tail as proof, but I think we both know there's only one scenario where this could be dug out of a body."

I begin to shake, a tremor that starts in my hand and spreads over my whole body. I grip the chip in my fist as I sink to the floor. Nothing matters. I can't even remember what seemed so important moments ago. He's gone. My partner, my best friend. My lover. He was everything to me. Everything that should have mattered, and I risked his life to get to the top of a broken ladder.

He stood by me because he *loved* me. I treated him like an animal, like he was less than human. I pushed him away because I was too fucking damaged to see how whole we were together.

Come back, Damon. Come back to me and I swear I'll love you like you deserve.

I feel it now. The emptiness of the Link that meant I was never really alone. He's not there. He's not there because he sacrificed himself to save me.

A drop lands on my hand, and I swipe at my face with a clenched fist. Tears. I swipe them away frantically, but more cloud my eyes and stream down my cheeks. I thought I was broken before, but here I sit in a place worse than death, and I realize I never really knew what broken was.

"Well, I can see that you were very attached to your Shifter. For what it's worth, I am sorry it had to end this way."

I don't feel any anger, any urge to fight back or take revenge. I just want to sit here, sink into the floor and fade into nothing.

"There's still one little matter we have to settle. Your Shifter's body will never be discovered, that's not an issue. But you on the other hand... you have the potential to cause me a lot of headaches I don't care to deal with."

He pauses, as if expecting me to comment or have an opinion. I'm listening, but only so I can hear the punchline. The part where he says this is all a joke, a test, anything at all that means Damon isn't really gone.

"Let's be reasonable, shall we? You attacked me, and your Shifter died as a result. I think we can call that even. I'm even willing to offer you a second chance. You can keep your job, and I won't say a word about this to anyone."

I look up at him, and the smug grin on his face says he thinks he's giving me an offer I can't refuse. I keep my title and my reputation, and he keeps me close enough to ensure I don't cause him any more trouble.

He keeps talking, but I can't focus on his voice. After a while, I'm left alone. My world has been reduced to darkness, my consciousness revolving around the tiny, smooth chip in my hand.

What have I done? What was the point of any of this?

I entered the Academy to escape my life; to become an Agent and make sure I never had to live under the heels of men ever again. I accomplished my goal. I graduated, got steady jobs working under Charles. I found Damon and bought us a home.

I had everything.

Why couldn't it have been enough? What childish, naive, pathetic part of me actually thought that I'd get here and be content? How could I have honestly believed a title and a change of address would change anything that really matters?

The things I said to him.

I crawl up onto my bed, burying myself in the covers and wishing I could turn my mind off. He was my Shifter, and I loved him. Then he became a man, and I treated him like something less than human.

I pushed him away until he finally listened, and he left.

If only he had stayed gone. But he would never have done that. He loved me, and I was too selfish to see what that meant.

～

I OPEN my eyes to a dim room, the lights of the city spilling through the windows along with the perpetually cool breeze. I feel numb. Drained. Pointless.

A memory slices through the haze, something I haven't thought about in a very long time.

"What's the point?"

My brother's thin lips twist into a smirk. I lower my eyes, focusing on a crack in the floorboards so I don't have to look at him. I hadn't planned to tell any of them, not yet. But he pushed me too far, and I opened my big mouth.

He laughs at my silence.

"Because when I'm an Agent, I'll be able to protect innocent girls from dick-less assholes like you."

That makes him laugh even harder, and I clench my fists and grind my teeth to keep from saying more.

"You honestly think they'd ever let you in? Even if they did, you'd never make it through. You don't have what it takes to become a Protector."

I lift my chin, raising my eyes to meet his. "Yes. I do. I will do whatever it takes to make a difference."

I brace for his response, but none comes. He shakes his head and walks away.

I rub my temples, feeling the ache of a rare headache. I remember my thirteen-year-old self thinking he had finally taken me seriously. That they would all take me seriously now that I was on my way to becoming an Agent. It had been a foolish thought.

But that's not what sticks with me now, when I think back to that day.

I said I wanted to become an Agent to help people. I said I would do whatever it took to make a difference. I don't remember ever thinking about what I would get out of it. I knew without ever having stepped foot out of my hometown that there were others like me... girls whose lives were made hell by the men who were supposed to love them. I wanted to help them.

Somewhere along the way, I lost sight of that goal. It became about me and what I deserved. Being an Elite on Solar One... it became a beacon in the darkness, the ultimate symbol of freedom from oppression and abuse. I stopped thinking about what I could do for others. I never thought about being happy. I only cared about being powerful. Untouchable.

Then I had a brief taste of happiness in Damon's arms. A few precious moments when he showed me what it felt like to be loved. No amount of power could compare to that. I didn't let myself believe it was real, and now it's gone. He's gone.

I care nothing about being a part of this fucked-up system. Not anymore. But I set out on this path, I became a weapon, for a reason.

A soft knock against my door makes me pull the blankets over my head. I stay quiet, hoping whoever it is will move along, but the door slides open anyway.

"Whisper?" Tanikka's hushed voice calls into the room.

She's the last person I want to see. I consider pretending to sleep, but a new idea begins to take shape. It's crazy, it's...

"I'm here."

She steps cautiously into the room, dressed impeccably as usual. There's no sign of the stressed-out, beaten-down woman I saw last time we talked. She stops, standing in the middle of the floor and fidgeting awkwardly on her feet.

"I'm sorry about Damon."

I cringe at the sound of his name on her lips.

"You never told me about his Shifter." I watch her expression closely in the dim lighting, catching the flash of guilt that crosses her face as she sucks in a breath. "You told him I was coming."

Her eyes drop to the floor as she crosses her arms.

"I... I didn't think..."

"I loved him."

Her eyes snap to mine, and I don't even know why I'm saying this, I just know I need to. I owe it to him to say it out loud at least once.

"Damon wasn't just my Shifter. He was a man... we were... I loved him."

I wait for the grimace of disgust on her face, but it doesn't come. Her lips part slightly, as she moves to perch on the edge of the chair near me.

"Oh, Whisper." The sorrow in her voice makes the breath catch in my lungs.

"I know it's not right... I know they're not supposed to take human form..."

"No, stop."

She sits up straighter, her hands clasped in tight fists and a new look of determination on her face.

"Before I married, I worked as an assistant at BioSol Labs. I would have stayed on as a researcher, but Isaac wanted me home and I wanted to make him happy." She sighs, shaking her head at the memory. "I found something in the Shifter's DNA that didn't fit with the explanations of where they come from. Do you know the official story?"

"I know they come from off-world, that they're genetically modified animals." My voice hitches at the last word, as fresh pain shoots across my chest.

"Yes, essentially. They're shipped in as embryos from Centauri B. Technically, they're a genetically modified race of symbiotes, unable to survive without being bonded to a higher lifeform."

"So, they're not animals?"

"Well, not exactly, but it's a bit of a grey area. Every new civilization we discover has a different way of classifying life... so we're finding more and more grey areas. If the difference between animals and people is intelligence, then no, they are not animals. They are definitely not the animals they appear to be... the embryos are implanted in either a cougar, wolf or bear and so the young are born mimicking their surrogate mother's form."

"What do they really look like?"

"I don't know. I'm not sure if anyone does, or if they even have their own unique forms. The Centaurians likely know, but they claim that Shifters as they are now only exist in labs, and only survive with a bonded host."

How could I not have known all this? I took the simple, one-line public statement and never bothered to ask questions. I never even tried to learn who he really was, I just accepted that he was there to serve me and didn't care about anything deeper.

I brace my fingers against my temples, rubbing at the pressure building behind my eyes.

"By three months of age, the bond with their surrogate mother fades. If they don't bond with another at that point, they experience rapidly deteriorating health and death within a week or two, at most. Once bonded, they very quickly learn the language, thought patterns, and even cultural nuances of their bondmate. Their growth, both physical and psychological, accelerates dramatically until they are at par, then slows and keeps pace. No matter what species they bond with, their lifespans will sync. When the host dies, the Shifter experiences brain death within about forty-eight hours."

I can't sit still anymore. I slide out of the bed and give in to the urge to pace the floor.

"I'm sorry. I'm being insensitive. I shouldn't be talking about this, I just wanted-"

"No." My voice carries a shrill edge that gives away how desperate I am. Desperate to know everything about him, to know that what we had was real... to turn back time and tell him... "I need to know."

She nods her understanding, but when she continues her voice is a shade lower.

"I questioned why Shifters couldn't take human form. They seemed to be designed to grow and take the form of their bond-mate. It seemed obvious to me, but every time I brought it up, I was given the same speech as everyone else. *It doesn't work. It causes insanity. It's illegal because of the danger to the public.* I wanted to look deeper, focus my research, but I was denied at every turn.

I told Isaac what I thought. I told him that there appeared to be no reason Shifters couldn't take human form. I told him it seemed to me that taking their bondmate's form was a natural part of their growth, and my theory on why there was such a vast cover up about the whole thing. He got angrier than I've ever seen him. He told me to let it go and never bring it up again. I tried to argue with him, but he... that was the first time he hit me." She clenches her jaw, her face reddening in anger or shame. "I didn't mention it again. Not to him. Not ever."

"It was awkward at first, same as any new form, but each time he seemed more comfortable, more... human."

I tip my head back, refusing to cry anymore. I don't need tears. I need anger. I push away the memories, like shards of glass in my heart. I want to feel the pain, I deserve it after what I did to him, but I won't let it take me down. I need to use it.

"What does it all mean?"

I know there's something deeper in all of this, I just can't quite put the pieces together in my foggy, pounding head.

"Did he argue with you?"

"No," I reply immediately, but I feel the sting behind my eyes as I'm taken back to the night at Kelsey's, and to the fight that ended with him leaving. "Yes. But he was right. He had good reason."

"Yes!" She clasps her hands together. "It's exactly what I hypothesized would happen! It's not insanity, it's independence. In human form, with a human brain, they no longer require their bonded host. They lose their symbiotic traits and can thrive on their own. Maybe even reproduce naturally. That's the reason it's illegal, and why they go to such lengths to convince us of the horrible consequences.

Without the symbiosis, there is no control. The Shifters stop being accessories and become a unique species worthy of rights and protections. It threatens the entire military system we've established and the trade relationship with Centauri B. For the Centaurians... they've built their entire economy around this technology; these creatures that only they can provide.

The repercussions of this becoming common knowledge, of accusing them of misleading us, goes beyond my level of understanding. I do know that our relationship with them is on shaky ground as it is, and they're far more advanced technologically than we are."

"So, pissing them off would be a bad idea."

"Yes, I expect that would be a very bad idea."

"He said he loved me." I blurt it out, instantly regretting how pathetic and naive I sound. But if what she said is true, if Damon had broken our bond by fully adjusting to his human form...

"I'm sorry. I'm rambling about these things and you're grieving. I shouldn't be so selfish."

"He said he loved me, and I told him it was only the bond. That he didn't really know what love was."

Tanikka stays quiet, her enthusiasm seeming to be drained as she sits with her hands folded in her lap. I resume pacing, but when she speaks again it stops me in my tracks.

"I think he knew how he felt, Whisper. I might not have brought this up again to Isaac, but I kept searching for proof. I found two other cases. Names I will never repeat. My theory isn't just a hopeful figment of my imagination. I know it's true."

For a moment all I'm aware of is the breath entering and exiting my lungs. Then the memories come crashing into me like a wave. All the love he gave me, and I brushed it off like it wasn't even real. Like it didn't count. I fucked up, and now, it's too late.

I take a deep, shaking breath.

How do I move on from this? How do I keep working, keep breathing, without Damon? Why would I even want to?

There was a time when I wanted to help others; when I wanted to make a difference. Now, I'm grabbing that thread and trying desperately to form it into something I can work for. Something I can live or die for. If I don't, I'll kill Isaac for what he did, and then his Shifter will kill me.

I can't say that sounds like a bad ending right about now. I also can't bear the thought of Damon's sacrifice being for nothing. I owe him more than that.

"I need to do something. Something real. I need to take down Horizon Zero. I need to kill those bastards, all of them. I've been so selfish, but I can do this... I can get taken again. I can stay undercover until I get in front of someone big. I can..." My words are spilling over themselves as my mind spins and struggles to grasp the plan that's forming.

"Whisper, I... I have an idea. Something I've been thinking about for a long time. It was just a thought, nothing I could have ever put into motion myself."

I step toward where she still sits, her eyes lowered as her fingers fidget in her lap. I crouch down, impulsively grabbing her nearest hand. Her honey eyes snap to mine, and I try to show her how serious I am. I need a purpose. I need a mission. If she knows something. If she has a way in...

She sighs, her shoulders slumping as her forehead creases with worry. She nods, slowly at first and then with increasing confidence. She straightens up and an expression of cold determination takes over her features.

"Have you heard of the Pharaoh of Gliese?"

LOST AND FOUND

"*T*his bitch is the reason my niece is dead."

"Gideon, I-"

The back of his hand connects with my cheek and I don't need to fake the yelp of surprise and pain that escapes. Fuck, he's really owning this role.

Good.

I was counting on him being low enough, desperate enough for the taste of revenge, that he'd be able to channel his anger so convincingly.

I look up at him as I cower at the end of my restraints, and his pale green eyes hold no hint of compassion. Maybe part of him does blame me for Camilla's death. She had adapted to her captivity, done what she needed to do to survive. It was freedom that forced her to face the reality of what she had lost, to see the abuse for what it was and feel those wounds all at once.

"Her implants have been removed. She won't be much trouble, though I still wouldn't underestimate her if I were you."

Just hearing those words makes my gut twist. No more changing my clothes with just a thought. No more Medic to save my ass when shit hits the fan. Thanks to Tanikka's connection with BioSol Labs, I've got a clean neck and a fresh scar along my top three vertebrae.

I run my tongue over the back of my teeth, feeling the slight ridge at the edge of my gumline. A little bit of hidden tech that I'm saving for a particularly special occasion. Then there's my hair, which has been dyed a deep scarlet. Even my lashes and brows are dyed with immaculate care, so that no one could suspect it's not my natural color.

"She doesn't look so tough," Gideon's contact replies, his voice as neutral as if he were talking about the weather. He's a slim, mid-twenties man with the look of someone who lives behind a desk. He's clean and well-groomed, but there's nothing original or interesting about his appearance.

Gideon laughs, the sound not quite his usual pitch. "No, she doesn't. Don't worry, she'll break easy. She's lost everything; her Shifter, her title, her implants. She's more likely to off herself than try to escape."

That's harsh. I don't have to fake the shudder in my breath as I inhale, or the moisture that blurs my vision.

He tugs the nylon rope that binds my hands, making me stumble toward him. He fists a hand in my hair, looking for a moment like he might kiss me. The thought passes, and he pushes me away again.

I hate that I'm putting him through this. The last thing he wanted was to have to deal with Horizon Zero again. He knows what I'm risking by going back in, even if he doesn't know the full scope of this mission Tanikka envisioned. Hell, I'm not even convinced all the pieces will fall into place. If they don't, I'll still get to put a dent in their business. If they do, if everything goes as planned, I'll be a fucking nuke.

"Time for you to get what you deserve."

His choice of words makes me snap my eyes to his, and for a moment I see a touch of softness in his expression. Revenge. Justice. Yes, I will get what I deserve. What we both deserve along with every life that's been touched by these assholes. I sense the reluctance in his movements as he hands the end of the rope over to his contact.

"Dude, are you sure about this? I know you're pissed about your niece, but..."

"This is what you do, right? You take the deliveries up the chain."

"Sure, but... you're an Elite. You're pissed off now, but what happens when your conscious kicks in? You're not going to be able to get this chick back if you have a change of heart."

"You want her, or not?" Gideon crosses his arms over his broad chest, his jaw flexing as he narrows his eyes at the smaller man. He's impatient to get this over with, one way or another.

"Yeah, man, she'll be a good payday."

"Great." Gideon drops his hands to his sides, his eyes flicking to mine for just a moment as he turns toward the door of the rundown shack he uses for his meetings with this particular contact. "Consider her payment for all the intel you've given me over the last year."

Then he's gone, the door slamming in his wake. I look back at the man holding the rope. His amber eyes are bright in the dim, dusty room. His mouth curls into a thin smile as he stands a little taller. In Gideon's absence, his confidence seems to be taking a leap.

"You are a pretty little thing, aren't you?"

I step back as far as the rope will let me, and he gives a half-hearted laugh. "Don't worry, I'm just here to take you to your next stop."

~

THE SHARP CRACK of a stick concealed beneath the thick carpet of needles sends my latest attempt at a meal leaping effortlessly away through the trees. My growling stomach urges me to give chase, but the continuous throbbing pain at the base of my neck reminds me that the effort would be wasted.

I curse my failure, wishing I could manage the energy to shift to human form just so I could have the satisfaction of hearing the profanity out loud. The urge to communicate with words is something new. Before taking human form, I only used words when I needed them. I always enjoyed hearing Whisper talk, but having a conversation wasn't that appealing to me.

It's just one of many things that have changed. Not all at once, and some so slowly I barely noticed. It's more than just the thoughts and emotions, it's something deeper. I suspect my bond with Whisper might be broken.

I love her. As sure as I breathe, I love my Whisper. Getting back to her is my only desire. If she's been harmed because of my absence... I can't even think about that.

It's different than before. I've always felt compelled to be near her; unsettled and agitated when she got too far from me. But it was different, like a pull in my gut, an instinct that made me never question my need to be within her reach. It also guided me to know how to find her if she strayed, like part of my own being existed within her.

I don't feel that now, but I wish I did. If I could find even a hint of that tug, I'd know which direction to go. I wouldn't have been walking in this cursed forest for days that feel like weeks.

My stomach growls again. I can track a human with perfect stealth. Catch a meal like an apex predator should be able to do? Apparently, that's not in my skillset. Not that this infuriating injury helps matters any. I guess I should be grateful. I assume the intention was to tear out my implants, but somewhere along the way they must have assumed I was dead and dropped me out here to rot.

Clearly my Medic is still functional. The fact that I'm up and walking is proof enough of that. It's definitely a bit sluggish, judging by the speed I'm healing and the unmistakable stench of infection. No way to tell if my Link works... I tried reaching out to Whisp, but the silence in return hurt as much as my wounds. Better not to try, so I can hold on to the hope that she's still there.

The things I said to her. Fuck, I wish I could take those moments back. If I hadn't left her. If I had only been by her side.

There's a break in the canopy above, and I'm able to confirm that I'm still headed west. I don't know if that's taking me farther away from Moridian, or closer. I just had to guess at a direction, since staying still didn't feel right. Whoever dropped me here must have been on wings, because there was no trace of their scent on the ground around me.

I keep pushing forward, my mind wondering from memories of Whisper to hopes of finding her again to thoughts of diving into a proper home-cooked meal. There's something I won't take for granted again. Ever.

Another twig snaps, but I don't pay it any attention. I'll never catch anything anyway, unless I can find a creature unfortunate enough to be in worse shape than I am. My nostrils flare, trying to determine what forest creature has happened upon me this time. The scent that wafts in on the still air makes me pause. I breath deeper, second guessing myself.

Wolf. Why would a wolf come this close? I certainly can't smell like a meal, with the infection that's likely coursing through my blood. I'm not even edible at this point. But there's something off about the scent. Shifter, I think, but still something different. Maybe that means I'm getting close to civilization.

I inhale deeply once again, and the scent is sharper. Closer. I widen my stance, turning slowly. I bare my teeth, ears flat as I growl a low warning. Not a challenge, just a warning for whatever or whoever it is to keep their distance.

A rustle of branches to my left, and a fresh wave of the odd wolfish scent reaches my nose. I turn, trying not to show that my neck won't bend, though I'm certain the creature that emerges is well aware that I'm in no condition to defend myself. The white wolf is tall and healthy, his thick coat covering an obviously muscular frame. He's in his prime no doubt, with blue eyes so vibrant they're violet. Eyes that hold the intelligence of a Shifter.

Meeting him here can't be a coincidence. I wait, not breaking eye contact and not offering any submission or challenge. His nostrils flare as he scents the air in my direction, his eyes moving to the back of my neck and over the rest of my body. I try to stand a little straighter, expand my chest, but I'm at the end of my strength as it is. I can only imagine the matted, dull condition of my coat and the smell of infection and filth.

I lower my head.

Let him attack, if that's why he was sent. I'll die fighting, however feeble it may be. He dips his own head even lower in response. The gesture takes me completely off guard... to what purpose? What game is this? His head is low, nose nearly to the ground. His eyes are lowered too, though he flicks them up to mine every few seconds as if to gauge my reaction.

I just stare, until he turns to leave the way he came. He looks over his shoulder, tipping his head in a clear invitation to follow. I can think of no good ending to this odd turn of events, but my aimless path wasn't exactly destined for great success either.

I follow, if only because the alternative would be to die of curiosity. He slips silently along through the brush, as I trudge clumsily behind. I dig deep, trying to sense if this change in direction is taking me farther away from Whisper. There's still no hint of the connection that kept my body so tuned to hers.

I'm not sure how long or how far we walk. I'm moving in a haze, focusing only on the thick, white tail that leads the way. From one step to the next, the brush parts and brilliant light washes over my face, leaving me blinking away the temporary blindness. When my vision clears, I stop and sit on my haunches at the edge of the forest. The wolf retraces his steps to join me.

We're at the outskirts of a camp, or maybe a small village. A wide clearing is carved out of the forest, surrounded on all sides by tall, thick trees. I'm guessing a couple hundred people could live here. Nothing seems permanent; no wood or stone buildings. It's all tents and brush, like the entire place could pack up and leave at any moment. They haven't though, not in a long while judging by the worn paths and the way the grassy ground cover climbs the sides of some of the tents.

People and animals are scattered all around. Not animals; Shifters. A tawny wolf and a lion walk together, heading away from the village. They glance curiously in my direction before continuing on their way into the forest. A woman walks between the tents, three little kids in tow. A young man chops wood, stopping to greet a black bear that ambles over to join him.

The smell of roasting meat makes my stomach growl. Just the scent of it gives me a surge of energy, and the thought of filling my belly is far more appealing than solving whatever mystery this place is.

I look to my right, and the wolf is watching me with those odd, violet eyes. He's a Shifter, but beyond that I know nothing about him. His scent is odd, but I can't quite put my finger on why. He holds my stare for a few minutes, no doubt trying to figure me out as well.

His body begins to twist, and from one breath to the next the wolf is replaced by a human. A female human. She continues to stare at me with the same violet eyes, her pretty face framed by blond hair so fair, it's nearly white. She sits cross-legged beside me, wearing work-worn jeans and a thinning t-shirt over a pleasantly curvy frame.

She's impossible. Her very existence is impossible. Female Shifters don't even exist. I let my eyes travel slowly over her, as I breath in her scent along with the heavy smell of the roasting meat. This beautiful girl. This place. It's proof that I've reached the end. I look around again, expecting to see Whisper walking toward me at any moment. If my mind has constructed this fantasy in its last delirious, dying moments she will surely be here.

"My name is Hope." When she speaks, the sound of her voice sends a shiver down my spine. I haven't heard a human voice in so long. "I want to help you. We have medical supplies. I can patch you up and give you some antibiotics. Can you trust me?"

I don't even trust that she's real, let alone that she will help me. I've got nothing to lose, so I might as well play along. I give her a slow nod, and a bright smile spreads across her face.

"Good," she says as she stands, brushing the dirt from the seat of her pants. "Follow me."

I do as she asks. We pass well-tended gardens and tents of all shape, size and material. A few look like they came right out of a department store, though faded with time and sunlight. Some are fashioned from animal skins and some are barely more than blankets and brush tied together. Anyone on the same path swerves to give us a wide berth, their curious stares snapping away whenever I make eye contact.

Hope slips through the flaps of a dull, green tent. It's one of the sturdier dwellings, with wide posts and thick canvas. Inside is a clean, organized and seemingly well-stocked medical facility. Not that I've been in many medical facilities, but the layout and equipment remind me of my few visits to BioSol Laboratories. Many of the objects and equipment around the room even sport the familiar stylized microchip logo.

This room is definitely out of place in the primitive camp. The more I look around, the more unease creeps through me. I also start to consider that this strange Shifter female might actually be able to heal me. She's watching me with a cautious expression, and when I meet her eyes, she gestures to a low platform in the corner of the room.

"Get as comfortable as you can, so I can give you a mild sedative before I clean you up." I growl at that suggestion. If she thinks I'll willingly let her sedate me she can think again. "You've got a nasty wound, and it's very infected. I'm going to need to cut away some of the surrounding tissue before I can patch you up. I know you don't like the idea, but if I don't sedate you, you'll pass out from the pain anyway. Probably after taking a chunk out of me. It's safer for both of us this way, ok?"

I know she's right. Besides, what have I got to lose at this point? I grudgingly step up onto the platform, settling down onto my belly and heaving a resigned sigh. Let this all be over or let me wake up restored. Either option sounds pretty damn good.

"That's great. Thank you."

She kneels in front of me, reaching out a tentative hand to touch my paw. When I don't react, she gets a little bolder and moves up my foreleg, her thumb kneading in slow circles until she finds what she's searching for. I look away when she produces a syringe with a long, thick needle.

A tiny pinch precedes a pleasant warmth that spreads through my body, pushing the pain away in its wake. I'm almost clear-headed for a moment, long enough to hear her call over her shoulder.

"Biorn, he's ready."

I don't like the sound of that. A dark figure pushes through the tent opening, and I push myself up. At least I try to push myself up, but instead I feel my head loll to the side.

"You sure about him?"

"I tailed him for a day, I'm sure. Just help."

"Okay. It's your hide if this goes bad."

TRAINING

*B*reakfast cereal. Grain and preservatives processed into crunchy lumps resembling... flowers? Stars, maybe. A few weeks ago, I would have gladly gone hungry to avoid such garbage, but for the first time since I learned how to cook for myself, I remember what hungry really means.

I eat quickly, refusing to let my mind focus on the slightly sour taste of the oat milk. It's a little worse than yesterday, but not nearly as bad as it's going to be tomorrow. The fridge has been on the fritz for three days now, and it doesn't sound like there's any plans to replace it in the near future.

"Good morning, ladies." The soft, almost feminine voice carries down the hall moments before Paul's round form enters the small dining room.

"Good morning, Paul," the four of us say in unison. Our combined voices sound almost happy to see him, though none of our faces reflect any joy.

It's a practiced routine, one that's been played out since well before I came here. Paul likes us being happy to see him. Paul also likes to touch our hair as he makes his morning loop around the table before settling into his own bowl of empty calories. Any time he passes us, his chubby fingers seem to automatically reach out and touch a stray lock or gently tug a ponytail. It's a simple fetish. A little disturbing, but easy enough to endure. My room-mates tell me he's never taken his attentions any farther.

"Still no word on the new fridge?" Paul sticks his nose in the milk carton and makes an exaggerated expression of disgust. It's not far gone enough yet to pass up the nutritional value, but our guards don't face the same rationing as they impose on us.

"Nope." The response comes from Chris, sitting at the opposite end of the oak table. His deep voice sounds as distant as it always does. He's tall and well-built from spending hours each day working out. Honestly, he's the most entertaining thing here. There's no exercise equipment in this starkly furnished bungalow they use for our holding house. Instead, he gets creative with the furniture and door frames. In his mid-twenties with a handsome face and chiseled body, I watch him out of the corner of my eye while the others are passing the time in front of the television.

He catches me looking sometimes, and the spark in his eyes is one I know too well. Our guards aren't allowed to hurt us, not in any serious way. But Chris is a man on the edge of doing something stupid. He's my ticket to where I want to go, if I play my cards right. It's too soon though. It needs to be his idea.

"May I clear the table, Sir?" Mary's voice is barely a whisper as her eyes stay focused on her empty cereal bowl. And so begins another day of phase one training.

This phase is all about obedience in the day-to-day. We don't do anything without being told. We don't even get to take a piss without asking in a very specific manner; low voice, eyes down. It's simply about control. Our ability to practice self-control in all things at all times, and our ability to accept that we are controlled by our masters in all things and at all times.

Any lapse in obedience, however insignificant, is met with immediate punishment. Solitary confinement in a locked closet...

no food, no water, no pot to piss in. Each incident is met with a longer sentence. Sounds easy enough to avoid. I came here with every intention of towing the line and getting passed up the chain, and I still managed to spend most of my first three days in there.

"Yes, Mary," Paul waves his hand dismissively. "Ann will help. The two of you can clean out that fridge when you're done, so it's ready to swap when the new one arrives. Laura, you can see to the laundry. Hanna, it's your turn for the shower."

He lists our simple orders as casually as if he were commenting on a grocery list. He always has our actions planned in advance, able to set us up on our next task without even taking a moment to think about it. I imagine him up at night, pouring over a spreadsheet as he calculates the time each will take and the best order to make everything run smoothly.

And it does run smoothly, for the most part. Mary and Ann rise in silence to begin clearing the dishes, their matching ginger hair in identical ponytails. They are both tall and slim, with angular features and a dusting of freckles. They aren't related, but they could pass as sisters easily. I doubt it's a coincidence they were placed together... no doubt there's a market for matching pairs. My stomach turns at the reminder of the future in store for these girls.

Not if I can help it.

Laura rises next, her curvy, five-foot-nothing frame topped by a shock of curly, copper hair. She's a little less obedient than the twins, though a huff of irritation at her assigned duty is the only protest she makes before shuffling off. She, too, learned her lesson the hard way. I wasn't here to see it, but apparently she nearly died in her first week from all the time she spent in the closet. Now, she walks a fine line... doing as she is told, with just a hint of the attitude that still simmers under the surface.

Then there's me. Hanna. I don't say much. I don't complain, or talk about being rescued, or cry in my pillow at night. I'm not homesick, because I have nothing to go home to. I'm basically neutral, indifferent to my surroundings. Except for when one of our keepers gets angry...

Paul never loses his temper. If one of us disobeys, he deals with it without emotion. No, when it comes to anger issues, that prize goes to our third keeper, Zephyr.

"Well, well, I hope I didn't miss breakfast?" Mr. Cool Breeze himself strides into the room just as I rise from my seat. His chosen name says a lot about him; overly dramatic and not as tough as he thinks he is. I'm pretty sure he believes the word means something fierce, but no one bothers to point out otherwise.

He makes a loop around the table, giving my ass a stinging slap on the way by. I squeak in surprise as if I wasn't expecting him to do the same damn thing he does every time he gets behind one of us. He takes any opportunity to push, pull, slap or restrain us... and it's blatantly obvious he wants to do a lot more than that.

Unfortunately for my master plan, his physical advances aren't sexual. Not even a little. He likes to terrorize women the same way some sick fucks like to torture animals. The only time Zephyr gets a little heat in his gaze is when Chris' shirt comes off during a workout session... but that's a fantasy that's never going to materialize.

The sting of the slap is still fresh as my eyes dart to Chris. As always, he's looking back at me. It's a fleeting connection before we both turn away; quick enough that no one else ever notices. It's progress.

We aren't permitted to make eye contact with our keepers, ever. The first few times I tried, it got me thrown into the closet. Then Chris caught on... I only look to him when pain is involved. It's such a subtle gesture that he would never suspect it's intentional, but it's reinforcing the connection in his subconscious.

The way he handles us, the way he looks at us; Maybe he's a

dom, maybe he's a sadist. The exact definition doesn't matter for my purposes. He gets turned on when we're getting roughed up. The heat in my eyes, the hitch in my breath, the way I bite my lower lip... they're all cue's that I like that, too.

It's just a matter of waiting, of keeping up this little dance, until they finally get the clue that I just happen to be exactly the kind of plaything a certain wealthy client is waiting for.

I leave the table in silence, padding down the hall on bare feet without a backward glance. The bathroom is tiny, with a pedestal sink, low toilet and water-stained shower stall. Still, only being able to shower every four days makes it a sweet, blissful luxury. The water isn't hot, and the five-minute timer by the sink is as good as Paul's voice in my head; *if the water's not off by the time that bell rings, you'll be spending a cold, wet night in the closet.* I don't think any of us has risked testing his sincerity on that one.

I pull the thin, gauzy dress over my head and brace myself for another thing that only happens once every four days. I look in the mirror. It's full length and only slightly warped, hanging on the inside of the bathroom door. My eyes instantly blur with tears that won't fall, as I force myself to take steady, deep breaths.

It's not the dark circles under my eyes and unfamiliar waves of red hair. It's not the ribs and hip bones that jut out slightly where soft curves used to be. It's him. I see him every time I look in this mirror. First, it's just eyes in the shadows. Silky, black fur as he walks toward me on silent, feline legs. Then, human hands and strong arms wrap around me as his face nuzzles against my neck.

I cover my mouth with my hand to stop the sound of my grief. It's a cruel joke that whatever psychosis lets me see him so clearly, won't also let me feel his touch. I'd gladly give up my remaining sanity to feel those hands against my skin. To feel his lips and his body pressed against me.

I love you, I say though the Link that was gone even before they removed it from my body. His mouth forms the words without sound as I reach out to touch his reflection. Then he's gone.

Once every four days.

My heart is filled to bursting by just the sight of him, before shattering all over again with his loss. My grief gives way to anger, and I'm ready to endure whatever comes next to get to my goal.

I STOP the timer at four minutes and fifty seconds. I've got showering down to a science at this point, with not even a second wasted. I pull my towel-dried hair back into a limp pony and slide a fresh dress over my head. It's identical to the one I took off, and to the one I'll put on tomorrow. When I graduate out of this phase, I'll have a new rising sun tattoo on my wrist to go with it.

I take a calming breath, averting my eyes from the mirror as I open the door. A hand grabs my wrist, and I nearly shout before catching myself. Chris. He pulls me down the hall behind him. He's sweaty from working out, dark stains around his collar and armpits. I've been in the bathroom for twenty minutes tops, so he must have been going at it pretty hard to get this heated up.

Oh, shit. I thought he was leading me to the closet, but we veer toward his room instead. The keeper's rooms are off limits. I dig my heels in, and he immediately spins to grip my neck with his free hand, shoving me roughly against the wall.

I close my eyes, forcing myself to imagine that the rough hands on my wrist and neck belong to Damon. That he is here, angry for the danger I'm putting myself in and desperate to prove that I am still his. A moan escapes my parted lips, as my back arches toward my captor. My imagination has convinced my body, and my core ignites at the prospect of having Damon again.

"Fucking witch." Chris's seething voice breaks the illusion, and I open my eyes to see his hazel gaze burning into mine. I swallow against the nausea rising in my stomach. I press my throat into his hand until I'm close enough to dart my tongue out and taste his mouth. His eyes widen in surprise, the expression fading to something more sinister as a grin spreads across his face.

Now, he gets it.

"You're not allowed to touch me..." I whisper. It's the first time I've spoken directly to him. It's a risk, but I definitely want him to remember that little rule.

Anger flashes again in his eyes.

"Why is that?" I ask, my voice as low as I can manage as I reach a hand out to grasp a fistful of his shirt. "Why do Paul and Zephyr get to have the girls they want, but you have to follow the rules?"

His stops breathing for a moment before taking a slow, deep inhale that makes his already broad chest expand impossibly wider.

"Are you fucking with me?"

A valid concern.

My doe-eyes speak for themselves, I hope. But just in case he doubts my sincerity, "I... I thought you knew?"

He licks his lips, his mind working out the new information as he tries to figure out what to do next. The tent in his jeans tells me problem solving isn't going to be his strong suit at the moment.

"If you talk to them, I'm sure they'll cover for you, too. Just like they're covering for each other. Then you can punish me for talking to you. For touching you." I slide my hand down his firm torso, slipping it under his shirt to scratch my fingernails along his abs. "For disrespecting you."

He slides an arm around my waist, his hand slipping down and then up under the hem of my dress until he can grab a bare ass cheek. He squeezes, hard, as he presses his teeth against my neck. I use the pain of his grip to channel another convincing moan. He shudders in response.

Go, asshole. Go talk to your buddies. See how they respond when you accuse them of fooling around with Horizon Zero property.

THE MEADOW

The scent of roasted meat is the first thing that reaches me through the thick blanket of sedation. My stomach growls as I blink away the dopey haze to discover the smell is coming from a huge platter of steaming meat laid within my reach.

I don't question it, I just dive in.

"Easy there, buddy."

Hope's voice is close, but I don't bother to glance her way. I've never been this hungry. Never tasted food this good. It's gone too quickly, and I lick the platter and my lips until every bit of flavor is gone.

I look up now to find Hope sitting cross-legged on the edge of the platform, with a cougar at her side. I push myself up onto my haunches, testing my strength and moving my head from side to side. Stitches pull, but it's a minor pain. A surge of gratitude rises in my chest, and impulsively I move toward my rescuer.

The cougar rises to its feet and growls a warning. I'm happy to respond in kind, making sure he knows that even in my current condition, I could take him easily.

"Okay, that's great. You're both strong, vital, alpha-males who could easily take the other in a fair fight."

Hope rolls her eyes as she shoves a hand against the cougar's shoulder. He responds by shifting into the dark-skinned form of the man I saw just before the sedative kicked in.

Now there's two of them that can take human form. This doesn't make sense. I want answers, but I don't know if I've recovered enough to shift, or if showing them what I can do is a wise idea.

"You can go, Brom. He's not dangerous."

"I don't like leaving you alone with him... we don't know anything about him."

"He'll be more comfortable with only me here."

He narrows his dark eyes at me. Then he does as she told him to, backing out of the tent and leaving us alone. I have so many questions, and no voice in this form to ask them.

"I know this must be more than a little confusing for you." Hope reaches her hand out to rest her fingertips on my paw. The delicate contact commands my full attention. "I don't know who or what did that to you, but luckily your Medic implant was still functional. It just needed a little repositioning. Your Link was exposed, but it didn't have any visible damage, and your tracker was removed. I'd guess someone didn't want your body found."

So not only am I clueless to find my way back to Whisp, but she has no way of finding me. I have to get back to her. I need to know where I am, and how to get out of this damn forest.

I grit my teeth against the pain of tearing stitches and force my body to take its human form.

"Holy shit!" Hope jumps to her feet, scrambling through a series of cupboards before rushing toward me with bandages and tape. "That was a dumb move! You're not healed enough to..."

She stops in her tracks, then drops down in front of me where I sit now in human form. Reaching over my shoulder, she presses a bandage against the back of my neck. Her violet eyes stay locked on mine.

"This isn't your first time taking human form."

"What is this place?"

She pushes me to the side, moving to get better access to my back as she tapes the bandage in place. She smells like pine and mint. The heat of her small body against mine makes me ache for Whisper even more.

"We call it the Meadow. It's our home." She finishes her work with the bandage and slides backward off the platform. "Walk with me, if you're feeling up to it. I'll tell you our story."

I stand with stiff knees. "Who are you?"

She ignores my question and grabs my hand to pull me through the heavy flaps of the tent, out into the pale light of a cloudy morning. I wonder briefly how much time has passed since I last saw Whisper, but the days and nights have been slipping by in such a haze that it could be a week or a month.

We're in the midst of her village of tents, on a dirt path running between them. Cook fires are lit here and there, struggling to stay alight in the crisp breeze. They're being tended by older women and men whose eyes scan me as we walk, a wariness there that makes me think strangers aren't a welcome sight.

Hope laces her fingers with mine, trapping me in a tight grip. "People are scared of you. Walk with me like this, so they see you're a friend."

I do as she asks, relaxing my hand in hers. The contact feels good. Comfortable.

"Who are you?" I ask again, because her very existence is impossible. There are no Shifter females. We are genetically modified animals, created and grown in BioSol Labs from off-world tech. They don't make females. We have no language to communicate with each other. We can't shift to human form. All of these facts are the truths I've known without question since the beginning of my memory.

Yet here I am. And here she is.

"First, tell me your name."

I think about the question long enough that she stops walking to stare at me, studying my face. Perhaps wondering if I've lost my memory. Maybe it would be better that way. If I'm supposed to be dead, announcing my name to anyone might not be the best way to stay alive. I expect her to push, but instead she takes a long breath and resumes walking.

"My mother was born in the laboratory, same as you." She digs into her jeans pocket, pulling out a tie to restrain her long hair. "They like to tell people female Shifters don't exist, but really it just sounds better than 'we euthanize them at birth'. Lucky for her, it was my father who had the job of incinerating the biological waste. He saw that she was still breathing and saved her life."

"Did he save you as well?"

She lets out a quick laugh, squeezing my hand as she lifts it with hers to point. I look where she indicates to see a grizzly lumbering along the path ahead. A small boy rides high on its back, a warm blanket around his shoulders and a bowl full of berries in his hands.

"I was born here, just like all the children you see. My parents founded this colony almost thirty years ago. Along with a few others who realized the truth."

"What truth?" I ask automatically, but I'm already starting to see.

"That Shifters aren't animals. We aren't weapons or accessories. We're our own species, able to live and love and raise families. That the only part of us that's genetically modified is the part that makes us dependent on the bond. Without that, we grow as individuals, at a normal rate."

That information makes me pause, pulling my eyes away from the worn tents and occasional beast or human that comes and goes from view. "How old are you?"

She smiles, understanding the weight of my question. "I'm twenty-four. I was born twenty-four years ago."

I let that sink in, and the heat of anger rises in my chest. I realize I've been cheated out of a life I never knew I was missing. I've never thought about it before, never questioned it. My first clear memory is of meeting Whisp. I have blurry memories of life in the lab before that, but nothing I can really grasp.

"How old are you?"

"I was born almost five years ago."

Just saying it out loud sounds absurd, as the image of that little boy riding the grizzly flashes behind my eyes.

"You grew fast, until you reached the age of your bondmate. You used his experiences, education, and beliefs to form your adult self instead of having those things for yourself. It's not natural. It's not the way we were meant to live. You're content, happy even, and you'll live a long life... as long as your bondmate lives, of course. You'll be dependent on him, compelled to obey and follow him anywhere, providing you stay in a lesser form.

It's why they tell you how dangerous it is, and why they've made it against their laws to try. Once you take human form, that bond begins to break down. It dissolves and you become your own person. They lose their control over you. They can't use you anymore."

I take a few more steps and sit on the low stump of a tree, resting my elbows on my knees. Even though this is the first time I've heard most of this, I don't feel surprised. Since I started taking this form, it's only felt more right each time. In this body, with Whisper in my arms... but even she couldn't really accept me as a man, as something more than just *her* Shifter.

"They all just want us to be their pets." The deep voice interrupts my thoughts, and I look up to see a man standing beside Hope.

He's tall and leanly muscled, wearing thin cloth pants held up by a drawstring tied around his waist. I stand up, rising to equal height. Something in his yellow-green eyes makes me brace myself. I don't know what it is, but I don't have a good feeling about this male.

"Luke," he states his name as he holds out a hand to shake. I ignore it.

I've never paid much attention to other Shifters. We give each other a wide berth in passing, or just ignore each other if our Agents are working in close quarters. I never had a desire to attempt communication, not that we had any direct way of doing so. Whisper was always enough for me, and I assume the other Shifters felt the same about their bondmates.

"Lucky for me, I started taking this form before my Agent got himself killed." Luke seems unfazed by my refusal to shake his hand. "Figured I'd go crazy, or just keel over. When neither of those things happened, I realized the truth. I headed to BioSol Labs to show them what I thought about this little show they've got going. Ran into the right person, at the right time, and they brought me to the Meadow."

"How long since you started taking human form?" Hope squints at me as if she's trying to work something out. She also sidesteps, putting a little more distance between herself and Luke.

"A month, maybe two." I think I know what she's trying to determine. My bond with Whisper is broken. She could be hurt or killed, and I wouldn't feel it. I wouldn't know. "I need to go back."

Luke nearly chokes on a laugh. "His bond is broken, yet this pet's still loyal to his master!"

I step toward him, my lips peeling back in a snarl as the shift starts to ripple across my skin. Hope plants herself between us, putting her hands flat against my chest.

"Ignore him."

Her bright eyes are pleading. I grab her hand and pull her behind me as I put some distance between myself and Luke. I can hear him laugh as we turn a corner.

"I need to go back," I repeat once we're alone again.

The wind is gaining strength, making the tents shudder and flap under a darkening sky.

"Why?" She asks, her tone conveying only curiosity. Tendrils of hair are pulled lose, whipping around her face. She ignores them, watching my face, waiting for my answer.

"Just point me in the direction of Moridian. Please."

"Why go back to living like someone's property? You could stay here with your own kind and be free. Why go back to your Agent?"

Her hand is on my arm as she looks so intently into my eyes that I almost think she can see my thoughts. There's a deeper meaning to her question, something she's trying to figure out for herself.

"Because I love her."

Hope's eyes go wide, and when she speaks again there's a hitch in her voice. "North," is all she says.

It's all the information I need. This place calls to me, answering questions I hadn't even known to ask. But my Whisper calls to me even stronger. Not as my bondmate; as my mate.

"It'll take days through the forest in your cond-"

Her words cut off as my wings extend. The thought of finding Whisper, the desperate need to know that she's safe, it fills me with raw energy. I jump from the ground, the wind catching me as I set my eyes on the northern horizon.

PRESUMED DEAD

The sound of arguing wakes me up from a restless sleep. I tiptoe out of the bedroom I share with the other girls, each of us with a single foam mattress on the floor.

"What's going on?" Laura's voice sounds groggy in the darkness.

"Nothing. Just their usual bickering." I hope she's tired enough to not question the fact that their 'usual bickering' doesn't happen in the middle of the night. "I just have to pee." I add, and she grunts a response that sounds agreeable.

I close the door behind me, creeping up the hallway until I can make out the keeper's words. After our little encounter, Chris avoided me for the remainder of the day. Not an easy task in such a small house. I have no doubt this midnight staff meeting is directly related, and I want a preview of the consequences I'm going to face tomorrow.

"She needs to go, there's no question about that." Zephyr's voice sounds emotionless and confident. He's clearly done arguing and made up his mind about the topic.

"I agree. She's clearly trying to turn us against each other, or just get you fired. Who knows what she thinks she'll accomplish." Paul is on Zephyr's side... that's rare.

"Or I give her what she wants, see if she thinks twice about causing shit after I'm done with her." Chris's vote. No surprise there.

"Oh, no. What a sacrifice. You're such a team player." Zephyr's voice is dripping with sarcasm, earning a caveman grunt from Chris. "How about we all just say fuck it and do whatever we want with them? I'm sure the company will forgive us, maybe give us a nice severance package instead of a severed head like they do to anyone else who breaks their contract."

I guess Horizon Zero treats their employees as well as they treat their products.

"Fuck off, both of you." Paul's tone says the discussion is over. "I'll deal with her. There's a client on the special-order list who might be looking for something like her. I'll contact head office, leave out the part about her trying to turn us against each other, and let them know we might have found a match. If you two keep your mouths shut, and you keep it in your pants, we'll be rid of her by tomorrow night."

"Sounds good." Zephyr's voice.

No response from Chris.

I turn to slip back to my room, but then a thought enters my mind, bringing with it a rush of adrenaline. The three of them are there, off their guard and assuming we're all asleep. I could take them out. I've been acting like a weak, defenseless child for so long I find myself believing it. But it's still there; years of training and honed instinct. I could kill them all and set us free. Tonight. Right now.

The thought is dizzying. I've had opportunities before, but none so clean. The other girls are safe in their beds, not floating around to potentially get caught in the struggle. The keepers are all together, not spread out around the house.

I could be free of this, save some lives, draw attention to the organization and live to tell anyone who will listen... like I should have done after I burned the last house. But there was no evidence left that time, nothing concrete anyway, and Gideon hadn't wanted any possible retaliation aimed at Cam.

I could do it now. I wouldn't have to face the consequences of my deception when Chris finds me tomorrow, or deal with the next phase of training. Getting to the client would be a bigger statement, but this could be big, too, if I do it loud enough.

I start to turn back to the kitchen, but my feet don't obey.

No. No, I won't take the easy way out. I can do better. I can save these girls and more. I just have to endure this a little longer. As long as it takes. I've got nothing to lose, save for my pride... and after losing Damon, pride doesn't mean a whole hell of a lot to me anymore.

I WATCH as the light of the morning sun grows slowly brighter, seeping through cracks in the heavy blinds. Sparks of light drift across the white walls and ceiling, slowly illuminating the small bedroom. I'd normally be asleep, like the three young women tucked into their meager beds around me. Not this morning.

I couldn't sleep after listening to the keeper's conversation during the night. Not because I'm afraid or worried, well, maybe I am a little. I'm more awake and alive than I've been in weeks. Something is going to happen today, for better or worse.

If I'm lucky, Paul will follow through with contacting whoever's in charge of making the decision to move me along to the next phase. I don't know exactly what that will look like, but I do know it gets me one step closer to my end goal.

If that doesn't happen, if they're told to keep me here, I'm not sure Chris will keep his anger to himself. I heard him stop outside our door before he went to bed, breathing with a rough edge that spoke of seething anger. I expect he will get his revenge, but he's got his own safety to consider if he breaks the rules.

When seven o'clock comes at last, I'm ready and eager to get the day started.

Ann stirs first, a slender hand reaching out to turn off the chirping alarm. No one moans or complains about the day beginning. No one fights the urge to linger in the warmth of a comfortable bed. We all simply stretch out our stiff limbs and rise to go through the motions of another day.

At the breakfast table, it's business as usual. Zephyr's on morning watch, ready and waiting at the head of the table when we arrive. His beady eyes give each of us a once-over, his thin lips pressing into a cocky grin as he starts giving out instructions for each task that needs to be completed before we sit to eat.

When the others are busy with their simple tasks, he turns his attention to me. I can feel his eyes on me, though I keep my head bowed, eyes on the floor. I wait for my instructions.

"Sit down, Whisper."

My blood runs cold at the sound of my name on his tongue. They weren't supposed to figure out who I am. The temperature in the room seems to spike, and before I can wrap my mind around the possibilities of what's happening, hands grip my arms from behind.

"Sit." Chris's voice is in my ear, his breath cooling my neck.

He pushes me roughly to obey, guiding my steps until he presses me down into the seat beside Zephyr. When he takes the empty seat to my right, I glance toward the kitchen. The other girls are gone, their tasks abandoned. I swallow past the lump in my throat.

The heavy weight of fear presses down on my lungs, and my nerves are blazing.

I bite my lip to keep from grinning.

Let them do their worst. Give me the excuse to show them who I really am.

I keep my gaze down, my posture slack. I won't break character until I've got no other choice. There's still a chance I can get to-

"Elite Whisper." Paul's feminine voice has a self-satisfied ring to it as he joins us at the table, sitting his flat ass down across from me, at Zephyr's left. "I had an interesting conversation with my co-worker today. Do you know what we talked about?"

I look up at him, and Zephyr's hand shoots out to slap the back of my head. "Answer."

I lower my eyes back down, my hands curling into fists on my lap. "You talked about me. About who I am. Who I was."

"Seems you were a bit of a celebrity, before you died."

My eyes flick to his of their own accord, and this time it's Chris's meaty hand that cuffs me. Deep breaths.

"Did you honestly think we wouldn't find out?" Chris asks, the hand that slapped me now resting on my shoulder. He pushes my hair aside, his fingers tracing along the skin of my neck where my tattoos used to be.

I fight the urge to swat him away. They know who I am, so what's the point of keeping up this charade? They want to provoke me. Why not give them what they're looking for and show them who their dealing with?

But I don't. I keep my head down, because it's not over yet. I don't move a muscle as Chris's hand drifts from my neck, down my arm until it rests on my thigh. The seconds crawl by as I wait for their next move. But they're watching me, waiting for me to answer.

"I didn't-" My words are cut off when Zephyr's foot kicks the chair out from under me. Searing pain vibrates through my skull as it connects with the tile floor, and I'm scrambling to roll out of their reach and gain my footing. A boot connects with my ribs, and I can't stop the cry of pain that escapes me.

Fuck, I miss my Medic right about now. The pain in my head and ribs is intense, and I fight the urge to panic at the knowledge that it's not going to get any better without the synthetic aid. I finally get my feet under me, and I lunge at the nearest body. I grab Chris's shirt, and land a punch to his cheek that makes him shout in surprise.

His response is a slap across my face that sends me sprawling into the wall. A dusty frame dislodges from its anchor to join me in a heap on the floor. I stay where I've landed, tucking my feet under me and pulling at the hem of my dress to cover as much of my legs as I can.

I keep my eyes shut, waiting for another blow, but it doesn't come. Moments pass, and I hazard a glance, peeking up through my lashes to see Chris standing between me and the table. Zephyr and Paul are on their feet, having stood from their chairs but not moved after that. Paul's face is twisted in a grimace. He's not enjoying seeing me treated this way. Zephyr face is just the opposite, his eyes wild and his chest rising and falling with quick breaths. He's hoping I'll keep fighting back.

The expression on Chris' face is harder to read. His forehead is creased and his jaw set tight... confusion, resolve.

"She hits like a girl," he comments, breaking the silence that's making my ears ring.

"It's true, then." Paul lets out a long breath, the tension visibly melting from his posture.

"Did they tell you what she did to get them removed?" Chris asks, his expression softening slightly.

"Apparently she tried to off her employer. Fucked it up and got her Shifter killed in the process." Paul sums up the worst moments of my life as if he's reciting the plot from a movie. "They took her implants as punishment and left her fair game for everyone else she's crossed. One of them decided to take his revenge by turning her in to us, and now she's missing and presumed dead."

Presumed dead. Didn't take them long to write me off. I shouldn't be surprised they didn't send out a search party. There's plenty of people out there that would have been happy if I disappeared long ago. Kelsey's face flashes behind my eyes. I should have asked Gideon to let her know I was okay, but I suppose it's best if she thinks I'm dead, too.

Hell, it'll probably be true once I'm done here, anyway.

"So, what do we do with her?" Zephyr asks, rubbing his palms together as if he has plenty of ideas about what they could do.

"Exactly what they told us to do with her. Nothing more, nothing less." Paul sits back down at his chair, palms spread out on the table as he seems to think for a moment. "Put her in the closet until they get here, so she doesn't do anything stupid."

"TIME TO GO." Chris's voice cuts into the silence along with the piercing hall light.

It's only been a few hours, maybe six, but each stay in that fucking closet gets more distorted than the last. He helps me to my feet, my legs weak and shaking from being unable to stand up in the four-foot-high space. I expect him to shove me along, but his arm snakes around my waist as he pulls me to lean against him. I stiffen, expecting this to lead to something much less pleasant.

"For what it's worth," he speaks in a hushed, almost comforting tone, "I'm sorry it's come to this. I didn't recognize you, but I know who you are. Who you were. You were a fucking badass, and you deserve a hell of a lot better than this shit."

I look up at him, expecting to see a smirk on his face. His expression is dead serious. I start to pull out of his grip, and to my surprise he lets me go. We stand there for a moment, just staring at each other. It's weird. I'd rather him slap me upside the head than leave me questioning my sanity like this.

"What's going to happen now?" I venture to ask, hoping this little interlude will earn me a straight answer.

He lets out a stunted laugh, shaking his head. "Nothing you or I can do anything about."

With that, the moment's over and he's pushing me down the hall. I don't bother resisting, because as unhelpful as his answer was, it's very true. All I can do now is go along for the ride.

The narrow hallway empties into the sitting room, where two soldier-types are waiting. Tall, muscular builds, close-cropped hair, identical at-ease postures, and matching don't-fuck-with-us expressions on their ugly faces. If I had any plans to escape in transit, I'd be thinking twice right about now. The other two keepers are here as well; Zephyr looking bored and Paul looking worried. All eyes turn to me, and I lower mine obediently.

I don't resist as Chris ties my hands behind my back. One of the new guys walks across the room, fitting a cloth bag over my head and tightening it firmly around my neck. Without any words, I'm pushed forward.

Big, bruising hands grip my arm as I stumble down concrete stairs in my bare feet. The outside air on my exposed arms and legs feels amazing, and I wish I could breathe it in. I feel grass under my feet, and a ridiculously giddy sensation sweeps over me. I must be delirious. When's the last time I had food or water?

Whisper

The familiar voice in my head stops me in my tracks. I trip over my own feet as the mountain of a man guiding me keeps us moving forward, pulling me along with little effort.

Damon? I send out the thought, but it's the same empty

feeling as always. There's no way I heard him. I don't even have my Link anymore. I start to struggle against the hands that hold me, suddenly desperate to return to the house. I need to get to the bathroom, to the mirror.

He'll be there waiting for me. He's always there.

A heavy hand on my head shoves me into what must be the trunk of a vehicle. They can't take me away. Not now. I need to see him.

I kick out, panic flooding my veins as I feel more out of control than I ever have. Voices shouting, more hands, then a searing pain in my arm followed by a wave of heat that sweeps away all the fear and pain until there is nothing but blackness.

COMMANDER

*M*y talons grip the familiar railing, high above the metal city. I cling tightly, my body swaying as I fight against the sheer exhaustion from the effort of the flight. My Medic has clearly been pushed to its limit. My body needs more rest than I'm willing to give it.

The glow of the city at night filters through the swaying curtains, casting shadows around the room that Whisper and I called home for a little while. It's empty now, the bed neatly made. I inhale deeply, but no trace of her scent comes through the open doors.

The shift to my panther is brutal as my body stretches and molds to my will with a slow, agonizing burn. I push past it, needing my feline sense of smell. There's still no sign of Whisper, or anyone, as I move silently around the room. Even the bed holds no lingering memories of her presence.

Fear rises in my chest, as I'm forced to accept that I don't know where my mate is. I don't even know if she's alive.

No. That isn't an option. I would feel it if she were gone. I would die along with her, even if I am free of our artificial bond. I simply cannot exist in a world without my Whisper.

Exhaustion grips my body and my mind. I need to find her. I need to find my mate. I drop to my belly on the floor of the dark, unfamiliar room.

There is no home without Whisper.

MY RELIEF at being out of the stinking trunk is short-lived. My legs are crampy, and my head buzzes like a swarm of bees have taken up residence. I get a quick flash of black sky before they put the cloth bag back over my head.

I'm pushed around by one of the meatheads, through doors and winding hallways. When we stop, heavy hands on my shoulders shove me to my knees.

"What are you doing here?" A new voice speaks with authority and a hint of something familiar, though it's muffled by the heavy cloth over my head. "You know it's too late to add any more to this shipment."

"Yes, Sir, we know. But this one's special order."

"Of course it is." That voice again.

The cloth bag is pulled off my head, and I know what I'm going to see even before my eyes have adjusted to the sudden light.

Charles. I bite my tongue. How the fuck did he get involved in all of this?

We're in a room about twenty feet square. A metal table and four plastic chairs are pushed into one corner, but other than that it's empty. Mold creeps along the bottoms of the walls, where faded paint peels from years of neglect. The air is thick with dampness and decay.

I hang my head, focusing on the cracks between the dirty floorboards, playing my role. I hear him suck in a breath of surprise, hesitant footsteps, and then a warm hand on my neck. He touches where my tats should be. Where a screen would be if I were hiding them. He moves my hair aside, a single finger brushing the scar at the top of my spine.

"Get out."

"But Sir, I..."

"I've got her from here. Go home."

"Yes, Sir."

A door closes, and I stay still for a moment. He's backed away, and I slowly raise my head until my eyes meet his. I ignore the pistol in his hand. He looks older. Tired. I hope the guilt has been eating him alive.

"What happened to you?" His forehead wrinkles as he looks down at me with concern, even as he keeps a finger hovering over the trigger. I can't say I blame him for the precaution.

With one foot, he pushes a chair toward me. I'd love to take that chair and beat him to death with it. Instead, I push myself awkwardly to my feet, hands still tied behind my back, and perch my ass on the edge of it.

"Why did you do it?"

"Whisp," he scrubs his free hand over his face, "It's not that simple."

"I deserve an answer, Charles." I stand up, and even though he has the gun and I'm tied, he still backs up half a step. He knows what I'm capable of. "You were the closest thing I had to family, and you turned on me. I deserve to know why."

"Yes," he says immediately. "Yes, you do. You deserve more than that."

He reaches for another chair, pulling it around so he can sit. His elbows rest on his knees as he slouches forward, his grip on the pistol relaxing.

I sit back down, waiting for him to speak.

"They wanted to take you. You threatened their system, and they wanted to fix the problem by taking you and selling you off-planet. I was a low-level recruiter, but I stood up for you. I convinced them that you wouldn't be a problem. That I could keep you in line."

I laugh, the sound coming out more like a choke. "Keep me in line? You drugged me and tried to kill me, Charles. And you know damn well if someone tried to take me, I'd-"

"No, Whisper. When you first came to the Academy. Do you remember the Cadet you met before I came along?"

I definitely remember him. Agent Cunt. He met me at the front doors, where I showed up with a black eye, busted lip and a broken arm. The night before I had gotten the bright idea to tell my brothers that I was headed to the Academy the following morning. They thought it was hilarious that I believed I had a chance, but just in case, they decided to lower my odds even farther.

The handsome cadet at the front door put his arm around my waist and guided me to the Medical wing. He told me he wanted to help, that they could heal me fast so I wouldn't lose my chance to earn my way into the Academy.

He was willing to help all right, in exchange for a blow job. I opted to introduce my knee to his balls instead, and he called me a cunt as I walked away... right into Charles.

I never told Charles that story. He saw me beaten, but he knew what my brothers were like. I didn't want to start off by complaining about a little altercation. I was well aware there would be plenty more and plenty worse over the next two years.

"Yeah, I remember him. I didn't tell you about him, though."

"No, you didn't. But he was already involved with Horizon Zero, as was I. He let them know that you were going to be more trouble than they wanted, and they instructed me to bring you to them. I made a deal for your freedom, promising that I'd keep you well away from discovering any part of their operations.

I told them you wouldn't make it through the Academy, but

you did. Then I convinced them you'd never make it past Enforcer, but you made me a liar there, too. When you got the offer from Gideon, that was it. As an Elite, you'd be out of my hands. Out of their reach. That couldn't stand.

Then there was that whole mess with Gideon's niece... that should never have happened in the first place. They never take girls that well connected, but her mother found out about Horizon Zero's operations. They murdered her and made it look like a suicide, then took Camilla. Gideon tracking you down for his Apprentice was clearly no coincidence.

You were too close. Too much of a threat. They told me to kill you to prove my loyalty. I tried to refuse; I swear I did. I begged for your life, but they would have killed us both anyway."

A single tear runs down his face and he ignores it. It gets lost in the scruff of his week-old beard. I've never seen him go a day without shaving. His clothes are a size too big.

"I'm going to take them down."

He looks up at me, his blue eyes are tired and dull. "Who?"

"Whoever I can. I won't live as a prop. I won't be a puppet in this little show. I've got nothing left to lose. The Elders are corrupt. The Elites are a joke. Damon's... gone. I can tear a hole in this. I can cripple them before they take me out."

He shakes his head slowly, reaching behind him to set the pistol on the table with a metallic thud that echoes in the empty room.

"So that's it, then? You want to die?"

"I don't particularly care if I live. But as long as I'm breathing, I plan to make it count."

"And how far do you think you'll get without your implants?"

"As far as I can."

No reason to tell him more than he needs to know. I'm already risking this whole plan by letting him in on it, but I can't help but feel his remorse over what he did is real. Not that I forgive him or any shit like that. Bastard can go to hell as far as I'm concerned. No matter what he tells himself to sleep at night, he could have told me what was going on and given me a chance to make a run for it. Not that I had anywhere to run. Damon and I could have lived in the woods, kept away from the cities... hell, I was screwed either way.

"I can't be a part of this. I just can't."

"Get me on the shipment to Gliese."

"And then what? You can't take down an organization this massive simply by killing a few people... even if they are upper-rank. You're asking me to plant a bomb that's going to piss off a lot of people I don't want pissed off."

"I'm asking you to plant a bomb that's going to draw attention to places they don't want people looking. I want to kill someone important. Gliese is the best place to do that."

"Whisper, please. You're upset, and you have every right to be. You want revenge, I get that. But you're just one girl. You have no Shifter, no implants... you can't do what you used to do."

"Look, I get it, Charles. I get why you did what you did. I don't like it, and if I never see your face again it'll be too soon. But I forgive you. Losing Damon has... it's given me a different perspective. You risked a lot to keep me safe for a long time, and I'm grateful for that."

He opens his mouth as if to respond, his jaw working but no sound coming out. His eyes are suddenly glassy.

"I have a plan. Get me on that shipment, and I swear no one will know we talked. You can put that hood back over my head, and none of this ever happened. I swear. It's the least I can do after all you've done for me."

He nods, and although I'm saying what I need to say to get what I want, my own words are ringing truer than I expected. He did do a lot to keep me safe, in his own twisted way. He gave me the best chance he could, I suppose.

I'd still like to break his face.

But he's nodding, picking up momentum as if the idea is growing on him. "Okay," he announces as he stands from his chair, all at once seeming less like the worn-down old man and more like the Charles I knew. "I know where I need to take you."

SEARCH

*T*he morning sun wakes me with a jolt, followed by a rush of guilt at having wasted so many hours in sleep. I jump to my feet, listening, watching and scenting the air to ensure I'm still alone. Thankfully, no one discovered me while I was in such a vulnerable state.

I shake my body, stretching and yawning and pleased to find the pain in my muscles all but gone. Time to find my mate.

I head toward the door that leads to the rest of the building, but then have second thoughts. What would be the point in seeking out Tanikka? I wouldn't trust a word she said anyway. I'd be just as likely to stumble across her husband or his Shifter.

Whisper. I project her name in my mind as if our Link still connects us. How could I not have known there was another Shifter here? How had I not scented the tiger on Isaac, if not throughout the house? The only scent I had been concerned about was Whisper's. I'd been so preoccupied with her. With us. I'd been so comfortable with our new positions that I'd grown complacent, neglecting the core purpose of my existence.

To protect her.

I shift to my human form, needing the logic of my human

mind to consider my options. There's only one course of action that makes any reasonable sense, and just the thought of it makes my stomach turn.

Jeffries. That fucking traitor. He tried to kill Whisper, and I've regretted not tearing him apart ever since. As much as I hate the idea, he may be the only one who can help me now. If he ever really cared about her, if he ever gave a shit beyond his own personal gain, he will help me find her.

I start to take my phoenix form, but opt for a common falcon instead. I head west to feed. Rodents and smaller birds are plentiful in the fields outside the city, and in my avian form the thrill of the hunt from above is undeniable.

With a full belly, I head back toward Moridian. A deserted alley just a few blocks from Base serves as the perfect spot to swap from my falcon to human form. The stench of rotting garbage and alcohol infused vomit is a stark contrast to the immaculately maintained streets and alleys of the sky city.

It makes me think of the boy.

It says a lot about human nature to see how they divide their own kind, casting away their lower ranks like garbage while their upper ranks live in comfort and excess.

My thoughts turn to Hope for the first time since I left the Meadow. The tiny Shifter village seems more like a dream now, and I can hardly believe that such a place exists in this world.

I fluff up my feathers, confident that there are no witnesses as I take human form. Walking toward my destination along the crowded streets feels strange, and though I keep expecting someone to shout an alarm at my presence, not one person bothers to look twice in my direction.

I stroll up to the front doors as I have countless times before, though it's very different now. I've only ever been here on four legs. Only ever at Whisper's side.

My pulse quickens with each Agent and Enforcer I pass. Even

more so when they have a Shifter at their side. One lumbering black bear stops to stare, sniffing the air as we pass each other. I can only hope he doesn't draw any conclusions.

These Shifters are like I was not so long ago; oblivious to the potential they have to be more than mere tools to be used by humans. The bear seems to lose interest, hustling to catch up to the Agent that didn't bother to wait.

I reach the gated elevators, remembering only now that Whisper had a card she would scan to get through.

"Can I help you, sir?" The nearest receptionist is watching me with a disinterested expression.

"Sargent Jeffries. I'm here to see Sargent Jeffries."

"Okay, let me find your appointment. What was your name?"

Fuck. Humans piss me off sometimes.

"I don't have an appointment, but I need to speak to him now."

"I'm sorry, sir." She speaks like a recording, her face remaining expressionless even when her eyes dart to the side. I follow her gaze, to see a security officer heading our way with carefully measured steps. Fuck.

"Can you tell him someone's here to talk about Jane?" I hate that I've used that name. It feels wrong on my tongue.

She holds up a hand to the security officer, who stops a few strides away to wait. "I'll see if he's reachable by comm," she offers, her hands moving across the keyboard in front of her with practiced speed.

I look toward the elevators, finding a familiar angle that I've viewed from the monitor in Jeffries office. He won't recognize me, not like this. But if I give my name...

"He says to take the elevator to the twenty-second floor. You'll find his office to the right, four doors down."

As soon as she gives me the message, she's moved on to the next person waiting for attention. The gate in front of me clicks open, and the security guard has faded into the background as he was.

I don't waste another moment. Once the lift is moving, I brace myself against the back wall. I'm expecting the doors will open to more security. They will know what I am.

But the doors open to reveal an empty hallway, and as I exit the lift to move toward Jeffries office, there is nothing but the ticking of a clock on the wall to disturb the silence. I knock twice, then open the door.

Jeffries is behind his desk, as always. Pushing papers like nothing has changed in his world.

"Hello, young man." He greets me with a practiced smile, but I can see the tension in his posture, the way his eyes keep me in their periphery even as he pretends to keep sorting whatever he was sorting. "Jillian said you need to speak with me?"

His voice sounds casual, unconcerned. But I know him enough to hear the strain beneath the words.

"Where is Whisper?" I cut right to the point, and he looks directly at me for the first time. His right hand moves to rest on the pistol at his hip. I take a step closer. "The last time I saw her she was bleeding and unconscious under that fucker, Isaac. Where is she?"

Jeffries' face is shades paler as he braces his palms on the top of his desk. "Who are you?"

"I'm the one who had your skull between my teeth and didn't end you like you deserved."

He lets out a long breath, sagging back onto his leather chair. He looks years older all at once, and the only emotion I can read on his face is relief.

"You can't be in this form, Damon, you know the consequences."

"You can skip that bullshit, whether or not you actually believe it. Where is she?"

"She's alive, your presence proves that at least."

His words make my stomach turn to stone. My presence proves nothing, not with our bond broken. I growl as I step toward his desk, slamming my fists down onto the hardwood.

"Tell me what I want to know!"

He doesn't even flinch, just stares at me with fucking pity in his eyes. Pity for me, or for her? What the fuck isn't he telling me?

"It was her idea. Her plan. She had it well in motion before she came to me." He's speaking, but all I hear are excuses.

"Where is she, Charles?"

"Have you heard of an organization called Horizon Zero?"

TOBIAS

*C*onsciousness returns to me with a sudden jolt, my eyes flying open to strain against the brightness. My nerves are lit up with a wash of adrenaline, and it takes a great effort to stay still. I listen, slowly scanning the room to try and make sense of my surroundings.

A soft bed; silk sheets, pillows and down comforters. Everything crisp, white and softly scented. There's no sound save for the trickling of water, and I turn my head slowly to find its source. A splash of tropical green in the corner. Broad-leaved plants climb the wall, up through an opening in the floor and continuing through another in the ceiling. A trickling cascade of water flows from above, disappearing down through the same opening.

I push myself up, confident that I'm alone in this room for the moment. A hotel maybe... certainly an upgrade from the holding house. My clothes are unchanged. The faded, gauzy slip of a dress seems out of place in the modern surroundings.

Charles reluctantly handed me off to yet another delivery man, who felt the need to recreate the whole hood-trunk-sedative routine. I expected to wake up in a container headed off-world, not an upscale hotel.

I stretch my limbs, doing a quick head-to-toe assessment to find no trace of injury. Not even a bruise remains to mark my recent struggles. Someone decided to hit me with a shot of Medic. I absently rub a thumb over the crease of my elbow, unsettled by the thought that someone pushed a needle into my veins while I was unconscious. I run my tongue over the undisturbed ridge behind my teeth.

Walking to the door, I test the handle to find it unlocked. I consider returning to the bed... an unlocked door seems like an invitation, and I'm not so eager to meet the one who's waiting on the other side.

My curiosity wins out, and I turn the handle to crack the door. Peering through a thin opening, I find myself looking out into a kitchen. White and modern like the bedroom, splashes of living green climb from nearly every corner and nook.

The entire room is washed in golden sunlight that pours in through a wall of glass. Beyond is a garden, lush with all shades of green and flashes of vibrant color. Wide, glass doors are braced open, letting in a warm breeze that smells like springtime. I'm clearly still on Earth.

A man's voice reaches my ears. I hold my breath, clutching the door handle, ready to retreat back to the bed if he comes this way. Better he finds me asleep, so I can learn something of his motives before we actually interact. The thought that he may have already interacted with me plenty while I was unconscious makes my stomach turn, but I push it away. Nothing I can do about that now.

A moment later, the source of the voice comes into view. Elder Tobias. I recognize him, and yet he looks different from the stern, grey-haired patriarch I met briefly at the Atrium.

Here he's at ease, comfortable. His voice has an edge of laughter as he prattles on about a child's birthday party and the antics of twin girls. His grandchildren.

Why the hell am I here and not on my way to Gliese? Fucking Charles.

As I watch unnoticed from the doorway, a woman comes into view. She's the one he's been talking to, and she responds with a light-hearted laugh of her own as she comments about the trouble-making habits of one of the twins.

Something about her appearance is unsettling. She's wearing white, flowing pants and a snug sky-blue shirt. Minimal, modern and comfortable... just like the house. She's about the right age to be his daughter, or even granddaughter, but the way she talks about the twins doesn't make me think she's their mother or aunt. She's very familiar in the way she talks to the Elder, but not in a romantic sort of way. I keep watching, expecting one of them to look my way at any second.

The young woman flits about the kitchen with ease and familiarity, prepping food and washing dishes as if she were at home. It's all very domestic, very casual, and yet I can't shake the unsettled feeling in my gut. Maybe because I know what he's hiding in this little bedroom.

Does she know I'm here?

A wide, amber eye blocks my view, peering back at me through the crack in my door. We both jump in surprise, and I scramble back to the bed. Too late to pretend I'm asleep, but I can at least maintain the ruse of being a scared, fragile thing.

The door pushes open farther, and the girl slips into my room. She's wearing the same loose, white pants with a snug, lavender shirt. She looks to be barely twenty years old. Her chestnut hair is pulled back and tied at the nape of her neck. She seems healthy, clean, well fed... but I catch a flash of a tattoo at her wrist. The familiar curve of the rising sun symbol that I haven't yet earned.

"Hi, Whisper." She speaks with a soft voice and a smile to match. "I'm Stacey. Are you feeling okay?"

I keep quiet, watching her face and body language for any

hints about this place. Waiting for her to volunteer more information to fill the silence.

"I know your scared." Her brow creases with concern. "We all were when we first came here. You won't believe me yet, but you're safe now."

I raise my eyebrows in response, impressed that she's able to deliver that line with a straight face. Her smile deepens, and she turns to go.

"Wait!" I call out to her in barely more than a loud whisper, but she pauses to look back at me. "Where am I?"

Her smile lights up her eyes, as if she's thrilled at the question. "You're in the home of Elder Tobias Moreau. You're very lucky that he chose you. We all are. I can't tell you much... he'll want to talk with you about all of it. But you really are safe here. We help out with whatever he needs, and he makes sure we have everything we need."

I cringe at her description. She sounds like she's in love with the man who owns her. Her way of coping with the situation, I suppose. I can only imagine what his 'needs' are. I shudder at the images, pushing them out of my mind.

I don't know why I ended up here. Maybe Charles ran into problems getting me on the shipment to Gliese, or he knows something I don't... maybe taking out Elder Tobias will make an even bigger statement. I can't see that being the case, though. Not with everything Tanikka told me about the Gliesen Pharaoh.

I only hope this girl can find her way back in the real world. Cam couldn't. Maybe the same thing will happen to this poor creature. She certainly seems more fragile, more innocent than Camilla had.

"Do you feel okay?" She asks again, and I nod. "Good. Elder Tobias gave you a Medic injection, so we were hoping you'd be well again before you woke." A darker emotion flickers in her eyes for a moment before her smile returns. "Will you come with me? There's a washroom around the corner with everything you need to get cleaned up. It's just you and I in this part of the house, no one else will disturb you until you're ready."

I watch her face, searching for some hidden agenda or ulterior motive in her words. She seems genuine. The thought of a hot shower that lasts for more than four minutes and fifty seconds sounds like a dream.

"The water's hot," she adds as if reading my mind. "And we have scented soaps, bubble bath, six different shampoos... I won't spoil all the surprises for you. There's also a lock on the door. On the inside. You can take as long as you like."

I laugh, and her eyes widen with surprise. She's describing a trap, that much is obvious. But hell yes, I'm in. I can deal with whatever plans they've got for me. I'm back to full health, thanks to that Medic shot. Just let them try.

It's amazing how something so simple can bring such joy. A hot shower, something I took for granted not so long ago, has become a luxury beyond compare. Thirty minutes, an hour, two hours... I don't know how long I stand under the wide jets of water, but the temperature and pressure never once falters. I try all the shampoos, all the soaps... stretching the moments for as long I can.

The girl was right, the door locks from the inside. Not that I honestly think they don't have a key within easy reach. Still, the measure of privacy is enough to give me a sense freedom I haven't felt in a long while. Let them sneak in and find me naked and pruney, I don't care. This might be the last shower I get, and I'm sure as hell going to make it last for as long as their patience does.

No such intrusion comes, and eventually I shut off the water and step out onto a plush, pale grey mat. The room is huge, with the spacious marble shower stall in one corner and a bathtub big enough for at least six people in the other. Like the kitchen and bedroom, this room is bright, modern and accented with thriving tropical greenery. Wide windows of frosted glass let in plenty of natural light, and a skylight set into the ceiling directs a patch of glaring sunlight down onto a cushioned bench.

I wrap myself in a terrycloth towel that reaches my knees and remind myself again that I'm a captive here. At the moment, it's hard to imagine I'm anything less than royalty. I consider staying here until they force me out, but my rumbling stomach reminds me that I haven't eaten in... well, it's been a while.

I take the pile of clothes Stacey left for me, pulling on the simple cotton underwear and a sports bra that happens to fit perfectly. I won't think about how they got my measurements so accurate. The white, flowing pants are an exact match to the ones the other girls are wearing. The snug, long-sleeved shirt is a comfortable, relaxed fabric in a pastel green.

I catch myself before nearly glancing in the mirror. It's big and hard to avoid, but I've managed so far. I think I'm more afraid I won't see him. Like maybe I left him behind in the holding house. Like he's tied to that mirror instead of being a symptom of my own insanity.

I could look. Just take a quick peek. Seeing his face makes me whole again, even as it breaks me apart. But I can't lose my focus. I need a clear head. I need to think my way through this new place, figure out how it works.

I stop thinking about it and force my legs to move. Opening the bathroom door slowly, I see Stacey sitting at a small table in front of the open, glass doors. She's reading a novel, looking relaxed and carefree.

I scan the room carefully before stepping through the door, confirming that no one else is around. A wide sitting area separates the bathroom from the kitchen, with a recessed floor, plush carpeting and deep sofas. I walk toward where Stacey sits, hopping down the two steps to cross the soft carpeting before climbing the two steps on the other side.

She smiles up at me as I sit across the table from her, my eyes darting to the open door and the illusion of freedom.

"Hey there," she chimes, as she sets the book down and rises from her seat. "How do the clothes fit? I thought we looked about the same size."

"Fine, thank you."

"Let me grab you something to eat."

She shuffles through the double-wide refrigerator before returning with a plate full of little sandwiches, cut veggies, hummus, fruit, sliced meat and olives. She sets it in front of me, along with a tall, frosted glass of orange juice.

I don't make a move to touch it. I just stare at her, and she sighs as she reclaims her seat.

"Please, I know you don't trust us yet, but you must be starving. Enjoy the food, no strings attached. Okay?"

Her face is so concerned, so genuine, I almost want to tell her I'm not as weak and wounded as I appear. That would be foolish, to confide in this gullible girl who honestly believes this is a safe home.

"Thank you." I reach for a sandwich. "I don't mean to seem ungrateful, it's just-"

"No." She shakes her head slowly from side to side. "You don't need to explain. We've all been where you are. When I came here, it took me weeks to accept that it was real. To finally stop watching my back and suspecting every word I heard was a lie. You'll get there, in your own time. No one blames you for being cautious."

Wow, she's good at this.

"How many of you are kept here?" I ask between bites. The

sandwiches are the best thing I've tasted in forever. The veggies are so fresh and crisp I'm sure they were grown right outside.

She sits up a little straighter, her eyes lighting up. "There's six of us, but we're not kept. Not in the way you mean. This isn't a holding house, Whisper, and you're not in training anymore. Elder Tobias and his wife, Meredith, they bought you. Just like they bought all of us. You're free now."

I cough around the bite of sliced turkey, taking a long gulp of orange juice that tastes like it was growing on a tree moments ago.

"Free?" I choke out, but her face is serious. "You're owned by a rich, old man. You dress how he wants you to, do what he tells you to, and you wear the mark of the organization that made you a slave. None of this is freedom."

Fuck, she is too far gone. I shudder at the thought of how hard it will be for her to transition back into the real world. I hope the other five aren't so broken.

"Whisper."

The man's voice from across the room makes me jump to my feet, the chair scraping loudly across the tiled floor. Elder Tobias. I stare at him for a moment too long before schooling my expression and lowering my gaze to the floor. I'd be stupid to show my hand, to show any defiance at this point.

"I'm sorry to disturb your meal. I intended to give you as much space as you needed, but if you'll allow me, I'd like to talk with you."

The fuck?

"Yes, sir." I sit back down in my chair with my hands folded in my lap.

He walks slowly across the kitchen, pulling out a chair to sit at the table. He's a few feet away from me now. I could take him out with my bare hands, and the thought of it is intoxicating. I glance over at Stacey, and she gives me another one of those soft smiles she seems to have no shortage of.

"I know your story, Whisper. At least, I know the media's version of it."

I get the impression this is going to be long-winded, so I test my limits by reaching for another sandwich. He doesn't comment, and so I resume eating slowly while he recites the abbreviated story of my career.

"You came out of nowhere, planning to take on the Academy. Unlike any other woman before or since, you did exactly what you set out to do. You graduated with your male peers, scoring above them in everything except brute strength. You earned your title as Enforcer. Within a few months, you advanced to Agent.

For four years you ranked high in the stats, winning nearly all your missions. For four years you were passed by when openings in the Elite program came along. Agents with less experience and less qualifications were promoted above you. Until Elite Gideon came along. He took you on as his Apprentice, during which time you liberated his niece and three other girls from a human trafficking ring. He vouched for you, and you were officially inducted into the ranks of the Elites. Tanikka Durant then requested you specifically for her employ."

He pauses, as if waiting to see if I have any objections. He's got all the highlights right, but what comes next in my story even I don't know. Not the so-called media version at least. Hopefully it doesn't continue with *and then you went undercover to destroy the previously mentioned human trafficking ring*.

When he continues, his voice is a shade lower. "You had everything you worked for. You were at the top. Then you suffered a psychotic break. You attacked your employer's husband, the son of an Elder and future Elder himself. Your Shifter was killed in the fight. You were wounded. You should have been jailed, tried and likely executed for your crimes. Lucky for you, Isaac Durant is a compassionate soul like his Elder father. He took pity on you and offered to keep you under his roof and within his employ. He gave you a second chance.

You were devastated by the consequences of your actions. Actions that caused the death of your own Shifter and nearly cost Isaac his life. You couldn't live with what you had done. You left a note stating your intentions to jump from the edge of the Solar, though your body was never found."

Minutes pass after he stops his story, and I realize I'm gripping the arms of my chair. I force my white knuckles to relax.

"Would you like to know how I think that story actually ends?" He looks concerned, and I want to get up and walk out those open doors. See how concerned and polite he is when I'm not giving him the audience he expects.

But I can't move. I'm rooted to this spot, and I want to know what he's working up to. There's a reason for this conversation. The story he tells of how things went down with Isaac isn't surprising... of course he would need to save face and paint me as the problem. Faking my suicide to prevent anyone from looking too closely... I didn't see that one coming.

He leans forward, elbows on his knees as he looks at me with a weathered yet handsome face that could belong to a man much younger than his seventy-odd years.

"I think you found out what Isaac was involved in, and you did what you had to do. You likely had no one you could turn to for backup, but you couldn't ignore it once you had seen the truth. I think you underestimated him, though what cards he had up his sleeve to defeat you and your panther, I can't imagine." He pauses again, and I know he can see that I'm shaking. "I don't think you gave up. Not for one second. The system betrayed you. Your friends betrayed you. You were stripped of your rank, your implants and your freedom. But the woman that's looking at me now, she hasn't given up just yet, has she?"

His eyes are wild, tempting me to agree, to stand up and claim the version of the story he's offering. And it's damn close.

"What do you want me to say, Sir?" I ask as I fold my hands back onto my lap. "You bought me. You own me. I'll go along with whatever story you prefer."

"Yes, Elite Whisper. You're still in there." He chuckles, shaking his head. He leans back in his chair, folding his arms across his rounded abdomen. "Would you like to hear my story now?"

I shrug my shoulders, but my eyes stay on his.

"Ten years ago, roughly, I learned of an organization called Horizon Zero. It had grown up seemingly overnight, dabbling in this and that, to suddenly become one of the wealthiest entities on the planet. Unlike other organizations of such magnitude, this one was never mentioned in the media. Never cited in court. Never spoken of by anyone, other than those directly involved.

I learned of it because a few of my fellow Elders had founded it. They nurtured it in silence for years, and now needed more hands to keep it running smoothly. I wasn't the only Elder they approached at that time. Two others were also propositioned. One was eager to get involved once he saw the financials. The other refused, as I had intended to, and he met his fate that same day in an accident involving the mechanical failure of an elevator.

It was clear that refusing the 'offer' to join them wasn't an option. Instead, I showed interest, asked questions and learned more about the darker side of their business. They weren't afraid to share, because they had no intention of letting me live if I refused them or tried to speak out. Ten Elders, and four of them were involved. Drugs, murder, smuggling, slavery, prostitution, human trafficking... you know the worst, I'm sure.

I talked with Meredith about it. We wanted to do what was right, but we had our own children to think of. Our grandchildren. It sickened us, but we knew we had no choice. Protecting our family had to be our top priority, even if that meant we helped commit unspeakable sins against other families. It's not right, but I'd make the same decision again to keep my children safe."

He looks at me in silence for a while, as if waiting for my judgement. I stare back, offering nothing.

"Meredith had the idea first, beautiful soul that she is. Four years ago, she said, 'we can't help them all, but why can't we help one?'. So I requested a girl. Specifically, a girl who was strong-willed, combative, hard to break. They took the request to be an appetite of mine and didn't question. That's how Emily came to us. She would not have survived her training... her will was too strong and she would have died before letting anyone own her. It took a while, but we finally convinced her that we only wanted to offer her a safe place to stay, recuperate, and when she was ready, a new identity to start a new life. We intended to claim that she had died, that we had burned all traces of the body to keep our secret. It would have worked, I believe, but Emily had nowhere to go. No life to return to, and no friends or family to speak of. As is the case with so many of the homeless girls they prey on.

She also felt the strong desire to help others like herself. So, we came up with a new plan together. We switched our main residence here, to our summer estate. I requested another girl, claiming the first was still useful around the house, but that she no longer interested my wife and I in the ways we wanted. The words themselves disgust me, but for our plan to work we needed to play this role convincingly.

Clara came to us shortly after that. Like Emily, she chose to stay. Each girl here has decided to stay, and we've modified our home and guarded our privacy to great lengths to keep them safe. I do not own them, though they keep their marks and play that role whenever someone who is a part of the organization pays a visit. To our family and to any public eye that happens past the gate, they are live-in help. And to be fair, they do help... this property is vast, and to preserve our privacy we must handle all the maintenance ourselves. I'm away a lot for work, so I'm afraid the bulk of the chores around here fall to the women. My wife is happy with that arrangement, though. Keeps her busy and gives her plenty of company. She was a bit lonely after our own daughters left home."

He's looking around the room now, lost in his memories for a moment before he turns back to me. I see only honesty in his face, and my mind is going over everything he has said. What does it all mean for my own mission? If what he's saying is all true, killing him to draw attention to the organization would be like killing a homeless man to raise awareness for homelessness.

He's waiting, watching my face and giving me time to think. I feel like I just drove full throttle off a cliff, and now I'm suspended in the air like a cartoon character, waiting to see if I fly or fall.

"Why don't you rest?" He offers, when I'm still lost in the maze of my own thoughts. "You can use that little guest room, or Stacey can show you to something a bit nicer. You can meet the other women tomorrow and get a good look around if you like."

I don't answer, but Stacey pushes to her feet and flashes me a grin. She starts away from the table, and I follow because what else can I do? I glance back at the Elder just before we leave the bright kitchen, and he's simply staring out the windows. His jaw is flexing. Grinding his teeth.

There's more he wants to say.

DRAGON

*A*s I knead my hands into the dark, fragrant earth I'm acutely aware of the eyes watching me. Elder Tobias has kept his distance since he told me the story of this place. It's been three days, and while I know he is giving me the space he thinks I need to process and consider, it's also clear that whatever details he held back are weighing on him.

Time's running out. I don't know why Charles sent me here, but it's clear Tobias isn't my target. I need to get on that shipment to Gliese. I'm just not certain if I can trust him. It seems ridiculous, given the fact that all of the women here have assured me that everything he said was true.

They've elaborated and filled in the blanks with their own stories. Julie was nearly dead due to untreated blood poisoning when he bought her. Kara would have been killed for breaking her keeper's nose when he tried to rape her. That was just the kind of feisty Elder Tobias is known for liking.

The girls who refuse to break, who would rather die than submit, those are the ones he takes in and gives a second chance to. And they love him for it. They love him like a father, and for most of them he's the only father figure they've ever known.

And then there's Meredith. I've never spoken to a woman so genuinely in love with her husband. After forty-three years of marriage, this little mission of theirs has brought them closer than ever, according to her. And you can see it. You can feel it in the air around them. It's a spark that makes my heart burn and my fingers itch for the touch of Damon's skin.

Seeing them together makes me ache for what I almost had. What I threw away. But it also makes me feel a little better, just knowing that love like that really is possible. Like it confirms that Damon and I could have been great, if I'd only gotten my head out of my ass in time.

He's not in the mirror anymore. I thought for a moment he was with me, but the hazy image faded. Now he's really gone, and I wear that pain like a well-earned scar.

Fuck. I need to get out of here. I stop turning the earth, tending the garden like I'm actually part of this. I stand up, brushing the dirt from my hands onto the worn fabric of my gardening pants.

"Everything okay, honey?" Meredith's ever-cheery voice calls from the other end of the garden.

"Yeah."

I look up to the second story window where Tobias works at his desk. It's time to stop waiting. He's going to tell me what he's been holding back, and help me get on that shipment.

When I walk through the open glass doors, he's already sitting at one of the low, plush sofas. I take a moment to slip off my shoes and brush the dirt from my pants.

"Could you be happy here, Whisper?"

I don't respond. He looks at me after a moment, dropping his eyes to my bare neck.

"You worked hard to get through the Academy. Then to become an Agent, and an Elite. I'm willing to bet you worked at least twice as hard as the boys in those programs."

I swallow past a lump in my throat. Something about the way he's looking at me, the tone in his voice. I sit on the step that leads into the recessed sitting area.

"I heard that you were in one of the holding houses, and an idea came into my mind that I couldn't shake. Sleep was impossible that night, but when the sun came up, my better judgement returned. It was all the silly imaginings of an old man, and I pushed it aside as so. I paid for you and waited for your arrival as I had with all the others, fully committed to helping you recover and find the safety you deserve.

But since you arrived, I've been unable to stop myself from thinking about it. You're not like the others. The way you move, the look in your eye... you are every bit an Agent still, aren't you? They didn't break you, not for one second."

He waits for me to answer, but I just hold his stare. My gut tells me I can trust this person, but my head reminds me that I've never gotten anywhere by trusting anyone. He nods anyway, gleaning enough of an answer from the expression on my face, I suppose.

"I wanted to stop Horizon Zero. I wanted to expose the corruption and shut them down, as is my duty as an Elder. But I was too selfish. I am too selfish. I will not risk the safety of my wife, my children and grandchildren. I can't bring myself to sacrifice my family, even if it means saving so many more. That is my weakness and my shame."

His voice breaks at those last words, and he clears his throat.

"You want to protect your family. There's no shame in that."

He shakes his head. "No. I am ashamed because I sit here behind the comfort of these walls, doing nothing to stop this great evil that is only growing stronger before my eyes. I'm ashamed, because I vowed to protect you from them, and now I am about to ask you to risk everything again."

Sounds like we're on the same page. Time to show my hand.

"Horizon Zero is a business. To bring them down, I need to hit them where it hurts. I know they're funded largely by an off-world client. What do you know about that?"

Tobias leans back into the couch, clasping his hands together on his lap. The worry melts away from his expression, and for the first time since arriving here I can see the Elder I met at the Atrium.

"Roughly 65% of their income is from one client's distribution network. The Pharaoh of Gliese. A strange culture; technologically advanced yet archaic in their religion. They claim he's a demi-god. He buys and sells so-called exotic females like our royalty does with pure-bred horses. He's the true head of the snake. He might not own Horizon Zero, but his death would deliver a crippling financial blow."

I don't remember getting up, but I find I'm standing near the windows. Meredith, Clara and Julie are still at work tending the garden. They seem content, happy even. I can still smell the richness of the fertile soil that clings to my clothing.

"He's the reason I was in that holding house. I've got the right shade of hair and the right attitude. I just need to be on that shipment, so I can get close to him." I don't plan to mention Tanikka's role in this. Or even Charles. I look back at Tobias, but his expression shows no alarm. "I played along with their training, pretending to be weak, so I'd get passed up to him. I don't know why I ended up here."

A fleeting smile crosses his face. "When I inquired about purchasing you, I discovered you were already headed for the Gliese shipment. I figured you were out of my reach at that point But I got a call from a friend... a fellow unwilling accomplice in all of this. He said he didn't have the heart to send you along. Asked if I'd take you instead."

Charles sent me here intentionally. I don't know whether to be pissed off that he delayed my mission, or touched that he cared enough to send me somewhere safe.

"I want on that shipment."

"Whisper, what we're talking about is a one-way ticket. There's no chance they will let you live."

"I know. When does it leave?"

"Tomorrow."

"Tobias!" Julie's shrill voice precedes her panicked face as she rushes into the room. "There's a... there's a dragon outside. It's asking for Whisper."

~

"BRING... ME... WHISPER."

Making my dragon's tongue form human words is a challenging feat, but I think she gets the point. The terrified female scrambles to her feet the moment I release her from beneath my scaled foot. She trips over herself in her effort to get away from me and into the safety of the sprawling fortress in front of me.

I'll give her five minutes, then I'm burning this place to the ground.

I'm not certain if I can actually breath fire, but I can sure as hell level any obstacle that stands between me and my Whisper. I claw at the ground, high on the raw power and wishing for a worthy opponent to try and stand in my way.

That tiger. How good it would be to find him here. Let him try and outmuscle me now. I throw my head back and roar, the sound like fear and death as it erupts from deep in my chest. This strength, this power... it's consuming me with the urge to fight. To dominate. To destroy...

A scent invades my nose. Soft and subtle, yet it demands my full attention. I look toward the building and see my mate. Alive and whole and here. She stands at the doorway, her face twisted in confusion and concern.

"Tarek?" She says the name as if I could actually be that green reptile. Does she not see me? I am far more powerful than his dragon. And my scales, black as night, just the color she likes.

I flare my wings, swinging my long, spiked tail from side to side as a growl rumbles up from my throat. Still, she doesn't recognize me. She backs up a half-step, as if she would retreat into the building rather than run into my arms.

Maybe that's it... human arms to hold my mate.

I shift, and the earth tilts until I grip handfuls of grass to steady myself. Holy fuck. I thought taking human form for the first time had been a trip. Gideon hadn't been exaggerating when he warned me about trying a dragon. That beast's mind came with a temper I don't care to experience again.

I catch my breath, relieved when the world stops moving and I manage not to lose the contents of my stomach. I drop back onto my ass, not quite ready to stand.

Whisper hasn't moved. Her face is pale, her dark eyes fixed on mine with an emotion I can't decipher. She's thinner than when I last saw her, and my gut twists at the thought of all she's gone through. I should have been by her side. I should have protected her.

I push to my feet, ignoring the slight wobble in my vision. As I walk toward her, she stands absolutely still. Only her eyes change, widening as her expression melts into one of pure fear. What has happened that my Whisper could be so afraid of me?

I reach up, brushing her soft cheek with the tips of my fingers, bracing myself for her rejection. I breathe in the scent of her, wanting desperately to hold her.

"I'm so sorry I didn't protect you." The words don't even come close to expressing the guilt that threatens to tear me apart.

I cup her cheek with my palm, my gaze dropping from her

eyes, down to her full lips. They part as she sucks in a breath, her chin trembling. I move my hand to tangle in her hair, which is a new, vibrant shade of red. I wonder what made her decide to change the color. Or if the decision was made for her.

I press my mouth against hers, and the taste of her sends a shiver through my body. I kiss her, slowly at first until she begins to respond, leaning into me at last. Her hands slide along my stomach, and I groan as her touch makes me instantly, painfully hard. She responds by sucking my lower lip into her mouth, and I lose control.

Whatever intentions I had of treating her softly are gone, as I back her into the stone wall and devour her mouth without reservation. My hands are desperate to touch every inch of her, gliding over and under the thin material of her clothing. I press the hard length of my erection against her belly, and a delicious moan escapes her as she grasps fistfuls of my shirt.

I don't care where we are. I don't care who's watching. My Whisper. My mate. I need her now. All of her.

But she pushes against me.

"Stop."

She can barely say the word, but I obey. I brace my hands against the cool stone on either side of her and search the depths of her brown eyes. Eyes brimming with tears.

"Little one..." If I hurt her-

"Damon." She says my name like a prayer, and then the dam breaks. Tears stream down her perfect face as she buries herself in my chest. Her arms wrap around me as silent sobs make her body tremble and shake.

I don't know what to do. I've seen her angry and I've seen her sad. I've never seen her cry. I wrap my arms around her, kneading my hands along her spine, burying my face in her hair. I want to comfort her. Whatever she's been through without me, I want her to know it's over.

I will never leave her side again.

"I love you," I say, because even though she doesn't believe me, I still need her to hear it.

"I love you, too."

She says it back without hesitation, through her tears and with a shaking voice. But she says it. I grasp her shoulders, pushing her back so I can see her face. It's puffy, and red, and wet with tears... but she's smiling like a child. Pure happiness.

"I love you, Damon." She says it again as she looks me straight in the eyes. "I'm so sorry I couldn't... I didn't... when I thought you were dead..."

The realization of how my absence has affected her hits me like a kick in the gut. Never again.

"It's over now. I found a safe place. We can be safe, together. No more fighting. No more hiding."

She takes my face in both her hands, looking up into my eyes with a fierce intensity. "Nothing would make me happier," she says, but her eyes hold only sadness.

CAN'T

J'm a babbling mess, and I don't even care. He's here. Really here. I can see him. Touch his solid warmth. Hear his voice as it rumbles in his chest and across my skin. I can smell that fresh, crisp scent that always follows a shift. Like the air after an electrical storm.

He's really here.

I move my hands from his face, down over his chest, his stomach. Sweet fuck, he's hard as steel. I want to take him down right here in the front yard. I don't even care that eight pairs of eyes are likely on us right now. I need more of him. All of him.

He growls low in his chest, a dark rumble that's nearly a moan. "Let me fly you out of here," he says against my neck, and I shiver at the delicious promise within his words.

Yes, please, yes. There is nothing I want more than to fly away with him. To get lost with him, anywhere. Always.

"I can't. Damon, I thought you were gone." I swipe the tears from my face, stepping back and filling my lungs with air in an attempt to regain some control. "I was so cruel to you. I didn't understand. I didn't trust you. I am so sorry."

"Hey, easy, it's okay now." He steps forward, cupping my

cheek again in his big hand, brushing his thumb across my lower lip. "We're together now. I'll never leave you." His chocolate eyes look deep into mine, with such love and concern it makes my heart hurt.

How could I have ever thought he was less than human? He's so, so much more. I cover his hand with mine. How can I leave him? I want to be selfish. I want to forget everything I've learned, everything I've seen. Let Horizon Zero be someone else's problem. I can go with Damon and have everything I never knew I needed.

But I've been selfish for too long.

As HE PACES the floor in front of the glass wall, with a pink sky bathing everything in its fading light, Damon is every bit the panther. His body is all strength and feline grace. Black pants sit low on his hips, his grey t-shirt clinging to his biceps and broad chest. The conversation is deadly serious, but I can't stop staring at him, watching him move... imagining all the things I want to do to his body.

The image of his dragon form flashes in my mind. I hadn't thought for a second that the massive, beautiful creature had been him. But now it seems so obvious. He was barely in control, but he managed to take on the near impossible to save me.

An image flashes in my mind, of me in a dragon's saddle, flying alongside Gideon and Tarek as we patrol the Solars. Not long ago that would have been a dream come true. The ultimate goal realized. But nothing about that system or that life appeals to me now. Certainly not the idea of Damon being in service to me. I don't want a dragon, I want him. Just as he is now.

"No." Damon shakes his head for emphasis. "Just no."

Tobias invited him in, once we could keep our hands off each other long enough for me to open the door and introduce him. He quickly sent the rest of the household out of earshot despite their curious questions.

I filled him in on who Damon is, and we filled Damon in on the plan to take down Horizon Zero. The plan where I hop a one-way ticket to assassinate an off-world deity. Damon took to the idea about as well as I would have if the roles were reversed.

And I agree with him. Every cell in my body is screaming *no*. I can't leave him. I can't lose him again.

"It's the right thing to do." I say the words, because I know they're true.

Damon halts his pacing, baring his teeth in a growl. "The hell it is!" He snarls the words with such pure anger that both Tobias and I back up a step. I could never fear Damon, but he's never argued with me so vehemently.

"I thought he was bonded to you, as your Shifter. Shouldn't that make him more agreeable?"

I smirk at Tobias's question, but Damon doesn't quite see the same humor in it. He stalks toward the Elder, who somehow manages to hold his ground. Quite an impressive display of nerves, considering the man staring him down was a hulking dragon not thirty minutes ago.

"I am not bonded to anyone. Not anymore." His eyes flick to mine as he says it, and I know for certain that all Tanikka said was true. "I met others like me, far from here. There's a whole community, just living their lives. Real lives. Not accelerated versions of lives to suit a human master."

Heat rises in my cheeks. Shame. Shame at my part in keeping him from being his full self.

"I'm so sorry, Damon."

He abandons his attempt to intimidate Tobias, and in two long strides he's pulling me into his arms. "We can join them. We can help them. We can be apart from all of this human cruelty, together." His voice is pleading, and it breaks my heart.

I push away, wiping tears from my cheeks. Tobias has moved to sit on the couch, averting his gaze to give us a little privacy.

"I've seen what these girls are living through. I've only seen the holding houses, and that's bad enough. But the next phases, and after they're sold... Damon, I can't abandon this. Our plan could work. It could cripple the organization and save so many innocent lives. If I run away now, if I choose my own happiness over theirs... how could I live with myself? How could you?"

"I only care about you."

"And I love you for that. I will always love you. But you found a home, your own kind. And you've broken the bond so..."

"So I won't die when you do?"

"Damon..."

"I love you. That's our bond."

GOODBYE

*D*ammit, why does she have to be so fucking stubborn? I've always admired her ambition, her grit and determination to get what she wants. She never cared who she stepped on to get to her goals. But everything she had wanted had been for herself, to keep herself safe. Never before has she threatened to lay down her own life for others. As much as I admire her for this, as much as I could burst from the pride, I can't lose her again.

I can't let her do this.

But there's nothing I can do about it. Well, maybe one thing. My dragon form could pick her up and carry her so far from here she'd never make it back. I could force her to stay with me, to keep herself safe. But how long would she still look at me with love in her eyes if I resorted to that?

It doesn't matter. Even if she hates me, at least she will be alive. I can earn her love back after she cools down... but even I know how wrong that all sounds. I can't control her. I can beg, I can kiss her with all the passion and desperation I feel and beg her to stay with me. But I can't control her.

"Please." I've said that word so many times, I've lost count.

I hate the way she looks at me. The pity in her eyes makes me sick to my stomach, as if she's sorry for my loss instead of fearing for her own safety.

"Stay here tonight, Son," the old man offers. I hate him. I hate him for encouraging this. "If Whisper wants you to, of course."

"Yes. Thank you, yes." She sounds so relieved, her voice cracking with emotion.

She grabs my hand in hers, coaxing me to follow her through the wide glass doors. Out in the cool evening, she leads the way through a lush, blooming garden.

"Whisper, we need to talk more about this."

"No, Damon." Her words are final, the clipped tone leaving no room for arguing. But I plan to argue until my last breath.

We're out of sight from the house, weaving through a stand of smooth-barked trees. I plant my feet, our joined hands bringing her to an abrupt halt. She opens her mouth to speak, but I drown the words with a heavy, pleading kiss. She's breathless when I finally release her, but her expression quickly turns predatory.

She plants her hands on my chest and shoves me with a strength far greater than her small form should be capable of. She shoves me back into the wide trunk of a tree, and then she's pushing up the hem of my shirt.

Hell yes.

I pull the thin fabric over my head, as her hot mouth burns a slow trail down the center of my chest. Down over my abs. I'm shaking with anticipation by the time she reaches the waist of my pants, my cock painfully hard and straining against its confines. I hiss through my teeth as she stops her descent, trailing kisses off to the side until she nips at first one hip, and then the other. It's sweet torture.

I grip the tree trunk behind me to keep from grabbing fistfuls of her thick, cascading hair. I fight the urge to push her head down farther, to feel her mouth around my cock. The heat of her lips, her tongue... the image makes me mad with need.

At last she hooks her fingers in the waist of my pants, pulling them down until my erection springs free. Her little gasp brings a grin to my face, but then her hand grips me as her tongue runs a burning trail from the base of my cock right up to the sensitive tip. The moan that escapes me sounds more like a growl, and my head falls back against the cool tree.

The heat of her mouth closes around me, as her tongue flicks and swirls. She sucks me slowly deeper, and I lose my mind. I need her. Now. I need her to feel everything I'm feeling. Every sensation, every rush of pleasure.

THE TASTE of him is like a shot of adrenaline through my veins. His thick cock is hard and heavy in my hand, making my core ache at the thought of having him inside me again. But I'm not going there yet. I want to worship this man. I want to show him what he means to me. I want to kneel in front of him and make him roar with pleasure.

I've been so selfish. I want him to know without doubt how much I adore him. When I close my lips around his thick head, the sound of his pleasure nearly puts me over the edge. My panties are soaked as I clench my thighs together, trying to relieve the building pressure between my legs. It's sweet torture.

I take him deeper, but he's so big I couldn't possibly take him all in.

His hands grip me under my arms, hauling me roughly up to my feet. I'm not sure what happened, what I did wrong.

"Damon..."

"I need you." His words are a guttural command that I'm more than happy to obey.

He tears at my clothes. I try to help, but he's too impatient and the fabric shreds. My skin prickles in the cool night air, and then I'm wrapped in his warm arms. The trunk of the tree is rough against my back, but I'm lost in the feel of his skin against mine.

Fuck, I love this man.

He grips my thigh, pulling my leg up over his hip, and in one sure thrust he buries himself fully inside me.

We cry out in unison, my voice a song of pure pleasure as he fills me so utterly completely. His is a roar of deepening lust. He keeps still inside me, his hand brushing my cheek, fingers tangling in my hair. His eyes search mine, looking deep into my soul.

Then he takes me.

Hard and rough. His desperate, relentless pace takes us both crashing over the edge in a matter of minutes.

We're tangled together in the grass, and I'm reeling from the intensity of our lovemaking. My sweet, gentle Damon can fuck like a pro.

The laugh that escapes me sounds more like a snort, and Damon's body jerks in surprise, making me laugh even harder.

"Whisper?" His voice is filled with concern. For my sanity, no doubt.

I get control, sitting up as I sniffle and wipe the stray tears from my face. "I'm sorry."

He puts his hand on my back, smoothing my hair as he kisses my shoulder. "Did I hurt you? Was that-"

I cut off his words with a kiss.

I push him down onto his back, straddling his waist with my thighs. My tongue delves deep into his mouth and I bite his lip The softened length of his cock turns hard so fast, I can't help but break the kiss to look down between us.

Fuck, he's beautiful.

"You can't hurt me, Damon." I tear my eyes away from his body, back up to his face. He's looking at me with renewed heat, but he's holding it back. Waiting for my permission. "We were made for each other."

His abs flex tight as he lifts his shoulders off the ground, one hand threaded through my hair as he pulls my face to meet his. He takes my mouth in a deep, slow, burning kiss.

His other hand grips my ass, pulling me tight against him so that my core presses firmly against the length of his erection. I move my hips, grinding my clit along his hard length and making him slick with the proof of my arousal.

Our breathing grows increasingly labored, our kisses becoming sloppy as our attention focuses on our growing need. I expect him to maneuver so he can thrust inside me and find the same release I'm getting so close to. Instead, he moves his mouth down my neck, down my chest. He kneads one sensitive breast with his hand as he licks and sucks on the pebbled peak of the other. His free hand guides my hips to continue grinding along his cock, encouraging me to chase my own orgasm.

He releases the hardened bud of my nipple, moving to the other one. He swaps his hands, not missing a beat. I hold back, even though I'm so close to the edge. I don't want to be selfish. I don't want to come without him, but I can't bear to stop the sweet ecstasy of his mouth on me.

I reach between us, wrapping my hand around his cock as his moan of pleasure vibrates against my chest. I arch my hips to guide him inside me, but he grips my ass tighter, preventing me from getting the distance I need to maneuver him.

"Come for me first," he rasps against my chest, the hand on my ass moving around to press against my clit with quick, precise circles.

My orgasm is instant, the moment he says the words it crashes into me, the motion of his fingers taking me even higher. When I come down, he's staring at me, his dark eyes roaming over my face as if he's memorizing every detail.

He flips me softly onto my back, pressing his forehead against mine as he slides inside me. He braces his arms on the ground at either side of me, his hips taking a steady, unhurried rhythm.

I run my hands up over his arms, loving the feel of his biceps flexing to hold his body above me. I wrap my legs around his waist, giving him full access to thrust deep.

He keeps up the slow pace, as I let my hands explore every bit of skin I can reach. Soon, yet another orgasm is building inside me. I dig my fingers into his back, gripping him tighter with my thighs as I urge him into a faster pace. He responds immediately, picking up the speed so perfectly, it's as if he read my mind.

Then I'm detonating again, and this time he's right there with me. His roars of pleasure. His final, frantic thrusts. His cock throbbing inside me as he fills me. It's all so intense. Such utter perfection.

I can't imagine ever leaving him.

"Don't go." His thoughts are right there with mine, even as he still lingers inside me.

His chest is heaving with the aftermath of intense orgasm, but the look in his eyes is such sorrow I have to close mine to keep from falling apart.

"I love you, Damon. I love you more than I ever thought possible. But if I don't help them, who will?"

He flops down beside me, pulling me close so my head rests on his chest. I trace the scars on his skin with lazy fingers. The rapid beat of his heart is the most beautiful sound I've ever heard.

My Medic. I hadn't even considered. It doubled as my birth control, but I don't have it anymore. Can a Shifter and a human even... I don't know why I'm bothering to think about this now. I won't be around long enough to worry about the consequences.

"Promise me you'll come back."

I push myself up so I can see his eyes. He knows such a

promise would be empty. If the roles were reversed, if it were him leaving...

"I promise." I say it with conviction, even though we both know better. Saying the words makes this all seem a little less tragic. "Will you promise me something, too?"

"Anything."

I know what I need to say. I know what I would need to hear, if it were me being left behind. The words just don't want to come.

I want to tell him to be happy. To live his life, find someone new, fall in love, make a family. Seeing him in my mind's eye, surrounded by love and family, old and content. I want all of that for him. But I know I couldn't do any of that without him. I wouldn't even want to try. I know just as surely that he won't either. He'll die waiting for me.

"Destroy BioSol Labs." His body goes rigid, his steady breathing coming to an abrupt halt. I sit up, feeling the truth in my own words as the idea spreads through my mind. "Destroy it. Show the world who you are. Show them the truth."

"Whisper, without you..." There's a hitch in his voice, as a shudder ripples through his body.

"I know."

GLIESE

*D*ays and nights pass, the sun and moon slipping by above my head without fail, just as they always have. My world has ended, but the world around me continues to turn without so much as a flicker of the devastation I feel.

I shift my position, tucking my paws under my chest. My muscles are stiff, and my fur is dry and rough, but I don't care. Watching her walk away was the hardest thing I've ever done. I could have stopped her. I could have taken her away and held her until she gave in to my will.

But I didn't. I let her go.

This form dulls the pain just a little, the animal instincts taking precedence over human worries. Even that is getting weaker. Lately, my human mind seems to follow me into each form I take.

"Damon, will you come in for lunch?" The female's voice calls from below, and I growl in response.

I hear a window slide closed, and I'm alone again. From my perch on the Elder's roof, I can look past the well-tended garden and it's stand of birch trees. Past the high stone wall, and the rolling countryside beyond.

It's the direction they took her. I watched from here as a tiny spark of light rose from the horizon. A tiny spark disappearing into the atmosphere. My Whisper, gone.

I can't move. I can't move from this spot or move on with my life. I can't.

Destroy BioSol Labs.

Whisper's voice echoes in my memory. The idea she planted that I've been refusing to think about. She's always taken jobs, followed orders, gotten paid. There was never anything more to it than that. I followed her commands, and she followed those given to her. Now she's off planet, sacrificing her life for people she doesn't even know. And she wants me to do the same.

She knew that by leaving, she was sentencing me to a slow death. Not because of some artificial bond that would make my organs fail upon her own death... but because she understood how much I loved her. She understood because she felt the same.

But how? I've never planned a mission. I've never even asked what the next step is, let alone thought it through to completion. Protect Whisper. Do as she asks. That's the extent of my planning abilities.

I shift to my human form. I need all the focus I can get. What would she be expecting me to do? I could tear through the lab with dragon talons, destroying their facility and equipment. That would set them back. It would also show the world that Shifters are dangerous. Not the effect Whisper intended.

I think of Hope and the Meadow. They've been fighting for years. Not in any real sense of the word, but they've been saving Shifters, creating a place where we can be ourselves.

Show the world who you are. Show them the truth.

It's not about showing the humans, or teaching them any kind of lesson. Hell, they enslave their own kind readily enough, why bother trying to open their eyes to the plight of another species? It's the Shifters. They are the ones that need to see. Once they understand they can take human form and live independent of their Agent's, they'll be free to make their own choices.

Even knowing all of this, I wouldn't have left Whisper. Not all Shifters would feel that way if they had the chance to question their realities.

I could go back to the Meadow, but I need someone connected. Someone who's already dissatisfied with the system, and skilled enough to fight if it comes to that.

Ah, fuck.

THE FAMILIAR SOUND of a clock ticking lures me out of a thick, dreamless sleep. Something's not right. As I listen, focusing on the steady tic-toc-tic-toc, it occurs to me that it's far too slow to be a clock. I listen for other sounds, and one by one they filter through the fog. I hear voices, male voices, distant and muffled. I hear wind, as if through an open window, and the soft crying of a girl.

I focus on my sense of touch. I'm on a firm mattress, covered with a light sheet. I carefully flex each muscle group but find no injuries. I run my tongue along the edge of my gums, feeling the undisturbed ridge behind my teeth. They would have found my implants during the loading procedures, but this little toy was all but invisible.

The air smells like a stable; wood, hay and dampness. Tobias's words come to mind, that the Pharaoh deals with women like rich men deal with horses. Guess he meant that literally.

I can't hear any breathing nearby, so I peek through my eyelids, opening them slowly to adjust to the hazy light. I'm alone, and most definitely in a stable. My stall is about four feet by eight feet, containing a cot, bucket, and a small table with water and some sort of purple fruit. There's also a clock, the second hand ticking slowly around a face with fourteen symbols instead of twelve.

I guess I made it to Gliese.

I rub my temples, but I don't really have a headache. Actually, I feel pretty great. I'd heard cryosleep was a breeze, after the latest updates, but I'd never considered I might experience it myself. The last thing I remember, I was handed a paper cup with some sweet-smelling liquid. Now, I'm lightyears away.

About three days would have passed back on Earth.

My heart aches as I think of the torment on Damon's face when I left him. The evening before, and most of the night, he had shown me more love than I could have ever imagined possible. He had given me every reason to stay, and then some. But in the morning, when it came time for me to leave, he had stood strong. He had respected my decision, and whispered a final *Be safe, little one*, in my ear.

I don't deserve him. I never did. I only pray he finds some purpose, some reason to live.

I stand up, stretching my arms above my head to the sound of a shoulder popping. I feel the weight of the alien gravity, like I gained about fifty pounds along the way. It's a fraction of what I should be experiencing, with this size planet. I reach over and rub my left shoulder. A tender spot marks where the inoculations were administered on route. Everything from the common Gliesien cold to environmental variations, all counteracted with a series of nano-bot injections.

Fucking science.

I nearly jump out of my skin as a heavy knock rattles the door. Not a knock, it's the sound of a heavy chain being removed. The door slides open, and I stare wide-eyed at the strangest man I've ever seen.

He's under five feet tall, but his features look like they belong on someone monstrous. His long, straight hair is stark white, framing an angular and not quite unattractive face. His skin is a pale, powder-white that makes his red eyes stand out like pools of blood.

Is that two pupils in each?

His neck is thick and short, his shoulders wider than any human's. His chest is bare; a smooth barrel without any distinctive pecs or even nipples. He's wearing a wrap like a kilt around his waist, covering him from below that strange chest down to his knees. His legs are like tree trunks, his bare feet wide and flat.

I catch myself staring, forcing my gaze down to the floor. The girls I'm with completed all the levels of training. They certainly wouldn't stare. Thankfully, he doesn't seem bothered by my indiscretion.

He nods his head in a gesture I assume means I should follow, and sure enough as I head out into the center walk-way of the stable, other girls are emerging from their stalls as well. We're all dressed in the familiar gauzy slips, with Horizon Zero tattoos on our wrists. Mine with a slight pink tint around the edges.

Amongst the girls are many more of the strange Gliesien men, all wearing the same kilt-ish wraps in varying colors and patterns. Many of them have weapons strapped to their backs; odd devices that resemble high-tech swords.

I wish I'd spent a little time learning about their culture, but it hadn't seemed important. Not that it matters now, either. I know enough to finish my mission. What they use to kill me after is irrelevant.

I filter out of the barn with the others, the hazy air taking on a red hue as we step out into the sunlight. Make that *suns*. We're in an open field covered in thick, crimson grass. Trees and brush in all shades of red surround us on three sides. At the fourth side stands a looming A-frame building that blocks out a large chunk of sky. Its white siding is crawling with an intricate, black design. Its windows are round and blackened.

I suddenly feel very, very far from home.

I swallow the lump in my throat, forcing deep, steady breaths. I scan the men, looking for one in particular. The moment my eyes land on him, a heavy calm washes over me. Kle'Tar. Any worries I had about Tobias's intel disappear.

The Pharaoh looks mostly like the others, except for his chalky skin is covered in red tattoos. Every exposed inch of him is marked with the symbols and prophecies of their race. Even the unexposed inches, according to Tobias. When he blinks, even his eyelids are inked. Ouch. Might be a little bit sexy if he didn't look so much like a hobbit on steroids...

I know the moment he spots me. His double take is almost humorous. I don't let on I've noticed, but I do casually tilt my head to make my scarlet curls fall forward. Like a moth to a flame, he starts in my direction. He can't resist.

Red. It's the color of their sun, their world, and their gods. A female with this particular shade of red hair is a gift sent from above. A symbol of life and fertility.

When he gets close enough to touch, a meaty hand grips my shoulder from behind, pushing me down to my knees. He's certainly a lot more menacing from this angle.

My heartrate nearly doubles as adrenaline surges, every sense prickling with heightened awareness. A hand strokes my hair, tangles in it and tugs. The dye job's still good enough for this initial inspection, I hope. Even if he catches on, he's close enough for what I need to do.

With bowed head, I wait. His thick hand leaves my hair, dipping under my chin to tilt my face up. I summon all my strength and extend my knees. The motion propels me up into a squat, and then I lunge. Straight for his thick, veiny neck.

I bite him.

Like a fucking vampire.

The tiny hypodermic needle implanted in my eye tooth injects a swarm of nano-bots into his bloodstream. In the few seconds it takes his men to react and pull me off, the damage is done. The Pharaoh drops like a stone, blood trickling out of his ears, nose, eyes and mouth.

The sound of girls screaming mixes with the enraged battle-cries of the men. It's all a distant hum as I crouch on the ground, eyes closed, my conciousness far away in a stand of birch trees with Damon.

PHARAOH

I flare my wings, tilting them to catch the air and stall my decent. My wide back feet touch the rough pavement first, followed by my front feet as my wings fold back against my side. A perfectly graceful landing. Possibly due to the fact that I practiced about a hundred times before coming here.

Not that I'm vain, I just don't think a dragon belly-flopping at your feet instills much confidence.

Gideon appears appropriately impressed, nodding his head with a half-grin. Tarek looks almost wild with what I hope is excitement. His emerald eyes are wide, and his wings are poised for flight. The truth is I can't really read him that well. I can pick up on every little variation of Whisper's expressions and moods, but other Shifters are a mystery to me.

"Hello, Damon," Gideon shouts. "Good to see you're not dead!"

I snort, giving my head a shake. Elder Tobias wasn't willing to risk getting involved in this. His loyalty lies with the stolen girls. But he did agree to make one call for me... to Gideon, asking him to meet Whisper and I here.

"Where's our girl?" He looks around as if she would materialize out of thin air. His expression goes dark, and I fight back a surge of anger. Whisper told me his part in getting her involved in all of this. I can't let that affect my actions now. I need him.

I shift. Forcing it to be slow, I compress my massive dragon form down, reshaping into human form.

Tarek jumps as if electrocuted, a sound like a bark coming from him. Gideon goes a few shades paler, his jaw clenching along with his fists.

"Whisper is gone." I swallow back the emotion that comes with those words. I can't fail her now. "She found a way to save more girls. Maybe all of them. She left on a cargo freighter days ago."

Gideon doesn't move a muscle, even his expression gives nothing away. Then his lips peel back from his teeth as he nearly growls, "Why didn't you stop her? Why aren't you at least with her?"

I stalk toward him until we're nose to nose, the rumble of Tarek's guttural warning thick in the air. "I would gladly lay down my life to keep my Whisper from harm. I did everything I could to keep her safe in my arms."

Gideons eyebrows raise, the half-smirk returning. "In your arms?"

I ignore the comment, stepping back a pace as I turn my attention to Tarek. I tell him the story of our kind. I tell him all I know. All that I learned from the Meadow, what I've discovered on my own, and the details Whisp gave me from her conversation with Tanikka.

When I'm done, the green dragon seems to have lost some size. His wings are tucked tight, his eyes narrowed.

His gaze snaps to Gideon, who looks back at him. They appear to be communicating through their Links, so I stay quiet, waiting.

"Tarek's never questioned our bond. He's never wanted to be free or be anywhere else. He's loyal..."

"I'm sure that's true. But I'm also sure he's felt a nagging pull whenever he's gotten near another Shifter, like a forgotten memory he can't quite grasp. And when he sees you with a woman. I bet he feels a surge of anger, even though he doesn't know why." I look at Tarek, and his eyes are closed. "It's because we aren't meant to be isolated from each other. We're meant to live and work together. We're meant to find mates, real mates, and make our own families."

"Taking human form is illegal. The Shifter brain can't handle the deeper levels of thought and emotion." Gideon defends the actions of his kind with practiced lines. The same ones we all bought.

"The more time I spent in this form, the more my mind adapted. Now, I can think clearly in all my forms. My bond with Whisper is broken. I am my own man. I am not a weapon or a prop to display human power. Your people are killing my people... enslaving our males and murdering our females. Will you stand by and do nothing?"

I look directly at Tarek as I present my call to action, and he doesn't hesitate. His massive form compresses until a man takes his place. He lands on his knees, fists braced against the concrete.

His head is bowed, a mane of blond hair falling around his face. He's wearing cargo pants, steel-toes, and a black muscle top revealing a set of arms that give me the sudden urge to do some push-ups.

Shit.

My mental image of my human form mostly came from bits and pieces of Whisper's comments over the years. I didn't really think about it. I instinctively took the form that would please her eyes. This guy's clearly been fantasizing about some Greek mythology.

Even Gideon steps back, both of us watching Tarek as his monstrous back expands and contracts with labored breaths. He's trying to make sense of it. He's processing and sorting the flood of thoughts and emotions, as everything he's ever seen and heard comes rushing to the surface to take on new layers of meaning.

It'll get easier. It won't stop anytime soon, though. I still find my vocabulary and my knowledge is expanding, as Whisp's memories blend with my own. I might not have had a life before her, but I benefit from all that she learned. It's comforting to know that connection can never be taken away.

Tarek raises his head, his emerald eyes meeting mine. He uncurls to his full height; easily six inches taller than me. If he decides to go apeshit on us, I'll have to shift to something bigger to take him on.

"Your bond will start to break down now. Little by little, the more you take this form. You'll become independent, able to think for yourself and live your own life."

His broad, over-muscled chest heaves with each breath. His hands are clenched into fists that could take me out with one hit.

"Are you sure about this?" Gideon asks.

"Would you rather he stays as a servant, his life depending on yours?"

Gideon shakes his head, lowering his eyes as an expression like shame clouds his features.

"It's good to meet you, brother," I say to Tarek, and an awkward smile spreads across his face.

SILENCE SURROUNDS ME. Even the wind seems to be holding its breath. I open my eyes, tilting my head up just enough to see the wall of muscle and metal surrounding me.

The Pharaoh's men stand in a tight circle, surrounding me and their very dead god-king. Their weapons are drawn, held stiffly in front of them. But they aren't moving.

I stand, dread slowly replacing the calm. I had been prepared for a quick death. Tobias said they don't think much of trials and juries here... that an outright act of murder would get me beheaded on the spot.

I was ready for that.

When I reach my full height, the men move. They swing their swords above their heads, the hilts glowing with an eerie red light. As one, they thrust downward, imbedding the tips into the ground as the red glow flashes along the blades.

They kneel. Heads bowed, palms on the ground.

What. The. Fuck.

I just stand there like an idiot. I can't even...

"Great Pharaoh. Our lives are yours to command."

I don't know which one of them spoke, but he's bat-shit crazy.

"Your Pharaoh's dead."

I turn, looking at each of the twenty-four lethal warriors that surround me. I look past their bowed forms to find the girls are gone. Probably herded back into their stalls after the kill.

"You test us, Great Pharaoh." The voice comes from a warrior in a blue kilt, his white hair hanging in thick braids. He doesn't look up. "You are everlasting. This we know. We may not understand why you chose this form, but we will not question your wisdom."

I stand there stupefied, but they just wait. "So, ah, just to be clear... I killed your Pharaoh. So, that makes me the new Pharaoh?"

"We do not doubt your wisdom, Great Pharaoh. You chose to abandon the body of Kle'Tar, in favor of this human female. We will guide her and protect her, so that your mind may fully meld with hers to accomplish your holy purpose. We do not doubt your wisdom."

Okay. I think that... Maybe if I... Fuck. Think, Whisper. They believe their god inhabits a mortal host, who can only be killed if the god allows it. Or if the god wants to possess that new person instead. So, that's me now. I'm their god-king. I'm the Pharaoh of Gliese.

No fucking way.

"Stand." I say the word with all the authority I can manage, and in one smooth motion they all obey.

I take a deep breath. The men around me have their eyes fixed on the ground. My mind is spinning in a million different directions.

"Take the body away. Give him an honorable, ah, funeral. As per your, our, customs." The circle breaks up as they move to do as I've asked.

I catch the eye of the blue-kilted warrior, the one who was speaking to me, and motion for him to come closer. He obeys, bowing low when he reaches me.

"How many men do I command?" I ask, hoping such ignorance doesn't give me away as a complete fraud.

"Great Pharaoh, you command all of them."

Okay, try that again. "How big is my territory?"

"Gliese is yours, Great Pharaoh. Past, present and future. No one would question this."

I'm going to vomit.

I swallow repeatedly, feeling sand in my throat and snakes in my stomach. And then I start to laugh, which sounds like a gag, which turns into a coughing fit.

"Great Pharaoh?"

"This body is weak from travel." I pull the excuse out of my ass, hoping that's not an invitation to off me and take the role for himself.

"Come, I'll guide you to your chambers. You will be undisturbed while you recover."

I let out a long breath and follow his lead. Behind us, the other men busy themselves with their fallen leader's body. My eyes move to the barn. There must be a hundred girls in there.

I wanted to be an Elite. To get out from under the heels of men. When that failed, when I realized such an idea didn't exist, I thought that was it. That was the end of the line.

Now I'm a Pharaoh. A living deity in the eyes of an entire planet. I'll be worshipped. My every word obeyed. I wanted power. I wanted control. I have more than any human could ever dream of. I can send word to Earth, to the Elders, about the change in management. My brothers, my father if he still lives, everyone I ever met or worked with... they will all learn what I've done. They will all know how wrong they were to doubt my abilities.

I can bring Damon here...

"Did Kle'Tar have a wife? A mate?"

That question makes him stop and turn, giving me a quizzical look before schooling his expression and averting his eyes.

"Great Pharaoh, all are servants to you. The Pharaoh can take anyone he... she... chooses, at any time. It would never be required that you commit yourself to only one."

Well... perks of the job, I guess. We're half-way to the immense A-frame. Close enough to see that the walls are made of stone, the windows so black they're like mirrors. I want to finish this conversation before more ears are near enough to hear it.

"Do you have a wife?" I hope I'm not botching the terminology... I didn't come here expecting conversation.

"Of course."

"But I could still... take you? If I chose?"

"Of course."

"And your wife would be okay with that?"

"Of course, Great Pharaoh. We are all in service to you. Our lives are yours."

How sweet, except for the little fact that the moment I die you'll latch on to the next in line and forget me.

"What if I wanted to take just one. A King."

He stops in his tracks, turning to look me directly in the eyes.

Shit. I fucked up.

"Great Pharaoh," he says the title slowly, uncertainty creeping into his tone. "If this is a test, I assure you that I know your word as surely as I know my own name. There is no equal to you. You would never take another as your equal. Your core commands have been unchanged for as long as our world has existed and will remain unchanged for all eternity."

He's still staring me straight in the eyes. I hold his gaze, getting the distinct impression that looking away first would concede something vital.

"Perhaps this human body is still too weak to absorb your full greatness. Rest. Review the scriptures you wrote for us when we were mere figments of your imagination. You will emerge strong again."

Wow. Dodged a bullet there. "Your loyalty will be rewarded." That sounds like a godly thing to say.

He bows, continuing to lead the way to my new home.

FAR FROM HOME

"*I*t is blasphemy-"

"Silence!"

"But Tor'Heel, you must see. This cannot be what the Great Pharaoh intended."

"Who am I to question what the Great Pharaoh has intended? Who are you?"

"I don't question the Great Pharaoh. I question you. Is that not a wife's prerogative?"

"Come, we will talk in my office."

I remove my ear from the door as footsteps fade away. The blue-kilted warrior, Tor'Heel, led me to this opulent lounge with surprisingly high ceilings, considering the stature of its usual inhabitants. Rest, he said, as if I could even sit still while processing all this. I don't need rest. I need an instruction manual for how not to fuck this up.

He filled me in on a few more details along the way. This is my house, but not only mine. Kle'Tar lived here along with twenty-four warriors and their families. The heads of the entire planet's military. Traditionally, the Great Pharaoh chooses one among them as successor, which basically means one of them murders the current Pharaoh.

And I thought the Elders were sketchy.

There's just no way they'll keep this up. Tradition or not, a Terran woman as their leader makes no reasonable sense. The smart thing for them to do is pick a warrior and have him off me to claim the title for himself.

I pace the room, carving a path over coarse carpeting. Around the room, past sculptures, vases, paintings and even bones under glass casing. The couches might look comfortable, but the overall vibe here is closer to a museum than a home.

I walk for what feels like hours, my mind spinning and calculating and trying in vain to figure out all the potential outcomes. My thighs are burning when there's a soft knock at the door. I answer it immediately, not caring who it is, just eager for something to happen.

"Great Pharaoh." A woman, as stocky and pale as her male counterparts, bows as I open the door. Blue beads are threaded through her close-cropped dark hair. She's wearing a simple dress in the same color and pattern as Tor'Heel's kilt, and when she stands, her red eyes are bright and intelligent.

"Hello."

"I am May'Na. Wife of Tor'Heel. It is an honor to meet you."

"I... you as well."

She stares at me, waiting. She's looking at me like my next words carry a weight and purpose even before I've spoken them. This is more power than I could ever have imagined possessing, yet all I can think about is Damon. What is any of this without him? The sorrow on his face when I left... I would give anything to see that turned to joy.

Everything I need to do next comes to me in a rush. It makes my head spin and I grip the door frame to steady myself.

"You don't agree with the Great Pharaoh's choice."

May'Na's eyes widen, fear making a vein in her neck flutter beneath her powdery skin. I wait, allowing no emotion to filter through my eyes as I attempt to channel the confidence of a deity. We both stand a little straighter.

"I am troubled with doubts about your intentions. I am concerned about what this means for our culture and our faith. I expressed this to my husband, hoping he would also see reason to doubt you."

"Do you believe your husband would be a better choice?"

"I do."

Shit. She's not trying to backpedal or make excuses. She's owning her opinions and standing ready for the consequences. I let that sit for a bit, until the air between us is nearly sizzling with the tension.

"That's good. Because he is my choice."

Her forehead creases as her pale tongue flicks out to moisten her lips. I wait, letting her absorb what I've said.

"Forgive me. I do not understand."

"There is a problem that only this woman can help me fix. When I no longer require her, I will abandon her and embody your husband. No blood needs to be shed and the Terran woman can go back to her home planet. Will you help me with that?"

May'Na swallows, breaking eye contact for the first time to glance over her shoulders as if she is worried someone might overhear.

"Yes," she nods, clasping her hands in front of her waist. "I don't know how I can, but I will do as you ask, Great Pharaoh."

"You can start by convincing your husband."

～

FROM HIGH ABOVE THE TREES, I confirm we're still headed in the right direction. My hawk dives down, disappearing into the canopy to land on the forest floor with human feet. The six Shifters following my lead are waiting patiently, although they keep their distance from each other.

"We're getting close, brothers."

I shift to my panther form to continue leading the way.

Three wolves, a lion, a cougar, and a grizzly follow my lead. All of them trusting me to lead them into a future they couldn't have imagined just a few weeks ago. It's a heavy responsibility, and one I can no longer imagine turning my back on.

Whisper's last gift to me.

I glance up at the sky, flashes of blue through the green canopy. She's out there somewhere, I feel it in my soul. I don't know what that means, though I suspect it may just be my mind's way of coping. I couldn't survive if I knew for sure she hadn't. But I can cling to this thread of hope. I might see her again.

I force my thoughts away from her, and back to the Shifters behind me. The bear's been taking human form the longest. He was the first one Tarek reached out to. His Agent worked closely with Gideon. I approached the timber wolf and the grey wolf shortly after. We managed to get the lion and cougar alone outside Base.

With each it was the same. The moment we shifted to human form in front of them, a light came on in their minds. We told them the truth. After a few days of taking human form every chance they could, not one of them considered staying with their Agents. Even the lion, bonded to his Agent for twenty years, walked away without hesitation.

It took so much more than that for my bond with Whisper to break. Probably because I had no real desire to break it. I had nobody to tell me it was even possible.

I look behind me as I walk, making sure everyone still

follows. Tarek isn't with us. He revealed himself to an eagle the night before we left. As much as he wants to see the Meadow for himself, it was too soon to leave the newb without some support nearby.

A few more hours of walking, and I know we're close. The heavy scent of the forest begins to change, and my sensitive nose picks up hints of cut wood, smoke, and roasting meat. I'm not surprised when a low growl emerges from the brush ahead, a warning and further proof that I'm in the right spot.

I shift to my human form, and a gold-furred wolf emerges from the brush. The slope of the forest floor gives him the higher ground, and as he stares at me with bared fangs and narrowed, yellow-green eyes, I suspect I know exactly who it is.

A few growls join in from behind me, the cougar stepping up to my left. I raise a hand, gesturing for my companions to stay back.

"It's okay. Everything's fine," I say with false confidence. "Luke's just here to welcome us. Isn't that right?"

He shifts to his human form, bare chested and wearing the same drawstring pants. His expression is one of clear disdain. "What do you think you're doing?" His eyes move from me to the other Shifters in turn.

"I showed them the truth. They need a safe place to live."

"You what?" He steps forward until his face is inches from mine. "What the fuck gives you the right to think you can use this place as your own personal pet shelter?"

I swallow my anger, refusing to rise to his challenge. The last thing I need is for this to turn into a fight. "Is this not what you do here? Help Shifters live free of human control?"

"What *we* do to help *our* people is none of your business, pet. Last I saw, you were running back to your master with your tail between your legs."

I will not hit this asshole. I will not take my dragon form and watch him shit his pants before I crush him into the dirt.

"I want to speak to Hope."

He smirks. His face is still close enough that I could break his nose with my own head; a move I've seen Whisper pull on a couple occasions with cocky fuckers like this.

"You think playing the hero will get you into her pants? Been there, done that. Bitch doesn't struggle for long-"

The sound of my fist connecting with his jaw is a very satisfying sound. He stumbles backward but I follow and pound him again before he gets the chance to recover. Pain shoots up my arm as blood sprays from his mouth.

Hell yes, that felt good.

A chorus of growls and the bellow of a grizzly fills my ears.

"I got this asshole."

They back away but I sense they're ready and willing to jump in if I ask.

Luke regains his footing and makes like he's going to charge, then thinks better of it. I step toward him, and he backs up a step. Guess he's got a brain in there somewhere.

A moment later, he's back in wolf form and disappearing into the trees.

"I pictured these people being a little more welcoming." The grizzly steps up beside me, his human body almost as imposing as his bear.

"They will be." I'm having some serious doubts at the moment.

I shift back to panther form, leading the way on the final leg of our trek through the forest. I'm glad we can't talk amongst ourselves. In human form, they like to chat. It's understandable. They're full of questions and thoughts and ideas as their minds expand. I remember that feeling well.

I don't feel any of those things anymore. I have a task, a

mission, and I don't care to make any friends along the way. My body might have a purpose that keeps me busy, but my heart is elsewhere. They know enough of my story, between the media and whatever Tarek told them. I don't really care to elaborate.

We break through the trees into late afternoon sunlight. I shake the dewy moisture of the forest out of my fur and survey the sight in front of me. It's mostly unchanged from my last time here.

Shifters in all forms mill about the pathways between tents, tending to cook fires and children. Away to my left, a few men are chopping wood. Shirtless and gleaming with sweat, they talk and laugh as they work. In the open space between forest and tents, gardens are being tended. To my right, a black bear and a jaguar work together to haul a sizeable deer carcass out of the forest.

A woman in the gardens spots us, lifting her hands against the sun to get a better look. One by one, more people take notice of our colorful little pack. I shift to human form, turning to instruct the others to do the same.

We walk in silence past the onlookers, no one trying to approach us or prevent us from entering the village of tents. I expected a welcome party, considering the story Luke would have returned with.

When Hope rounds a corner into view, her violet eyes are blazing. There's a streak of blood on the front of her white t-shirt, and her hands are curled into fists. I guess he knew exactly who to take his story to.

"What do you think you're doing?" She points a finger in my face, then gestures to the six men around me. "I saved your life. I trusted you with our location. Now you come here with your friends and attack one of ours? What do you expect-"

On impulse, I grasp her face in my hands and kiss her forehead. She gasps in surprise, and maybe I do too because I did not expect to be this happy to see her. It's the most emotion I've felt since... A wave of guilt hits me. I didn't come here for myself.

She doesn't pull away, and so I keep my hands on her face and look into her eyes, making sure she's looking back at me. "And did he tell you what he said about you to earn that ass kicking?"

Her eyes narrow, but the anger fades away. "No. He didn't mention that part." She reaches a hand up, lightly covering one of mine that still grips her face.

"Has he hurt you?"

Her face turns to genuine confusion. "No... why would you say that?"

"If he laid a hand on you, I swear I'll-"

"No. He didn't. Never. You're scaring the shit out of me here, buddy. I don't even know your name and your acting like..." Her words trail off as she pulls out of my grip.

"Damon."

My sudden possessiveness of her is out of line. I don't know why I'm feeling this way. It's not sexual. I could never want anyone but Whisper that way. But I know in my gut that I would kill that bastard if his claims were true.

I owe this girl my life.

"Okay. Damon. Nice to officially meet you." She steps back a few paces, crossing her arms in front of her. Her eyes drift to take in the men standing with me, and I fill her in on who they are and why I've brought them here. I keep to the relevant facts, not bothering to mention that it was Whisper's request that I start this little venture.

She seems satisfied with my story. Unlike Luke, she welcomes them with genuine warmth.

"I'll introduce you to some of the Alpha's," she offers. "We can get you settled in somewhere for now, and talk about..."

I don't bother listening to the rest. I shift to panther form, and lope back the way we came. Out of the little village of tents and past the gardens. I reach the edge of the forest, then stop to wait.

I'm not interested in hearing about what comes next. Settling in, finding a place to sleep. This isn't my home. As far as I'm concerned, I don't have a home. And that's just fine with me. I do feel connected to these people, though. My people.

Hope's white wolf follows my tracks, her violet eyes catching mine as her tongue lolls out in a lupine grin. She settles down on her haunches beside me, close enough that her lush coat brushes against my dense fur.

We sit like that for moments, as I look out over the Meadow. She watches me, waiting, and then her wolf is replaced by her small, human form.

"What happened, Damon? When you left here you were going back to a female... to a woman you loved."

I heave a sigh, shaking my head to clear my thoughts. I waited here to talk to her, but now it's too personal. I shift, pulling a deep breath into my human lungs before I answer.

"She's gone."

A sharp inhale is her only response. She waits quietly, and I'm grateful for the space to think.

"Whisper's the reason I'm here. She's the reason I'm alive. The reason I'm free."

Hope sniffs, swiping at her cheek. "Whisper and Damon. I didn't make the connection."

I look at her with obvious confusion.

"You two are a little bit famous. Or, I guess infamous is the better word. She defied the system and earned the title of Elite. Then she turned on her boss and tried to kill him. I heard her Shifter was killed in the fight, and Whisper was fired. It drove her crazy, and she took her own life."

"It's bullshit." I growl through clenched teeth.

"I believe you."

She makes the statement so easily, that I don't doubt her sincerity.

"I want to destroy it. BioSol Labs. I want to burn it down and end this entire system once and for all."

"Woah." She rocks back on her hips, tucking her knees up under her chin. "That's a fantasy we've all had at some point. We'd need an army, and it would-"

I stand up and move away from her, feeling the rush of energy as my body stretches and bends to become the dragon. I flex the thick muscles of my legs, sinking sharp talons into the earth. I flare my wings as I look down at her, so small beneath me. Her eyes are wide, a hand covering her mouth, but she doesn't look afraid.

I bend my thick, scaled neck until my nose is close enough for her to touch. The human words are like gravel in my throat, but I force them out.

"I... Am... An... Army."

A rumbling growl travels up from my chest, and I feel something new. A burning sensation at the base of my throat. A tendril of grey smoke rises in front of my eyes.

Hell, yes.

I fight the urge to take to the sky and test this new ability. Instead, I release my hold on the dragon and shrink back down to sit again in human form. The expression on her face as she looks at me now is one of pure awe.

It feels good to be looked at this way.

Hope holds her hand up, and I realize that a crowd has gathered between us and the tents. She gestures for them to stay back. I look at them as they watch me, the same awe in their expressions as in Hope's.

"I think that's the most excitement we've had around here in a while." Her playful tone carries a hint of uneasiness.

"It's not a fantasy. I can bring that place down."

"It's not that simple."

"It could be."

"It isn't." She stands up, wiping the dirt off her backside before crossing her arms. "If we attack them, if we hurt them, what do you think that will tell them about us? Innocent lives will be lost."

"Innocent lives are already being lost." I stand to face her, my back to the tents. "What about the females who are culled at birth? The males that don't make the cut and die from not having a bond. Or the ones that live, and never amount to anything but a *pet*."

"We just want to live. We don't want to hurt them."

I growl, scrubbing a hand through my hair. I hear the truth in her words. My own truth. I've never had a stomach for fighting, for violence. I'm just so fucking angry.

"You saved those men. You gave them a chance at a life they didn't know existed. Isn't that good enough?"

I nod, opening my mouth to answer, but not able to find the words.

"And we have eyes in the Lab. We save the ones we can, without drawing attention. Keeping the Meadow safe is our priority, so we can live and protect our families in peace." She reaches up to place a warm palm on my cheek, coaxing me to look at her again. "Can this be enough? For you, I mean. Could you be happy here?"

"I'm not interested in being happy."

She drops her hand, nodding as she chews on her lower lip.

"But you need protection. More than just that jackass running around in the woods."

A grin spreads across her face as she rolls her eyes. "We've done all right so far. A few of the men, like Luke, were Protectors. They have implants. They can defend us if it comes to that. I've done my fair share of hunting, too."

I scoff at her statements. "You need more than that. It's only a matter of time before this place is discovered. The men I brought are good fighters. Tarek's more than comfortable in his dragon form, and the Eagle he's working with now is a pro. We can train your males, set up a better perimeter. Get ready."

"Sounds like you're staying, then?"

I ruffle her hair. She squeals and ducks out of reach, laughing as she punches me in the bicep with all the force of a bunny.

"Yeah. For a while."

I told Tarek how to get here, so he can find his own way easy enough. It's the best way I can think of to honor Whisper. I'll stay. I'll help them prepare for the worst. I'll keep helping more Shifters wake up. And I'll rain down hell on anyone who tries to harm this place.

I couldn't save her. I'll carry that pain with me until I die.

But I'll damn well die for something that matters.

HEAVY RAIN PELTS against the cab's windows, the steady drumming making my world feel very, very small. I rest my forehead against the cool window, my heart aching as I take in the blurry view outside.

Kelsey's bar. I haven't been back since that night with Damon. I haven't contacted her, either. Like everyone else, she thinks I'm dead. Though she's probably the only one that doesn't believe the official story. I'm tempted to reach out, to let her know I'm okay.

"Let's go."

The cab driver steps on the gas, and I breathe a quiet goodbye against the glass.

Our next stop hits me with a different kind of sadness, though I should have expected no less. The little home I shared with

Damon is bright and cheery, even in the face of the deluge pouring down from above. Warm light floods out from the windows, framing the silhouettes of a young couple sitting close together at the small kitchen table.

It would have been sold after news of my death. My possessions would have been picked through and auctioned off. Still, I'd held out hope I might get one more chance to step inside.

No matter. I wouldn't have been staying for long anyway.

"Take me to Base." The driver squints at me through the rearview mirror, his eyes tired and impatient. It might be early morning, but I get the feeling his shift is coming to a close. "The Headquarters of the United Army of Terran Protectors. Just drop me off there, please."

He nods, and we pull away from the curb. I've got nothing but the clothes on my back, and this little, red credit chip in my back pocket.

The only thing I took from Gliese was a small chunk of change. Barely a chip off the estate of a Pharaoh. Here on Earth, the conversion rate means I've got enough credits to cover me wherever I want to go, whatever I want to do, probably for as long as I live.

Technically, it's not stolen. May'Na helped me load it up before I passed on the title.

When we park in front of the familiar glass doors, I swipe my card to pay the driver, adding on the biggest tip I've ever had the means to offer.

"Thanks," I say, as I step out into the biting rain, sprinting the ten feet until I can duck inside.

I'm not worried about anyone recognizing me. If my red curls aren't disguise enough, I'm also wearing bright green contacts and a face full of makeup. I look more like my mother than myself, and that thought brings up a whole other dump of emotions I don't care to entertain just now.

My clothes most definitely paint me as far from home. My loose, crimson pants flow like an ankle-length skirt. My snug, black shirt is embroidered with the symbols of Gliese in gold thread. It's about as far as you can get from the worn-out dress I was shipped off in, or from the tactical gear I usually wear on these grounds.

I ignore the side-eyes and outright stares from the Protectors and civilians I pass. Chin high, shoulders back.

"Hello, beautiful lady," a distantly familiar voice speaks up behind me.

I stop, twenty paces from the front desk, and hold my breath. I turn slowly, to see none other than Agent Nutsack. I bite my tongue.

"Can I help you with something? You look like you're far from home." His voice is smooth. Polite even.

I glance around for the tawny wolf that's never far from his side, but it's absent. I look up at his face, waiting for him to add something disgusting to his greeting. His eyes look almost sad.

I try to feel some satisfaction at the idea that he might be suffering a measure of personal tragedy, but I can't manage to summon any pleasure from it. He's the product of the system we all live in. As am I.

"Yes, I..." I clear my throat, attempting to sound more aristocratic. "I'm looking for Commander Charles Jeffries."

"I can let him know you're here, if he's on site. Who should I say is looking for him?"

I open my mouth to answer, then hesitate. Agent Nu... Agent Thomas... catches my lapse and tilts his head slightly to the side.

"Jane. Tell him Jane's here."

He nods, moving away from me to talk privately on his comm. When he returns a moment later, his smile is warm.

"The Commander is in his office. I'll show you the way."

I follow him toward the elevator, waiting as he touches his

comm against the security gate. When he presses the panel beside the elevator door, he turns and looks at me with narrowed eyes.

"Thank you." I step in front of him as the doors slide open. "I can find my way from here."

I slide into the elevator, turning to find him considering me with a look that says he knows he's met me before, but can't quite place it. I give him a polite smile, averting my eyes. When the doors slide closed, I release the breath I was holding in one, long sigh.

ONLY YOURS

"*A*re you fucking with me?"

Charles chuckles at my reaction, but it's a humorless sound. I flip through the three pieces of paper he handed me, scanning my eyes over the black-and-white ink for the hundredth time. I hiss as the smooth edge of the last page slices a minuscule, stinging paper cut on the inside of my index finger. Fucking paperwork.

"I assure you, everything on those pages has been written with the blessing of the Elders."

"How did they know... who..."

"The Pharaoh of Gliese was assassinated by a Terran. A Terran who then took *her* place as a living deity and ruler of their entire race. That's the kind of news that travels fast."

I look up at him, feeling numb and utterly dumbfounded. I came back here expecting to dodge the law for as long as possible. To eventually be caught and tried for treason. Or maybe just eliminated quietly.

He gestures to the papers in my hands, sliding a fat pen across his desk. "Sign the papers, Whisp. You earned it."

"I don't... They..." I've lost the ability to speak or form

coherent thoughts. My mind is racing. On one hand, it seems so simple... sign the dotted line, and it all ends. On the other hand, I know that what I do in this moment will affect more than just my own future.

I set the papers down on the desk with an audible slap, then slouch backward into a padded chair. Elbows on my knees, I lean forward and try to make all this new information fit.

"It's all there in the report." Charles moves around his wide desk, picking up the papers as he leans against the solid pine. "The newly ascended Pharaoh of Gliese issued a public statement that the previous administration had been doing business involving human trafficking. She stated that Gliese would no longer take part in such ventures, condemned anyone who supported such things, and specifically named Horizon Zero as the primary offender. She also released a few specific names and addresses."

"I expected that would earn me more enemies." I gesture to the papers in his hands. "Not this."

"Well, there aren't too many systems confident, or stupid, enough to be at odds with Gliese. Within a matter of hours, Horizon Zero started to implode. They turned on each other. Clawing to be the first to come forward, to earn lenience for cooperation. Within two days, a quarter of the Elders themselves had either resigned or been forced into early retirement, pending investigations. Aid centers were set up to process the girls and women who had been taken, helping them to reunite with family or find housing if they had none."

I reach my hand out, and he passes me the papers. I skim the first two pages again, and it's all there. In this official report, I'm listed as 'an unknown Terran woman'. It's stated that I challenged the Pharaoh and won. According to their law, that made me the new ruler.

My pronouncements are all listed, including the orders to

return any and all purchased girls to their homes, if they chose. Any that opted to stay were granted freedom and autonomy equal to any other citizen of Gliese. I implored any other entity currently doing business with Horizon Zero to cancel their contracts.

It also mentions that for the first time in Gliese history, the Great Pharaoh chose to move from one living host to another. It took a lot of convincing, but eventually Tor'Heel agreed. He didn't really stand a chance, considering both the Great Pharaoh and his wife weren't taking no for an answer.

He was deeply honored, shed a few tears, and swore to continue enforcing the changes I set in motion. May'Na promised me she would keep him honest.

"What about you?" I ask, looking up at Charles's weathered face. His name was not among those I released. Whatever his sins, I would never have made it to Gliese without him.

He sighs, pushing off from the desk and turning to sit heavily in the chair beside me. "I expect they will come for me eventually. Justice will find me. Until then, I'll do what I can to help."

"Tanikka?"

"Her husband, Isaac, was charged along with Elder Marcus. Tanikka is campaigning to take a place within the Elders."

That makes me sit up straight. "A *woman* as Elder?"

"Don't get your hopes up... she still has a long way to go. But if a Terran woman can be a Pharaoh... well, maybe."

I can't help but smile at that. Out from under her husband's thumb, Tanikka will do great things. I have no doubt about that. I flip to the last page, the brief words and empty space waiting for my signature.

"Why did you come back?" Charles's tone is soft and curious. "You always wanted to be on top. I can't think of a higher position than god-Queen of an entire planet."

I look over at him, my vision blurring slightly as guilt washes over me. "I guess I figured out there are more important things than power."

He nods. "You made some other statements as well while you were there."

Hope rises in my chest. When I was sure I'd covered all my bases with Horizon Zero, and I'd done everything I could to shine a light on them, I had switched gears and started talking about Shifters. The Gliesiens weren't particularly interested. Shifters aren't something they have much knowledge of or any kind of dealings with. Still, I sent a message to Earth, detailing what I knew about their race and imploring the government to acknowledge them as a unique species deserving of freedom and protection.

"I never saw the message," Charles says. "Elder Tobias told me about it in confidence. He said it wasn't something the Elders were prepared to address or take public. The information about Horizon Zero was huge, and it spread like wildfire. The statement about Shifters was easier to bury. I tried to find a copy, but it's gone."

"Dammit." I crush the papers in my frustration. I look over at Charles, imploring him to believe me. "Everything I said was true. Shifters are not our *property*. They are intelligent and-"

"I know." He puts his hands up in a gesture of surrender. "I had a recent visit from a certain panther who made sure I knew exactly how things are."

My heart nearly leaps out of my chest, and I gasp out loud at his statement.

"Damon. Is he... is he okay?"

Charles shakes his head as he lets out a quick laugh. "Last I knew, he was headed to meet Gideon. Seems he's as determined to liberate his people as you were to save those girls."

My chest swells with pride, and for the first time in a long time I feel real, honest hope.

"Do you know where he is?" I hold my breath, waiting for his answer.

"I haven't heard anything from him or about him specifically. Not since he was here last month. I do know some Shifters have been going missing. The Elders have an idea about what's going on. How they'll respond to it, or what they'll do once the situation gets a little more public, remains to be seen."

I nod. Then stand and set the wrinkled papers on his desk.

"Thank you, Charles. For everything."

He pulls the bottom paper out from under the other two. He picks up the pen and holds both out to me. "Sign these, girl. You deserve it."

I shake my head.

A statement acknowledging that I was the one responsible for taking down Horizon Zero. A full pardon and reinstatement of my Elite status. I just have to sign my name, and the world will know what I did. Instead of going down in history as the first female Agent, who ultimately betrayed her employer and died a coward; I'll be hailed as a hero. I can only imagine the look on my brothers' faces if they read that headline.

It's a very tempting prospect.

"Will that help me free the Shifters?"

Charles's brow creases as he folds his arms across his round chest. "I don't doubt your ability to get what you want. Not after everything I've seen you accomplish. You took down a massive organization and dealt our government a serious blow in the process. They won't let you cripple their reputation or their profits farther."

Fucking politics. I can have my title, my reputation, my life... if I play nice.

"I think, Charles, that I can do far better if I stay dead."

He looks at me, lips pressed into a thin line as his sharp eyes grow glossy with emotion. "You've changed, Whisper."

"Absolutely."

$$\sim$$

SHE WRAPS her slim legs around me, gripping so tightly that her thighs tremble. I laugh, the sound coming out like a mix between a cough and a growl. The proud boasting of five minutes ago faded the moment her ass settled into the saddle. Now that I'm braced to take off, her fear is palpable.

I jump, and to her credit, Hope doesn't make a sound. I circle the Meadow, twisting and turning just above the trees to test the bindings and give her a good feel for how I might maneuver if we were actually in a fight.

I take the opportunity to survey the perimeter and note the fast progress of the builders, as the first stage of the wall sprouts up from the forest. It's just as tall as the trees, so it won't announce our presence to anyone from a distance. When it's complete, it will give us solid protection from ground attack, as well as strategic vantage points to defend against aerial attack.

It's overkill, considering we're a village made up of predators, including two dragons and three Griffons so far. It's preparation for the future. As more are liberated, our numbers grow, and the humans inevitably learn of our existence.

Some actual houses are being built, with wooden walls and thatch roofs. They're putting down roots, claiming their home, and preparing to defend it.

I feel at home.

Mostly.

My eyes drift from the wall up to the sky, as they do at least a hundred times a day. I live for these people. My people. But at the end of the day, I am alive because of her. My Whisper. I cling to the hope that she's still out there, that she found a home somehow. I refuse to think about how unlikely that is.

I roar into the wind, and Hope's small voice joins me in a battle cry of her own. I swoop downwards, relieved that she is one of the few who seems to have a stomach for dragon riding. If we ever find ourselves in a real battle, I'd rather have her strapped to my back where I can keep her safe.

When she falls to the ground beside me, she's all hysterical giggles. I shift to human form and hold out a hand to help her to her feet. I pull her into a tight embrace.

I've never had a real family before, but I'm certain this is what it's like. Hope and I share a connection, a closeness, that I haven't experienced with anyone else. It's never threatened to grow into something more. She knows that part of me belongs with Whisper, and I know she has her own walls that keep her guarded when it comes to males.

I catch a flash of gold fur and realize we're being watched. Luke's had his sights on her since long before I came along, and his attentions have always been unwanted. With her still wrapped in a tight hug, I meet his stare and let my hand drift down her back until I'm cupping one ass cheek in my hand.

His eyes flash with hatred, as he bares his teeth in a growl before loping off in the opposite direction.

Hope giggles, turning her head until her breath is hot against my neck. "Oh my, going right for the ass grab. Luke?"

"Yep."

I step back once he's out of sight. Most of the village thinks we're a couple, which suits us just fine. It keeps Luke off her tail and deters the handful of females that decided to vie for my attention in the beginning.

"Thanks." She grins, then grabs my hand with a shout of excitement. "Look!"

A massive green dragon swoops down into the clearing. Tarek's been back and forth with liberated Shifters while still keeping up appearances with Gideon back on Solar One. It's only a matter of time before the missing Shifters are noticed by more than just the Protectors. The longer we can avoid that, the more time we have to prepare the Meadow. This time, he wears his saddle, and as he lands, I lock eyes with the woman on his back. Her hair is red and curly, her clothes rich and proper.

But I would know her anywhere.

Hope grips my arm as if to hold me up.

"Damon?" Her voice is laced with concern. She puts a hand to my neck, then my chest. "Breathe. You're okay. What's happening?"

"It's her."

I SCAN THE GROUND, my eyes desperately hungry for the first glimpse of him. The wide clearing below is bustling with activity, as people and animals work, play and build. Tents and newly framed buildings are arranged like a small village, and a wall is being constructed around the perimeter.

Damon's idea, Tarek says. My Damon, who has not only taken up the task of spreading the word to other Shifters, but has also made it his responsibility to help defend their safe haven. I'm so proud of him, I could burst.

Charles pointed me to Gideon, who led me to Tarek, who agreed to bring me here. Every moment since has dragged on like an eternity. I'm so close to him, and to us.

Turning down that contract was the best decision I've ever made. Leaving that system behind for good, walking away without a second thought, was a perfect moment.

A group of shirtless men catches my attention, and I strain to see if one of them could be Damon. Another man walking alone, but no, not him either. A black wolf has my heart skittering for just a moment. I rub my eyes against the wind, trying to squint and push the limits of my vision.

From one moment to the next, he's right there. Right there in a grassy field between forest and tents. It's him, of that I have no doubt. But instead of shouting his name and announcing my arrival, I simply watch.

I watch as his hands roam over the beautiful woman in his arms. As she nuzzles into his neck, and his face breaks into a smile. She spots Tarek, and her excitement is obvious. Damon turns, and they hold hands as comfortably as long-time lovers.

The moment he spots me, it's like a bolt of electricity. His eyes bore into mine, his face a mask of shock as the woman on his arm touches his neck. His chest. I want nothing more in this moment than to sink into the earth and disappear.

How could I have been so naive? I've been gone how long... nearly two months now? Of course he would find comfort with someone else.

Tarek touches down with practiced grace, and I bend to release the bindings holding my legs. I feel almost empty as I stare at Damon, who stares back at me with pale shock. I don't feel anything. It's like all my emotions are vying for dominance, but none are able to surface.

Finally, my feet touch the ground. He's twenty feet away from me. Him and his... whatever she is. He's so close, and yet he seems as far away as ever.

I brush my hands down the front of my clothes, painfully aware of how overdressed, underprepared and just plain awkward I am.

He starts walking toward me, and in the next breath his arms are around me. His mouth finds mine and he kisses me with a desperate, starving intensity that reflects everything I'm feeling. I return his embrace with equal abandon.

It's beautiful. It's perfect. Everything else fades away and all that exists is us. We're both gasping for breath when he pulls back enough for our foreheads to rest together, his big hands coming up to cup my face.

"Whisper." He says my name, and I recognize the raw pain beneath the word. I'm helpless to stop the tears that stream down my face. "Is this real?"

"Yes," I choke out as I fling my arms around his neck, burying my face in his heat and his familiar scent. "I'm here. I'll never leave you again. If you'll have me."

I peek over his shoulder at the woman he was holding just moments ago. She's still rooted to the spot, a slender hand covering a wide smile that lights up her entire face. Stunning, violet eyes are brimming with tears. She looks... happy.

Damon pulls back as he touches my face, my neck, runs his hands over my arms. "Are you okay? How did you... how can you..."

He's so stunned by my presence that I can't help but laugh. I want to tell him everything, but it's such a crazy story I don't even know where to start. "It's over. Horizon Zero is gone. I'm here to be with you, to help you."

He looks stunned by my words, and I reach my hand up to touch his cheek. I run my finger over the silvery scar that runs down his neck. Images of our last night together before I left flash in my mind, heating me up like a fire in my belly. He seems to sense the direction my thoughts have taken, and he grips my hips to pull me snugly against him.

"Hi, I'm Hope." The woman's voice cuts through the moment, and I jump when I realize she's right next to us. Her violet eyes, a gorgeous shade I've never seen before, are dancing with joy. "I'm Damon's decoy girlfriend."

She holds out her hand for me to shake, and I accept it out of habit. "His what?"

She laughs with a deliciously feminine giggle, and I'm immediately at ease. "He basically took a vow of celibacy, because he was sure you would come back. And I had a particularly unwanted suitor... so we just let everyone think we were together. It made it simpler for both of us." She shrugs as if it all makes perfect sense.

Damon laughs, wrapping an arm around her shoulders and pulling her in for a quick kiss on the forehead. He's so casual and familiar with her. The Damon I knew didn't know anyone other than me. I was his whole world.

I look around and realize that I don't really know this man, not anymore.

And I am so eager to change that.

"We'll be in my tent," he states.

Hope giggles again, and then Damon is leading me away. I try to take in my surroundings and the people, but I can't look away from him.

"Is she a Shifter?"

"She is." He pulls me off the beaten path and into a small, square tent. "She's a good friend."

Inside the tent, the floor is canvass over flat, packed ground. A low, wooden pallet holds a thick layer of animal furs and a couple heavy, worn quilts. It smells like earth, smoke, and Damon.

"It's not much." Damon watches my expression as I survey the small space. "It's all I needed for just me. I can build us a cabin. Something bigger, if you-"

"It's perfect." I step closer to him, resting my hands on his stomach. I spread my fingers wide over hard, contoured abs. "All I need is you."

"You have me," he says without a moment's hesitation. "I am only yours."

"And I'm yours."

～

CURIOUS TO KNOW what's next?

FORGOTTEN desires ignite when Gideon meets the woman who makes him feel alive again. Can he risk giving in to temptation, or will the sins of his past keep him from the future he craves?

FIND OUT NOW, in *Hope in the Moonlight!*

A NOTE FROM THE AUTHOR

Thank you for reading Whisper and Damon's story!

Would you like to hear about my future releases and be the first to get freebies and sneak peeks? Subscribe to my newsletter at www.CharlenePerry.ca

If you enjoyed this book, please consider leaving a review wherever you can. As an indie author, reviews are critical for helping my books find the readers who will love them. I adore hearing what you think of my work. It gives me confidence, motivates me to push through the hard parts, and inspires me to keep adding to the series you love!

For more information about me or my stories, be sure to check out my website! (www.charleneperry.ca)

Find me on Facebook! @CharlenePerryAuthor. I love to chat and am always delighted to receive feedback :)

Thank you so much for spending this time with me,

Sweet Dreams!
    -Charlene

Guess my buddy got bored. I can't help but be a little disappointed at the wolf's absence when I return from the water. The clear morning air is still a bit chilly, and I hustle back into dry clothes as fast as my damp skin will allow.

The snap of branches brings an instant smile to my face. I'm a little surprised at how happy I am to have my companion back.

"Hey, I need to find something to call you other than-"

It takes a second too long for my brain to catch up, as a freight train of snarling teeth and gold fur barrels toward me. I have just enough time to block, before fangs sink into my arm and the weight of the ambush sends me sprawling onto my back with my attacker in tow.

I don't have my weapons, but I'm far from defenceless. I punch him in the ear with my free hand, using the arm in his jaws to pull him close enough to bite the sensitive spot behind his nose. He yelps in surprise and pain, letting go just as my white wolf plows into his side, sending both tumbling.

I scramble for my Glock, but even before I have it in hand the wolves have separated. My wolf stands in front of me, tail and ears down, growling a warning. The gold wolf is a dozen paces away, between us and the water, mirroring my wolf's stance.

My hand is on my weapon where it's stowed inside my pack, but I don't move to pull it into view. I wait, braced to act if this escalates. I can assume the Shifters know each other, but whether that works in my favor or against it is yet to be seen.

The gold wolf shifts. The man that takes his place looks even more furious. He's wearing only a thin pair of pants and looks like a wild thing just as much in this form as his wolf.

"What is this?" He ignores my presence, directing his anger at the white wolf. "Is this where you've been? With a *human*?"

My wolf's growl drops an octave, his body in a crouch, ready to attack. Ready to defend.

The man takes a step back, his stance faltering as he shakes his head. His features twist as he presses his hands against his head.

"You better get your ass back." He growls the words through clenched teeth. "Because I swear, if you don't show yourself at the Meadow before noon, I'll be telling your... our Alpha... exactly where I found you."

Whatever weight that threat holds, he seems satisfied. He shifts back to his wolf form, kicking up sand as he takes off for the forest.

"What the fuck?"

The white wolf turns, and those violet eyes are wide and bright. They snap to my arm, widening farther as a pitiful whine escapes him. I follow his gaze to my bloodied forearm, the shock and adrenaline making the wound painless.

"It's fine, I heal-"

Violet eyes hold mine as he shudders and contracts down into the form of a woman. My heart stops beating. Her hair is the palest blond, her features delicate. Her body is curved to perfection beneath ripped jeans and a sleeveless top.

Holy fuck. She's the most beautiful woman I've ever laid eyes on.

I'm dead. Or I'm delirious.

She grips my arm with firm confidence, my blood staining her flawless skin as she holds her small hands over the wounds.

"I'm so sorry, Gideon," she says with a tremble in her soft voice.

"It's okay. I have a Medic implant. I'll heal."

She looks at me with a desperate expression, her eyes searching mine. I reach out with my other hand, unable to resist touching her hair, her cheek, the gentle curve of her lower lip as it trembles under my thumb.

Fuck. I need to get away from this woman. This Shifter. If I don't, I'm going to do something stupid. Maybe it's the rush of the fight, but I'm really fucking close to kissing her. I've never felt this instantly drawn to a woman. She's not even human.

She's still looking at me, perfectly still as my hand refuses to stop touching her face. Those eyes. I pull my hand away, pushing up and away from her stare and her attentions.

What the fuck am I doing? Mercifully, the pain of the wolf's bite kicks in to distract me.

"I'll heal," I repeat, digging through my pack for first aid supplies.

I can't look at her when she crowds me again, swatting my hands as she takes over to wrap my arm with practiced skill. She's not the least bit concerned about the amount of my blood she has on her hands.

"Who are you?"

Read *Hope in the Moonlight*, available now!

Printed in Great Britain
by Amazon